The Holy War

John Bunyan

Publisher's Note

The Holy War, John Bunyan's account of the battle for the town of Mansoul, is told in the classic, allegorical style he perfected in *Pilgrim's Progress.* Revised for clarity, this updated version gives today's reader the opportunity to enjoy a fresh presentation of Bunyan's unique tale of the struggle for man's soul.

THE HOLY WAR

John Bunyan

Copyright © 1985 by Whitaker House
Printed in the United States of America
ISBN: 0-88368-165-X

CONTENTS

Chapter One

THE CONQUEST

As I traveled through many regions, I came upon that famous land called Universe. This spacious country lies between the two poles and amid the four points of the heavens. Adorned with hills and valleys, it is abundantly fruitful, well-populated, and splendidly situated.

The people of Universe are not all of one race, culture, or religion, but they are as different as the planets themselves. As I wandered throughout this land, I learned much about the native languages and customs of the people with whom I visited. The things I saw and heard among them were delightful. In fact, I would have lived and died there if my Master had not called me home to oversee some business for him.

In this gallant country of Universe, there lies a pleasant and peaceful municipality called Mansoul. The picturesque architecture of this town, its convenient location, and its superior advantages cannot be equaled under heaven.

According to the most authentic records, Man-soul's first founder and builder was one called Shad-dai. He built it for his own delight, making it the masterpiece of all that he did in that country. When first built, it was said by some that the angels came down to see it and sang for joy.

Shaddai made the town of Mansoul splendidly beautiful, as well as powerful, and gave it domin-ion over all the country. Everyone was commanded to acknowledge and reverence Mansoul as their cap-ital city. The town had absolute authority to demand allegiance of everyone and power to subdue any-one who refused to comply.

In the center of this town stood a famous and stately palace. It was strong enough to be called a castle and as beautiful as a paradise. King Shaddai intended this palace for himself alone, partly for his own delight and partly because he did not want foreigners to invade Mansoul. The palace was gar-risoned like a fortress, and Shaddai committed the keeping of it to the men of the town.

The walls surrounding Mansoul were strongly constructed and could never be broken down or damaged by even the most powerful adversary, un-less the townsmen consented to it. Shaddai had planned it this way.

This famous town of Mansoul had five gates which were also impregnable. They could never be opened or forced unless permission was given by the peo-ple within. The names of the gates were: Ear Gate, Eye Gate, Mouth Gate, Nose Gate, and Feel Gate.

Mansoul had the best, most wholesome, and excellent law in the world. There was not a rascal, rogue, or traitorous person within its walls. The townsfolk were all good men joined together in unity, and this you know is a rare thing. As long as the people kept true to Shaddai, their King, Mansoul enjoyed his presence and his protection; and the town was his delight.

Once upon a time, a mighty giant named Diabolus made an assault upon this famous town of Mansoul. He tried to take it and make it his own habitation. This giant was the terrible prince of darkness. He was originally one of the servants of King Shaddai, who had placed him in a very high and mighty position. Diabolus was given dominion over the best principalities and was called the Son of the Morning. His position brought him much glory and gave him an income that might have contented his Luciferian desires, if they had not been insatiable and as large as hell itself.

Seeing himself exalted to such greatness and honor, Diabolus aspired for a higher position. He began to imagine how he could be set up as lord over all the world and have sole power under Shaddai. This place, however, the King reserved for his Son and had already bestowed it upon him.

Diabolus considered how to proceed and discussed his plot with some of his companions. They decided to make an attempt to destroy the King's Son so that the inheritance would be theirs. The treason was concluded, and the time appointed. When the word was given, the rebels assembled, and the assault was attempted.

Now the King was all-wise and all-knowing and could see everything that took place in his dominion. Having great love for his Son, he was greatly provoked and offended at what he saw. The King caught Diabolus and his accomplices as they attempted to carry out their evil scheme. Shaddai convicted them of treason, rebellion, and conspiracy, then expelled them from their positions of trust, honor, and dignity. Having done this, the King banished them from his court and threw them down into the horrible pit. There they were to await the eternal punishment that he had appointed for them.

Knowing they had lost their positions and the King's favor forever, Diabolus and his rebels turned their pride into hatred against Shaddai and his Son. They roamed about in fury from place to place in search of something that belonged to the King on which to take their revenge.

At last they happened to find this spacious country of Universe, and they steered their course toward the famous town of Mansoul. Considering it to be one of the chief works and delights of King Shaddai, they decided to make an assault upon the town. Diabolus and his rebels knew that Mansoul belonged to Shaddai because they had been there when he designed and built it for himself.

When they found the place, they shouted horribly for joy and roared as a lion over its prey, saying: "Now we have found the prize and how to take revenge on King Shaddai for what he has done to us." So they called a council of war and considered what methods they should use to win this famous town of Mansoul for themselves. Four ideas were proposed for consideration.

First, would it be best for all of them to make themselves known to the town of Mansoul?

Secondly, should they make an assault on the town while in their fallen condition?

Thirdly, should they make their evil intentions known to the people of Mansoul or assault them covertly with deceitful words and ways?

Fourthly, should they give orders for some of their company to kill a few of the town's leaders? Would this promote their cause?

The first of these proposals was rejected since the appearance of too many of them might create alarm and fear in the town. A few or one of them was not as likely to do so.

"It would be impossible," said Diabolus, "for all of us to take the town, because no one can enter it without the consent of the townsfolk. In my opinion, only one of us should assault Mansoul."

Then Diabolus added, "Let me be the one."

Next, they came to the second proposal. Should they go against Mansoul while looking so dreadful? This was also answered in the negative. Although the town of Mansoul was familiar with unusual beings, they had never seen any of their fellow-creatures in such miserable condition as Diabolus and his crew. That was the advice of the fierce Alecto.

Apollyon said, "The advice is pertinent, for even one of us appearing to them as we are now would create a disturbance and put them on their guard. If that happens, then it is futile for us to think of taking the town."

Then that mighty giant Beelzebub said, "The advice already given is clever. Although the men of Mansoul have seen such creatures as we once were, they have never beheld such creatures as we are now. And in my opinion, it is best to come to them in a form that is familiar to them."

When this had been agreed on, they next considered in what shape or form Diabolus should show himself when he went to Mansoul. Someone said one thing, and another said the contrary. At last Lucifer answered that in his opinion it was best for his lordship to assume the body of some creature that the people of the town had dominion over.

"For," he said, "it would be familiar to them, and they would never imagine that one of these lowly creatures would attack the town. And to blind them to our tactics, let Diabolus assume the body of a beast that Mansoul considers to be wiser than the rest." This advice was applauded by all of them, and it was determined that the giant Diabolus should assume the body of a dragon.

They then proceeded to the third proposal which was whether or not they should make their intentions known to Mansoul. This also was answered in the negative because the inhabitants of Mansoul were a strong people, living in a fortified town whose wall and gates were impregnable.

"Besides," the famous Legion pointed out, "a discovery of our intentions may make them send word to their King for help. If that is done, it will all be over for us before we have begun. Let us, therefore, assault them with pretended fairness, covering up our intentions with lies, flattery, and misleading words. We can easily feign that which will never happen and promise things they will never find. This is the way to win Mansoul and to make them voluntarily open their gates to us and invite us to come in.

"This project will work because the people of Mansoul are all very simple and innocent, all honest and true. As yet they do not know what it is to be assaulted with fraud, trickery, and hypocrisy. They are strangers to lying and deceitful lips. Therefore, we are disguised by these tactics and by them we cannot be discerned. Our lies will go for true sayings, and our deceitfulness for upright dealings. They will believe what we promise them, especially if we pretend to have great love for them and convince them that we desire only their welfare and honor." There was not one reply against this idea, and it was unanimously accepted.

The last proposal they considered was whether they should give orders to some of their company to kill a few leaders of the town. This was carried in the affirmative. The man designated to be destroyed was Mr. Resistance, otherwise called Captain Resistance. The giant Diabolus and his band feared him more than they feared the town of Mansoul as a whole. But who should be the one to murder him? That was the next question. So they appointed Tisiphone, the terror of the Lake of Fire, to do it.

Having ended their council of war, these scoundrels rose up and secretly crept toward Mansoul. Diabolus, however, boldly approached the town disguised in the body of the dragon.

They came to the city wall and sat down before Ear Gate because that was the place of audience for anyone who desired to enter the town. Tisiphone came within bow-shot and prepared to ambush Captain Resistance. Then the giant Diabolus moved up to the gate and called to the town of Mansoul for audience. He took no one with him except Ill-Pause who was his orator in all difficult matters.

When Diabolus sounded his trumpet for audience, the chief men of the town of Mansoul—Lord Innocent, Lord Willbewill, Mayor Understanding, Mr. Conscience, and Captain Resistance—came up on the wall to see who was there and what was the matter. Lord Willbewill looked over and saw the dragon standing at the gate. He demanded to know who he was, the reason he had come, and why he roused the town of Mansoul with such an unusual sound.

Diabolus, as if he were a lamb, began his oration and said, "Gentlemen of the famous town of Mansoul, I am a neighbor of yours and one bound by the King to honor you and render what service I can.

There is a matter of concern I would like to discuss with you. Please grant me your audience and hear me patiently. First of all, I assure you it is not my own but your welfare that I seek. This will become obvious in what I have to share with you. For, gentlemen, I have come to show you how you may obtain deliverance from the bondage that, unknown to yourselves, you are captivated and enslaved under.''

At this the people of Mansoul began to prick up their ears. They thought, ''What is it? What is it?''

Diabolus continued, ''I have something to say to you concerning your King, concerning his law, and also touching yourselves. Concerning your King, I know he is great and powerful, yet all that he has said to you is neither true nor for your advantage. It is slavery to live in fear of death for doing so small and trivial a thing as eating a little fruit. If you do as he has forbidden, the terror he has promised will not come to pass or be fulfilled. In addition, his laws are both unreasonable, complex, and intolerable. They are unreasonable because the punishment is not proportional to the offense. There is a great difference between life and an apple, yet by the law of your Shaddai one must be given for the other.

''His laws are also extremely complex. He says you may eat of all the fruits, yet afterward he forbids the eating of this one. His laws are intolerable because that fruit which you are forbidden to eat will, by your eating, endow you with powers previously unknown to you. This is evident by the name

13

of the tree. It is called the 'tree of knowledge of good and evil.' Do you have that knowledge yet? No. And as long as you comply with your King's commandment, you cannot conceive how good, how pleasant, and how much to be desired to make one wise it is. Why should you continue to be held in ignorance and blindness? Why should you not be increased in knowledge and understanding?

"Inhabitants of the famous town of Mansoul, you are not a free people! You are kept both in bondage and slavery by an oppressive threat with no reason being given. Is it not grievous to consider that the very thing you are forbidden to do, if you were to do it, would yield you both wisdom and honor? Then your eyes will be opened, and you will be like gods.

"Since he has made this law, can you be kept by any prince in more slavery and in greater bondage than you are under today? You are enslaved and repressed as I have made it appear. What greater bondage is there than to be kept in blindness? Does reason not tell you that it is better to have eyes than to be without them and that freedom is better than being confined in a dark and stinking cave?"

While Diabolus was speaking these words to Mansoul, Tisiphone shot at Captain Resistance who was standing on the wall above the gate. The arrow hit the captain and mortally wounded him in the head. To the amazement of the townsmen and to the satisfaction of Diabolus, the captain fell over the wall to his death.

The slaying of Captain Resistance, the only man of war in the town, left poor Mansoul completely void of courage with no heart to resist. But this was as Diabolus had planned it. Then Mr. Ill-Pause, his spokesman, came forward and addressed the townsfolk.

"Gentlemen," said Mr. Ill-Pause, "it gives my master great joy to have the opportunity to speak with you today. We hope that we can persuade you to accept our good advice. My master has great love for you. Although he runs the risk of angering King Shaddai, his love for you will make him do even more than that. It is not necessary to say anything else to confirm the truth of what he has said. The name of the tree puts an end to all controversy in this matter. I, therefore, at this time only add this advice to you, with the permission of my lord," and with that he bowed low before Diabolus.

"Consider my master's words; look on the tree and its promising fruit. Remember, too, that you know so little and that this is the way to know more. If you do not accept our good counsel, you are not the men that I took you to be."

While Ill-Pause was making his speech to the townsmen, something terrible happened to Lord Innocent. It may have been an arrow shot from the camp of the giant or the stinking breath of that treacherous villain old Ill-Pause that caused him to collapse in the place where he stood. But Lord Innocent could not be brought to life again. Thus these two brave men, Captain Resistance and Lord Innocent, died. Brave men I call them, for they were the beauty and glory of Mansoul as long as they lived there. Now, not one noble spirit remained in Mansoul.

The rest of the townsfolk were like men who had found a fool's paradise. When they saw that the tree was good for food, pleasant to the eye, and a tree to be desired to make one wise, they did as old Ill-Pause advised. They took the fruit and ate it. And having eaten, they immediately became drunk with the nectar and opened both Ear Gate and Eye Gate.

The people of Mansoul let Diabolus in with all his hosts, forgetting their good King Shaddai, his law, and the judgment he had warned would come if they disobeyed.

Chapter Two

MANSOUL'S REBELLION

Diabolus, having obtained entrance at the gates, marched up to the center of the town to make his conquest as secure as he could. By this time the affections of the people were warmly inclined toward him. Thinking it was best to strike while the iron was hot, he made another beguiling speech to them.

"Alas, my poor Mansoul, I have done you this service to promote you to honor and to increase your freedom. But, poor Mansoul, you need someone to defend you. When Shaddai hears what has happened, he will surely come. He will be sorry that you have broken his bonds and cast his cords away from you. What will you do? Will you allow your new privileges to be taken away? What will you determine to do?"

With one voice the townsmen said to this imposter, "You reign over us." So he accepted the motion and became the king of Mansoul. Next, they gave him possession of the castle, and he gained power over the town. The castle which Shaddai had built in Mansoul for his own delight and pleasure became a den and hideout for the giant Diabolus. He made it a garrison for himself and fortified the castle against Shaddai or anyone who would attempt to regain it for their former King.

Thinking his position was not secure enough, Diabolus decided to restructure the town's government by setting up one person and putting down another at his pleasure. The mayor, whose name was Lord Understanding, and Mr. Conscience, the recorder, were removed from their positions of power.

The mayor had complied with the townsmen in admitting the giant into Mansoul, yet Diabolus thought it was not fitting to let him remain in his former exalted state because he was a man of discernment. Therefore, he darkened his situation not only by taking away his office and power but by building a high, strong tower between the sun's reflection and the windows of the mayor's mansion. This made his entire residence as dark as darkness itself; and being alienated from the light, he became as one who was born blind. Lord Understanding's house became his prison, and he could not go beyond the boundaries of his own property. He had a desire to help Mansoul, but what could he do or how could he be profitable to her? As long as Mansoul was under the power and government of Diabolus, the mayor was an impediment rather than an advantage to the famous town.

Before the town was taken, Mr. Conscience had

been the chief magistrate and a man well-versed in the laws of his King. He was also a man of courage and faithfulness who spoke the truth at every occasion. Although Mr. Conscience had consented to Diabolus' entering the town, the giant could not, with all his tricks, strategies, and devices, win him over completely. It is true that Mr. Conscience's allegiance to his former King had deteriorated and he was pleased with many of the giant's laws and services, but he would still now and then think about Shaddai and fear his judgment. At those times, he would speak against Diabolus with a voice as loud as a lion's roar. When his anger was aroused, the whole town of Mansoul would shake from the sound of his voice. For this reason, the new king of Mansoul could not tolerate him.

Diabolus feared Mr. Conscience, the recorder, more than anyone in Mansoul because his words were like booming thunder. Since the giant could not make him wholly his own, he studied how he could ruin the old gentleman with debauchery, stupefy his mind, and harden his heart in pride. As he attempted, so he accomplished his purpose. He corrupted the man little by little and drew him into sin and wickedness until his conscience was seared beyond all conviction of sin.

To further reduce the old man's influence, Diabolus thought of a way to persuade the men of the town that Mr. Conscience was insane and not to be taken seriously. The giant encouraged the recorder's fits of anger and said, ''If he is really in his right mind, why does he act this way? Like all raving lunatics, this doting old gentleman also has his hysterical outbursts.''

By one means or another, he quickly got Mansoul to despise and reject whatever Mr. Conscience said. Diabolus had a way of making the old gentleman, when he was in good spirits, deny what he had raved about during his angry fits. In this way he made him look ridiculous and kept anyone from seriously considering his arguments.

Mr. Conscience, however, never spoke freely for King Shaddai, but he always preached by force and constraint. At one time he would be vehemently against a matter, while at another time he would hold his peace. His behavior became extremely unbalanced. Sometimes he would act as if he were fast asleep or dead, while the whole town of Mansoul went chasing after vanity and dancing to the giant's pipe.

When Mansoul was frightened by the thundering voice of Mr. Conscience, the people would tell Diabolus about it. He would answer that the old gentleman spoke, not out of love for Shaddai or compassion for them, but as a result of his obsession for foolish chatter.

In order to leave no room for argument, Diabolus often said, ''O Mansoul! Consider that in spite of the old gentleman's ranting and the rattle of his thundering words, you hear nothing from Shaddai himself.'' (What a liar and deceiver Diabolus was, for every outcry of Mr. Conscience against the sin of Mansoul was the voice of God speaking to them.)

Diabolus went on and said, "You see that Shaddai does not value the loss or rebellion of Mansoul, nor will he trouble himself to call you to account for giving yourselves to me. He knows that, although you were once his, now you are lawfully mine; so leaving us to one another, he has washed his hands of us.

"Moreover, O Mansoul," he continued, "consider how I have served you with all my power and given the best that I have or could procure for you. Besides, the laws and customs that you are now under bring you more peace and contentment than the paradise you had before. Your liberty also, as you know, has been greatly increased by me. Remember, I found you an enslaved people, yet I have not put any restraints on you. You have no law or judgment of mine to frighten you. I call none of you to account for your ways, except the madman—you know who I mean. I have permitted you to live, each man like a prince in his own domain, with as little control from me as I myself have from you."

In this way Diabolus quieted the town of Mansoul when Mr. Conscience, the recorder, tried to stir them up. With such terrible lies as these, the giant could turn the whole town into an angry mob against the old gentleman. They despised his company, his words, and even the sight of him, especially when they remembered how he used to threaten and condemn them. Now, in his depraved condition, he terrified them even more. They often wished he lived a thousand miles away from them.

But all their wishes were in vain. I do not know how Mr. Conscience was preserved unless by the power of Shaddai and his wisdom. The recorder's house, moreover, was as sturdy as a castle and stood like a stronghold in the town. If any of the angry mob attempted to capture him, he could flood the moat and drown everyone surrounding his house.

Let us leave Mr. Conscience and come to Lord Willbewill, another member of the aristocracy of Mansoul. He came from a wealthy family and owned more property than many of the other men. In addition, King Shaddai had given Lord Willbewill special privileges that no one else in the town possessed. It may have been his position and privileges that caused him to avoid taking a stand against the tyrant. He, therefore, resolved to obtain an appointment under Diabolus as some kind of ruler and governor in Mansoul. Being the headstrong man that he was, he willfully pursued his ambition.

When Diabolus made his speech at Ear Gate, Willbewill was one of the first who consented to his words and agreed to open the gate. For this reason, Diabolus was kind to him and designed an official position for him. Recognizing Willbewill's strength and determination, Diabolus desired to have him as one of his chief advisors in matters of the highest concern.

Diabolus sent for him and talked with Willbewill about this secret matter, but there was little need for persuasion. Just as he had been willing for Diabolus to enter the town, so now he was willing to serve him. When the tyrant perceived this, he made Lord Willbewill the captain of the castle, governor of the wall, and keeper of the gates of Mansoul. In fact, there was a clause in his commission that nothing should be done in all the town without his consent.

Lord Willbewill was second only to Diabolus himself in Mansoul. His clerk was Mr. Mind, a man in every way like his master; he and Lord Willbewill were one in principle and in practice. Mansoul was now brought under control and made to fulfill the lusts of the will and of the mind.

What a desperate man this Willbewill was, when power was put into his hand! First, he flatly denied that he owed any service to his former Prince and Lord. Then, he took an oath and swore allegiance to his great master, Diabolus, and quickly settled into his new position of authority and ambition. You cannot imagine, unless you had seen it, the strange work that Willbewill did in the town of Mansoul.

First, he maligned Mr. Conscience, the recorder. He could not endure seeing him or hearing the words of his mouth. Willbewill shut his eyes when he saw him and stopped his ears when he heard him speak. In addition, he could not endure even a fragment of the law of Shaddai to be seen anywhere in the town. His clerk, Mr. Mind, had some old, torn parchments of Shaddai's law in his house. When Willbewill saw them, he threw them into the fire.

Mr. Conscience also had some of the laws in his study, but Lord Willbewill could not get at them.

Nothing pleased Willbewill except that which pleased Diabolus, his lord. He extolled the brave nature, the wise conduct, and the great glory of King Diabolus, praising his illustrious lord throughout all the streets of Mansoul. He even joined the ranks of the lowly, evil Diabolonian creatures and made himself like one of them—acting without permission and doing mischief without command.

Lord Willbewill had a deputy under him named Mr. Affection. He was also a man of low principle who was wholly given to the desires of the flesh; therefore, they called him Vile Affection. He married Carnal Lust, the daughter of Mr. Mind, and they had three sons—Impudent, Blackmouth, and Hate-Reproof. They also had three daughters—Scorn-Truth, Slight-God, and the name of the youngest was Revenge. These all married and yielded many incorrigible brats, too many to be named here.

After the giant, Diabolus, had garrisoned himself in the town of Mansoul, he began to destroy all reminders of the former King. In the marketplace and over the gates of the castle, there was a golden image of the blessed King Shaddai. Diabolus commanded that the image be defaced, and this vile deed was done by Mr. No-Truth. The order was also given that the same Mr. No-Truth should set up in its place the horrible and formidable image of Diabolus.

Moreover, Diabolus made havoc of all the laws

of Shaddai that could be found in the town. He destroyed anything that contained the doctrine of morals, along with all civil statutes. Nothing good remained in Mansoul which he and Willbewill did not try to destroy. Their design was to turn Mansoul into a wicked, sensual city by the hand of Mr. No-Truth.

When he had destroyed as much of the law and order as he could, Diabolus furthered his purpose of alienating Mansoul from Shaddai her King. He set up his own vain edicts, statutes, and commandments in every place of amusement and recreation in Mansoul. He did this with the purpose of giving free license to the lusts of the flesh, the lusts of the eyes, and the pride of life—all of which are not of Shaddai but of the world. He encouraged and promoted lasciviousness and all ungodliness. The townsmen were promised peace, contentment, and joy in doing his commands. They even believed his lie that they would never be called to account for their rebellion against their former King.

Mansoul was now thoroughly under the giant's control, and nothing was heard or seen except that which exalted Diabolus. Having disabled Mayor Understanding and Mr. Conscience from bearing office in Mansoul, he then chose a mayor and a recorder for himself.

The name of the mayor that Diabolus chose was Lord Lustings. He had neither eyes nor ears; and everything he did, whether as a man or as an official, he did as naturally as a savage. But that which made him even more vulgar was that he always chose evil over good.

The recorder chosen by Diabolus was named Forget-Good, and a sorry fellow he was. He could remember nothing except mischief and how to do it with delight. He was naturally prone to do things that were harmful to the town and its inhabitants. These two men, by their power, practice, and evil example, did much to introduce and settle the common people into harmful ways. We all know that when those who are in positions of authority are vile and wicked, they corrupt the whole country where they live.

In addition to these two men, Diabolus selected several representatives and aldermen from whom the town could choose officers, governors, and magistrates. These are the names of the most important Diabolonians: Mr. Unbelief, Mr. Haughty, Mr. Swearing, Mr. Hardheart, Mr. Pitiless, Mr. Fury, Mr. No-Truth, Mr. Tell-Lies, Mr. False-Peace, Mr. Drunkenness, Mr. Cheating, and Mr. Atheism. The eldest was Mr. Unbelief, and Mr. Atheism was the youngest of the company. There was also an election of councilmen, bailiffs, constables, and others, all of whom were either fathers, brothers, cousins, or nephews to the ones named before.

When the giant had thus far proceeded in his work, he next began to build some strongholds in the town. He built three that seemed impregnable. The first he called the Stronghold of Defiance because it was made to command the whole town and keep it from the knowledge of its former King. The second he called Fort Midnight because it was built to keep Mansoul from true wisdom. The third was called Sweet-Sin because it fortified Mansoul against all desire for good. The first of these strongholds stood close by Eye Gate in order to keep out the light. The second was built near Lord Understanding's house so that it might be made even darker. The third stood in the marketplace.

Diabolus appointed a governor over the first of these strongholds. His name was Spite-God, and he was a most blasphemous fellow. He had been among the mob that came with Diabolus to take Mansoul. The governor of Fort Midnight was one called Love-No-Light. He was also among those who first came against the town. The governor of the stronghold called Sweet-Sin was one named Love-Flesh. He was a very lewd fellow, and he could find more sweetness in lust than in all the paradise of God.

Now Diabolus thought he was safe because he had captured Mansoul and garrisoned himself within the city. He had put down the old officers and set up new ones. He had defaced the image of Shaddai and set up his own. He had spoiled the old law books and promoted his own vain lies. He had appointed new magistrates and set up new aldermen. He had built new strongholds and manned them with his own gang. He did all this to make himself secure in case the good Shaddai or his Son should try to invade the town.

Chapter Three

COMMISSIONED BY THE KING

You may think that, long before this time, word would have been carried to the good King Shaddai, telling how his Mansoul in the continent of Universe was lost. Surely he would have heard that the fugitive giant Diabolus, once one of his Majesty's servants, had rebelled against the King and taken the town for himself.

Yes, this news was brought to the King. He was told how Diabolus came upon the simple and innocent people of Mansoul and tricked them with deception, cunning, and guile. The messenger described how Diabolus had treacherously slain the noble and valiant Captain Resistance as he stood upon the gate with the rest of the townsmen. He repeated how Lord Innocent fell down dead when he heard Shaddai being abused by the mouth of filthy Ill-Pause.

The messenger further told how, after Ill-Pause had made a short speech in behalf of Diabolus, the simple townspeople believed that what he said was true. With one consent, they opened Ear Gate and let him, along with his crew, take possession of the famous town of Mansoul. He further told how Diabolus had removed Lord Understanding and Mr. Conscience from any position of power and trust.

The messenger also reported that Lord Willbewill had turned into a rebel along with Mr. Mind, his clerk. He told how these two roamed all over the town, teaching the wicked ones their ways. He said, moreover, that Diabolus had put Willbewill in control of all the strong places in Mansoul. He also told how Mr. Affection was made Lord Willbewill's deputy in his most rebellious affairs.

"Yes," said the messenger, "this monster, Lord Willbewill, has openly disowned his King Shaddai and has horribly given his allegiance to Diabolus. Besides all this, the new king, or rather the rebellious tyrant, has set up a mayor and a recorder of his own. For mayor he has appointed Mr. Lustings and for recorder, Mr. Forget-Good—two of the vilest men in all the town of Mansoul."

This faithful messenger also proceeded to tell that Diabolus had built several strong forts, towers, and strongholds in Mansoul. He told, too, how Diabolus had armed the town in order to resist Shaddai their King, should he come to subject them to their former obedience.

The messenger's information was not delivered in private but in open court before King Shaddai, Prince Emmanuel, and all the captains, and noblemen. When they heard the whole story, they were overcome with sorrow and grief to think that famous Mansoul was now taken. Only the King and his Son had foreseen this happening and had sufficiently provided for the relief of Mansoul, although they had not told anyone about it. Yet, they also greatly mourned the loss of Mansoul. The King said plainly that it grieved his heart, and you may be sure that his Son was also saddened. Everyone in the King's court knew of their great love and compassion for the famous town of Mansoul.

When the King and his Son retired to their private chambers, they again discussed what they had planned to do if Mansoul should ever be lost and how it could be recovered. They planned to rescue it in such a way that both the King and his Son would receive eternal fame and glory.

Emmanuel, the Son of Shaddai, was a kind and handsome Prince who always had great affection for those who were suffering affliction. But he had enmity in his heart against Diabolus because he had sought to take his crown and dignity. This Son of Shaddai, having promised his Father that he would recover Mansoul, stood by this decision and would not change his mind. He had agreed, at a certain predetermined time, to take a journey to the country of Universe. By means of justice and equity he would make restitution for the wickedness of Mansoul and would lay the foundation for her perfect deliverance from the tyranny of Diabolus.

Emmanuel resolved to make war against the giant Diabolus and drive him out of his stronghold, retaking Mansoul for his own habitation. The order was given to the Lord Chief Secretary to draw up an account of what was determined and to publish it in all the corners of Universe. A summary of the contents of this account is as follows:

"Let all men know that the Son of Shaddai, the great King, has made a covenant with his Father to bring Mansoul back under his dominion. Through the power of his matchless love, he plans to bring Mansoul into a far better and happier condition than it was before it was taken by Diabolus."

These papers were published in several places, to the annoyance of the tyrant Diabolus. "For now," he thought, "I will be overthrown, and my habitation will be taken from me."

When this purpose of the King and his Son first became known in the court, the high lords, chief captains, and noblemen were very interested. At first they whispered it to one another. But after a while it began to ring throughout the palace, and everyone was amazed at the glorious plan that the King and his Son had undertaken for the miserable town of Mansoul. The courtiers spoke fervently of the love that the King and his Son had for the town.

Diabolus was at first perplexed to hear of such a plan against him. But after thinking about it, he concluded that this news should be kept from the ears of the townsmen. "For," he said, "if they come to know that their former King and Emmanuel his Son are planning to help the town of Mansoul, what can I expect? Mansoul will revolt from under my government and return again to him.''

To accomplish his purpose, Diabolus renewed his flattery of Lord Willbewill and strictly commanded him to keep watch day and night at all the gates of the town, especially Ear Gate and Eye Gate. ''For I have heard of a plot,'' he said, ''to make us all traitors and put Mansoul under bondage again. I hope these are only rumors. Nevertheless, let no such news get into Mansoul, lest the people become disheartened. I think, my lord, this is not welcome news to you; I am sure it is not to me. At this time we must use all our wisdom and care to nip such troublesome rumors in the bud. For this reason, my lord, I hope you will do as I say and put strong guards daily at every gate of the town. They must stop and examine every foreigner who comes here to trade. No one should be admitted into Mansoul unless you plainly perceive that they are supporters of our excellent government.

''I command, moreover,'' said Diabolus, ''that there be spies continually walking up and down the streets of Mansoul. Give them power to suppress and destroy anyone they perceive to be plotting against us or talking about what Shaddai and Emmanuel intend to do.'' Lord Willbewill obeyed his master and, with all diligence, kept anyone from bringing this news into the town.

Next, Diabolus imposed a new law upon the townsfolk. He made them swear that they would never desert him or his government, never betray him, nor seek to alter his laws. They must confess and acknowledge him as their rightful king in defiance to any other who would, by pretense, law, or title, lay claim to the town of Mansoul.

The townsmen thought that Shaddai did not have power to absolve them from the covenant with death and this agreement with hell. Foolish Mansoul did not question this most monstrous arrangement; instead, they swallowed it hook, line, and sinker. Were they troubled about it? No, instead they bragged and boasted of their brave fidelity to their pretended king, swearing that they would never be traitors or forsake their old lord for a new one.

In this way, Diabolus put poor Mansoul into bondage. But jealousy never thinks it is strong enough, so Diabolus set out to corrupt the town of Mansoul. He had Mr. Filth, an odious, nasty, lascivious beast, write a proclamation and publicize it on the castle gates. This edict granted and gave license to all his true followers in Mansoul to do whatever their lustful appetites prompted them to do. No one was to hinder or control them without incurring the displeasure and punishment of their diabolical ruler.

His purpose in this was to make Mansoul weaker and weaker. Then, if the news of their redemption reached them, they would be unable to believe, hope, or consent to the truth of it. Diabolus reasoned, "The bigger the sinner, the less hope of mercy."

His evil mind thought that if Emmanuel saw the horrible and profane deeds of the town of Mansoul, he might change his mind about redeeming them. Diabolus knew that Shaddai was holy and that his Son, Emmanuel, was also holy. Yes, he knew this from experience. He had been cast from the highest realms because of his own iniquity and sin. For this reason, he concluded that Mansoul's sin would result in the same fate.

But afraid this knot would also break, he thought of another scheme. He planned to convince the town that Shaddai was forming an army to come to overthrow and utterly destroy Mansoul. He did this to forestall any news they might hear concerning their deliverance. "For," he thought, "if I first start this rumor, the news that comes later will appear to be false. When they hear that they are to be delivered, they will think, instead, that Shaddai intends to destroy them."

Diabolus then summoned the whole town into the marketplace and with deceitful words spoke to the people. "Gentlemen and my very good friends, you are all, as you know, my legal subjects and men of the famous town of Mansoul. You know how I have behaved among you and what liberty and great privileges you have enjoyed under my government—I hope to your honor and delight. Now, my friends, some troublesome news has come to my attention. I have received from Lord Lucifer reliable information that your old King Shaddai is raising up an army to come against you and destroy you. I have called you together to discuss what is best to be done in this crisis situation. I could easily escape and leave Mansoul to face this danger alone. But my heart is firmly united to you, and I am unwilling to leave you. I am willing to stand and fall with you, despite any harm that may come to me. What do you say, O my Mansoul? Will you now desert your old friend, or will you stand by me?''

Then as one man with one mouth, they cried out together, "If anyone deserts our king, let him die!"

Then Diabolus said again, "It is vain for us to hope for mercy, for this King does not know how to show it. True, perhaps, he may sit down with us and talk of mercy so that with more ease and less trouble, he may again make himself the master of Mansoul; therefore, do not believe one syllable he says. All such language is spoken to overcome us and to make us, while we wallow in our blood, the trophies of his merciless victory. We must resolve, to the last man, to resist him and not to believe him on any terms. Will we be flattered out of our lives? I hope you know more about the rudiments of politics than to allow yourselves to be fooled by him.

"But suppose he should, if he gets us to yield, save some of our lives or the lives of some of them that are underlings in Mansoul. What help will that be to you who are the rulers of the town, especially you whom I have set up and whose greatness has been procured by your faithful allegiance to me? And suppose that he should give mercy to every one of you; be sure he will bring you into that bondage under which you were captivated before, or even worse. Then what good will your lives do you? Under his rule, will you live in pleasure as you do now? No, no, you will be bound by laws that will inhibit you. You will be made to do that which at present is unpleasant to you.

"I am for you, if you are for me. It is better to die valiantly, than to live like pitiful slaves. But I say, the life of a slave will be considered a life too good for Mansoul now. Blood, blood, nothing but blood is in every blast of Shaddai's trumpet against poor Mansoul. Listen to me; I hear he is coming. Take up your arms so that now, while there is time, I can teach you some feats of war. I have armor for you from head to toe, and his forces will not hurt you if you keep it fastened about you. Come to my castle and prepare yourselves for the war. There are helmets, breastplates, swords, and shields that will make you fight like men.

"My helmet, otherwise called a headpiece, is hope of doing well in spite of the circumstances. Those who wear it say that they will be safe even though they insist on doing things their own way. This stubbornness of heart is a piece of approved armor, and whoever has it is protected against any arrow, dart, sword, or shield. If you wear it always, you will prevent many blows, my Mansoul.

"My breastplate is a breastplate of iron. I had it forged in my own country, and all my soldiers are armed with one. In plain language it is a hard heart, a heart as hard as iron and as unfeeling as a stone. If you get and keep it, you will have no mercy on others. This, therefore, is a piece of armor most necessary for all who hate Shaddai and who fight against him under my banner.

"My sword is a tongue that is set on fire by hell and speaks evil of Shaddai, his Son, his ways, and people. This weapon has been used successfully thousands of times. Whoever has it and uses it as I have told him can never be conquered by my enemy.

"My shield is unbelief—the calling into question the truth of the Word and all the sayings that speak of the judgment that Shaddai has appointed for wicked men. Use this shield to protect yourself. He has made many attempts against it, and it has sometimes been damaged. But in the record of the wars of Emmanuel against my servants, many have testified that he could do no mighty work because of their unbelief. To handle this weapon properly, it is essential not to believe things because they are true, in spite of the manner in which they are spoken or by whom. If the enemy speaks of judgment, do not worry about it. If he speaks of mercy, do not take it to heart. If he promises that he will do good to Mansoul if you repent, do not regard what is said. Question the truth of everything. This is the way to wield the shield of unbelief properly as my servants should and do. He who does otherwise will be considered my enemy.

"Another piece," said Diabolus, "of my excellent armor is a silent and prayerless spirit, a spirit that despises crying for mercy. Be sure, my Mansoul, that you make use of this piece of armor. What! Cry for mercy? Never do that if you want to be my soldiers! I know you are mighty men, and I am sure that I have clad you with strong armor. Therefore, do not even consider crying to Shaddai for mercy."

After he had furnished his men with armor and weapons, Diabolus addressed himself to them. "Remember," he said, "I am your rightful king. You have taken an oath and entered into a covenant to be true to me and my cause. Show yourselves as brave and valiant men of Mansoul. Remember also the kindness that I always showed to you and all the wonderful things I have granted you. The privileges, immunities, pleasures, and honors I have given you require your loyalty to me in return. What better time to show it than when another seeks to take my dominion over you into their own hands. One more word and I am finished. If we can stand against this one attack, I would not doubt that, in a short time, all the world will be ours. When that day comes, my true hearts, I will make you kings, princes, and captains. What great days we will have then!"

Diabolus thus armed his servants and vassals in Mansoul against their good and lawful King Shaddai. Next, he doubled his guards at the gates of the town and barricaded himself in his stronghold at the castle. His vassals, to show their supposed gallantry, trained and practiced every day, teaching one another feats of war. They also defied their enemies and sang the praises of their tyrant. They bragged about how gallant they would be if a war should ever arise between Shaddai and their king.

Now all this time, the good King Shaddai was preparing to send an army to recover the town of Mansoul from under the tyranny of their pretended king, Diabolus. But he thought it best, at first, not to send them under the leadership of brave Emmanuel his Son. Instead, he decided to have the army led by some of his servants. They were to determine the disposition of Mansoul and see whether they could be won back to the obedience of their King without a battle. So an army of more than forty thousand men was chosen by Shaddai himself from among his own court.

They came to Mansoul under the leadership of four brave generals, each man being a captain of ten thousand men. In all his wars, Shaddai placed these four captains in the forefront because they were very brave and rough-hewn men who were able to make their way by the force of the sword. To each of these captains, the King gave a banner to be displayed showing the goodness of the cause and the right he had to Mansoul.

Captain Thunder was the chief general. His ensign's name was Mr. Lightning, and he carried a black banner. The emblem on his shield was three burning thunderbolts.

The second captain was Captain Conviction, and his ensign, Mr. Sorrow, carried a pale-colored banner. The emblem on his shield was the book of law shown wide open with a flame of fire coming from it.

The third captain, Captain Judgment, had Mr. Terror as his ensign. He carried a red banner with the emblem of a burning, fiery furnace.

The fourth captain was Captain Execution. His ensign was Mr. Justice, and he also carried a banner of red. His emblem was a fruitless tree with an axe lying at the root of it.

These four captains each commanded ten thousand men, all loyal and faithful to the King and mighty in military action.

The King mustered his forces and gave the captains their orders in the audience of all the soldiers. Their commissions were basically the same, although there were some variations in position of authority. Let me give you an account of their commission.

"A Commission from the great Shaddai, King of Mansoul, to his trustworthy and noble captain Thunder, for him to make war upon the town of Mansoul.

"Oh! My brave and thundering captain over ten thousand of my valiant and faithful servants, go in my name with your force to the miserable town of Mansoul. When you get there, offer them conditions of peace. Command them to cast off the yoke and tyranny of the wicked Diabolus and return to me, their rightful Prince and Lord. Command them also to cleanse themselves from all that is his in the town, but make sure you are satisfied with the truth of their obedience. If they sincerely submit to your commands, then do everything in your power to set up a garrison in the famous town of Mansoul. Do not harm the least native who lives there, if they will submit themselves to me. Treat them as if they were your friends or brothers; for I love them, and they are dear to me. Tell them that I will take time to come to them and let them know that I am merciful.

"But if they resist, in spite of your summons, and rebel against you, then I command you to use all power, might, and force to bring them under your control. Farewell."

The commissions were the same for the other noble captains.

Having received their authority at the hand of the King, the day was appointed and the place of their rendezvous determined. On that day each commander appeared in great gallantry in keeping with his cause and calling. With banners flying high, they set out to march toward the famous town of Mansoul. Captain Thunder led the troops while Captain Conviction and Captain Judgment made up the main body. Captain Execution brought up the rear.

They had a long way to go because the town of Mansoul was far from the court of Shaddai. They marched through the regions and countries of many people, not harming or abusing any, but blessing everyone wherever they went. They also lived on the King's provisions all along the way.

Chapter Four

THE CAPTAINS' INVITATION

Having traveled for many days, at last the King's captains came within sight of Mansoul. When they saw it, the captains could do nothing less than mourn over the condition of the town. They quickly saw how it had fallen under the will of Diabolus and his ways.

The captains came up before the wall of the town and marched up to Ear Gate. After they had pitched their tents and entrenched themselves, they began to plan how to make their assault.

When the townsfolk observed this gallant company, so bravely outfitted and so excellently disciplined, wearing their glittering armor and displaying their flying colors, they came out of their houses and gazed. But the cunning fox, Diabolus, feared that the people might, on seeing this sight, open the gates to the captains. So he immediately came down from the castle and made the townsmen move to the center of Mansoul where he made this deceitful speech to them.

"Gentlemen," Diabolus said, "although you are my trustworthy and beloved friends, I must chide you for your uncircumspect action in going out to gaze on that great and mighty force which only yesterday entrenched themselves in order to attack the town. Do you know who they are, where they come from, and what is their purpose in encamping before the town of Mansoul? They are those whom I told you would come to destroy this town. It's against them I have been equipping you with armor for your body and great fortifications for your mind. At the first appearance of the enemy, you were supposed to cry out, 'Fire the beacons!' You were to send the alarm so the whole town would have been in a posture of defense, ready to receive them with the highest acts of defiance. I would have been pleased if you had done this, but instead you have made me afraid. I am worried that when we come to battle, I will find you lacking the courage to stand against them to the end.

"Why do you think I have commanded that you should double your guards at the gates? Why do you think I have endeavored to make you as hard as iron and your hearts like a piece of millstone? Was it so that you could show yourselves like a company of children gazing on your mortal enemies? Arise! Put yourselves into a posture of defense, beat the drum, gather together in a warlike manner so our foes may know that there are valiant men in the town of Mansoul.

"I will stop scolding you now and will not further rebuke you. But I charge you to let me not see such actions again. Let no one, without order first obtained from me, so much as show his head over the wall of the town of Mansoul. You have now heard me. Do as I have commanded, and we will dwell securely together. I will care for your safety and honor just as I do for my own. Farewell."

Now the townsmen were strangely affected by these words. They were stricken with fear. They ran to and fro throughout the streets of the town crying out, "Help, help! The men who turn the world upside down have come here, too." They would not be quiet, but acted like madmen, shouting, "The destroyers of our peace have come!"

Diabolus was pleased with them and said to himself, "This is as I would have it; now you are showing your obedience to me. Keep this up, and then let them take the town if they can."

The King's forces had been encamped before Mansoul three days when Captain Thunder commanded his trumpeter to summon Mansoul to give audience to the message that he, in his Master's name, was commanded to deliver. So the trumpeter, whose name was Take-Heed-What-You-Hear, went up to Ear Gate and sounded his trumpet. But no one appeared and answered, as Diabolus had commanded. So the trumpeter returned to his captain and told him what he had done and what had happened. The captain was grieved at this and told the trumpeter to go to his tent.

At a later time, Captain Thunder again sent his

44

trumpeter to Ear Gate to sound for a hearing. But the people would not come out or give him an answer because they were obedient to the command of Diabolus their king.

Then the captains and other field officers called a council of war to consider what else could be done to gain the town of Mansoul. After some debate over the contents of their commissions, they decided to give the town another summons. If they still refused to listen, they would try to force them to submit to their King.

Captain Thunder commanded his trumpeter to go up to Ear Gate again and, in the name of the great King Shaddai, to loudly summon them to come down without delay to give audience to the King's most noble captains. So the trumpeter went up to Ear Gate, sounded his trumpet, and gave a third summons to Mansoul. He said that if they still refused to obey, the captains of this Prince would come down upon them and endeavor to force them to submit.

Lord Willbewill, the governor of the town and the keeper of the gates of Mansoul, stood up to speak. He demanded the trumpeter to tell who he was, from where he came, and the reason he was making noise at the gate and speaking such insufferable words against the town of Mansoul.

The trumpeter answered, "I am servant to the most noble Captain Thunder, general of the forces of the great King Shaddai, against whom both you and the whole town of Mansoul have rebelled. The captain has a special message to this town and to you as a member of it. If you do not listen peacefully, you must take what follows."

Then Lord Willbewill said, "I will carry your message to my lord and will see what he says."

But the trumpeter replied, saying, "Our message is not to the giant Diabolus but to the miserable town of Mansoul. We will not even regard any answer made by him or for him. We are sent to this town to recover it from under his cruel tyranny and to persuade it to submit, as in former times it did, to the most excellent King Shaddai."

Lord Willbewill said, "I will take your message to the town."

The trumpeter then replied, "Sir, do not deceive us, lest in so doing you deceive yourselves much more. For we are resolved, if you do not submit yourselves in a peaceful manner, to make war against you and to force you to submit. As confirmation of what I have said, there will be a sign. Tomorrow you will see the black flag with its hot, burning thunderbolts mounted as a token of defiance against your prince and as a sign of our resolution to reclaim you for your Lord and rightful King."

Lord Willbewill came down from the wall, and the trumpeter returned to the camp. When the trumpeter arrived, the King's captains and officers gathered together to know if he had obtained a hearing and what was the effect of his errand. So the trumpeter told them, saying, "When I had sounded my trumpet and called aloud to the town for a hearing, Lord Willbewill, the governor of the town, looked over the wall and asked me who I was, from where I came, and the reason for my making this noise. So I told him my errand and by whose authority I brought it. 'Then,' said he, 'I will tell it to Mansoul.' ''

Then the brave Captain Thunder said, "Let us for a while, lie still in our trenches and see what these rebels will do.''

When the time drew near for Mansoul to give audience to the brave Captain Thunder and his companions, all the men of war throughout the whole camp of Shaddai were commanded to stand to arms. They made themselves ready to receive the town with mercy if Mansoul should submit, but if not, they were prepared to force a subjection. The day came, the trumpeters sounded, and throughout the whole camp the men of war prepared for the work of the day.

When the townspeople heard the sound of the trumpets throughout the camp of Shaddai, they thought it must be the order to storm the town. At first, they were thrown into great confusion; but after they were settled again, they also began to prepare for war in case the town was attacked.

When the time came, Captain Thunder was determined to know their answer. He sent out his trumpeter again to summon Mansoul to hear the message that they had brought from Shaddai. So he sounded, and the townsmen came up on the wall. But they made Ear Gate as secure as they could.

Captain Thunder desired to see the mayor, but Lord Unbelief came up instead and showed himself over the wall. When Captain Thunder set his eyes on him, he cried out aloud, "This is not he! Where is Lord Understanding, the rightful lord mayor of the town of Mansoul? It is to him I desire to deliver my message."

Then the giant Diabolus said, "Mr. Captain, you have by your boldness given Mansoul at least four summons to subject herself to your King. By whose authority, I do not know nor will I dispute that now. I ask, therefore, what is the reason for all this commotion? And what are you about, if you yourselves know?"

Captain Thunder, whose emblem was the three burning thunderbolts, took no notice of the giant or of his speech. He addressed himself only to the town of Mansoul: "Be it known unto you, O unhappy and rebellious Mansoul, that the great King Shaddai, my master, has sent me to you with a commission," and he showed them his broad seal, "to reclaim you as his own. And he has commanded me, in case you yield to my summons, to bring this message to you as if you were my friends or brothers. But he also has said that if, after summoning you to submit, you still rebel, we should endeavor to take you by force."

Then Captain Conviction came forward and said, "O Mansoul, you were once famous for your innocence, but now you have degenerated into lies and deceit. You have heard what my brother, Captain

Thunder, has said. It would be wise of you and for your happiness to accept the conditions of peace and mercy offered by the one against whom you have rebelled—one who has the power to tear you to pieces—Shaddai our King. When he is angry, no one can stand before him. If you say you have not sinned or acted in rebellion against our King, your deeds will sufficiently testify against you. Why else did you hearken to the tyrant and receive him as your king? Why else did you reject the laws of Shaddai and obey Diabolus? Why else did you take up arms and shut your gates against us, the faithful servants of the King?

"Submit and accept my brother's invitation. Do not let the time of mercy expire, but agree with your adversary quickly. Mansoul, do not allow yourself to be kept from mercy and to be run into a thousand miseries by the flattering schemes of Diabolus. Perhaps his lies may attempt to make you believe that we seek our own advantage in this matter. But it is obedience to our King and love for your happiness that is the reason for this undertaking of ours.

"Again I say to you, O Mansoul, consider if it is not amazing grace that Shaddai should humble himself like this. He reasons with you, using his message of entreaty and sweet persuasion, so that you will subject yourselves to him. Does he need you as much as you need him? No, no, but he is merciful and will not permit Mansoul to die. Turn to him and live."

Captain Judgment, whose banner was red and

whose emblem was the burning fiery furnace, came forward and said: "O inhabitants of Mansoul, you have lived long enough in rebellion against King Shaddai. We have not come with our own message or to take revenge for ourselves. It is the King, my master, who has sent us to enforce your obedience to him. If you refuse in a peaceful way to yield, we have been commissioned to compel you to submit. Do not allow the tyrant Diabolus to persuade you to think that our King is not able to bring you down and lay you under his feet. He is the Maker of all things, and if he touches the mountains, they smoke. But the door of the King's clemency will not always stand open, for the day of judgment is coming and will not be hindered.

"O Mansoul! Is it a small thing in your eyes that our King offers you mercy after all your provocations? Yes, he still holds out his golden scepter to you and will not allow his door to be shut against you. Will you provoke him to do it? If you say you will not submit, then judgment will come. Therefore, trust in him. Because of his wrath, beware lest he remove you with the stroke of his hand. Then not even a great ransom could deliver you. Will he value your riches? No, not your gold or all your forces of strength. He has prepared his throne for judgment, for he will come with his chariots like a whirlwind to render his anger with fury and his rebuke with flames of fire. Therefore, O Mansoul, take heed lest his justice and judgment should take hold of you."

Now while Captain Judgment was making this oration to the town of Mansoul, it was observed by some that Diabolus trembled. But the captain proceeded and said, "O woeful town of Mansoul! Will you not yet open your gate to receive us, the deputies of your King? Can your heart endure, or can your hands be strong in the day that he deals in judgment with you? Can you endure being forced to drink, as one would drink sweet wine, the sea of wrath that our King has prepared for Diabolus and his angels?"

Then the fourth captain, the noble Captain Execution, came forward and said: "O town of Mansoul, once famous, but now like the fruitless bough; once the delight of the high ones, but now a den for Diabolus. Hearken also to me and to the words that I speak to you in the name of the great Shaddai. Behold the axe is laid to the root of the trees. Every tree, therefore, that does not bring forth good fruit, is hewn down and cast into the fire.

"O town of Mansoul! You have become a fruitless tree that bears nothing but thorns and briers. Your evil fruit indicates you are not a good tree. Your grapes are grapes of gall, and your clusters are bitter. You have rebelled against your King, and we, the power and force of Shaddai, are the axe that is laid to your roots. What do you say, will you turn? Tell me before the first blow is given, will you turn? Our axe must first be laid *to* your root, before it is laid *at* your root. It must first be laid to your root in a way of threatening, before it is laid at your root by way of execution. Between these two your repentance is required, and then your time is up.

"What will you do? Will you turn? Or will I smite you? If I strike my blow, Mansoul, down you will go. I have commission to lay my axe *at,* as well as *to* your roots, and nothing except yielding to our King will prevent your execution. What are you fit for, O Mansoul, if you will not yield to mercy, except to be hewn down and cast into the fire and burned?

"O Mansoul! Patience and forbearance do not last forever—maybe for a year or two. But you have been engaged in rebellion for more than three years. And do you think that these are only threatenings or that our King does not have the power to execute his words? O Mansoul! You will find that when the words of our King are made light of by sinners, there is not only threatening but burning coals of fire.

"Will you continue in your rebellion? Your sin has brought this army to your walls, and will we bring judgment and execution into your town? You have heard what the captains have said, but you still shut your gates. Speak out, Mansoul. Will you continue to keep us out or will you accept the conditions of peace?"

The town of Mansoul refused to accept the speeches of these four noble captains. Instead, they wanted time to prepare their answer to these demands. The captains said they would give the townsmen time to consider their reply, if they would first throw out the villain Ill-Pause. But if they would not cast him out to them over the town wall, then they would give them no more time. "For," they said, "we know that as long as Ill-Pause draws breath in Mansoul all good consideration will be confounded and nothing but mischief will be accomplished."

Diabolus was very reluctant to lose Ill-Pause because he was his orator. He was resolved at first to give them an answer himself, but then changed his mind and commanded Lord Unbelief to do it, saying: "Give these renegades an answer and speak out so that Mansoul may hear and understand you."

At Diabolus' command Unbelief began and said: "Gentlemen, you have disturbed our prince and annoyed the town of Mansoul by camping against it. But where you come from, we will never know; and what you are, we will not believe. You tell us that you have this authority from Shaddai, but by what right does he command you to do it? Of that we remain ignorant.

"You have summoned this town to desert her lord and to yield herself up to the great Shaddai your King. You flatteringly tell her that if she will do it, he will have mercy and not charge her with her past offenses. You have also, to the terror of the town, threatened to punish Mansoul with terrible destruction if she will not consent to do as you have commanded.

"Now, captains, be informed that neither Lord Diabolus, nor I his servant, nor our brave Mansoul regard either your authority, message, or the King whom you say has sent you. We do not fear, and we will not yield to your summons.

"As for the war that you threaten to make against us, we must defend ourselves as well as we can. And we are not without the means to resist you. In short, for I will not be tedious, I tell you that we consider you to be some vagabond, renegade crew who has shaken off all obedience to your King. You are probably going from place to place to see if, through flatteries or threats, you can make some silly town, city, or country desert their place and leave it to you. But Mansoul will not submit to your lies.

"To conclude, we do not fear you, nor will we obey your summons. We will keep our gates shut against you to keep you out of our town, and we will not permit you to encamp before us any longer. Our people must live in quiet, and your presence disturbs them. Therefore, take your bag and baggage and be gone, or we will let our arrows fly from the walls against you."

This oration made by old Unbelief was seconded by desperate Lord Willbewill in words to this effect: "Gentlemen, we have heard your demands, the noise of your threats, and the sound of your summons. Yet we do not fear your force or regard your threats, but we will remain as you found us. And we command you to remove yourselves in three days' time, or you will know what it is to dare to arouse the lion Diabolus when he is asleep in his town of Mansoul."

The recorder, whose name was Forget-Good, added the following: "Gentlemen, as you can see, our leaders have, with mild and gentle words, answered your rough and angry speeches. They have, moreover, asked you to leave quietly and depart in the same way as you came. Therefore, accept their kindness and be gone. We could have come out with force against you and caused you to feel the blow of our sword. But because we love peace and quiet ourselves, we hate to hurt or molest others."

Then the town of Mansoul shouted for joy, as if Diabolus and his crew had gotten some great advantage over the captains. They merrily rang the bells and danced on the walls.

Diabolus returned to the castle, and the mayor and recorder went back to their places. Lord Willbewill took special care to secure the gates with double guards, double bolts, and double locks and bars. He especially reinforced Ear Gate for that was the gate the King's forces sought most to enter. Lord Willbewill appointed old Mr. Prejudice, an angry and ill-tempered captain, as keeper of the gate. He put sixty guards, called Deafmen, under his authority. They were very useful for that service because they could not hear the words of the captains or their soldiers.

When the captains heard the answer of the town's leaders, they realized that Mansoul was resolved to resist. So the King's army prepared to use force against them. Their first move was to strengthen their forces against Ear Gate. They knew that unless they could penetrate that gate, their efforts against the town would be useless. When this was done, they put the rest of the men in their places and sounded the battle cry: *"Ye must be born again!"* Then they sounded the trumpet, and the battle began.

The townspeople had placed two great guns called Highmind and Heady on the tower over Ear Gate. Diabolus' blacksmith, whose name was Mr. Puff-Up, had made these deadly weapons. The King's captains, however, were so vigilant and watchful that the shots from these guns whizzed by their ears and did them no harm. These two guns greatly annoyed the camp of Shaddai and helped secure the gate, but the townsfolk could not boast of killing many of the King's soldiers. Mansoul also had some other small weapons which they used against the camp of Shaddai.

The King's captains had brought with them several catapults and two battering-rams. With stones from their catapults they bombarded the houses and people of the town. They beat down the roof of the old mayor's house and almost killed Lord Willbewill, but he recovered. A notable slaughter was made among the aldermen, when with one shot the captains knocked off Mr. Swearing, Mr. Fury, Mr. Tell-Lies, Mr. Drunkenness, and Mr. Cheating.

The captains made many brave attempts to break open the gate with their battering-rams, but only succeeded in dismantling the two guns over Ear Gate. The people of Mansoul continued to fight fiercely, urged on by the rage of Diabolus, the valor of Lord

Willbewill, the lies of Mayor Unbelief, and the treachery of Mr. Forget-Good. In fact, that summer's battles were almost lost for the King's soldiers, and Mansoul seemed to have the advantage.

In the midst of the conflict a company of Lord Willbewill's men slipped out of the back gate of the town and attacked the rear of Captain Thunder's men. Three fellows from the captains' forces were taken prisoner and carried into the town. In a short time, the news spread throughout the streets of Mansoul about the three notable prisoners whom Lord Willbewill's men had taken from the camp of Shaddai. This news was soon carried to Diabolus at the castle.

Diabolus called for Willbewill to find out if this news was true and how it came to pass. Lord Willbewill explained, and then the giant sent for the prisoners. When they came, he demanded to know who they were, where they came from, and what they did in the camp of Shaddai.

Their names were Mr. Tradition, Mr. Human-Wisdom, and Mr. Man's Invention. They told Diabolus that they were not true soldiers of the King. They said they had offered their services to the King's captains when Shaddai's forces had passed through their country on the way to Mansoul. Diabolus then sent them back to the prison.

A few days later he called for them again and asked if they would be willing to serve him against their former captains. They told him that they did not live by religion but by the fates of fortune; and since his lordship was willing to retain them, they would be willing to serve him. Diabolus sent these fellows to Captain Anything with a note to receive them into his company. The content of the letter was this:

"Captain Anything, the three men who are the bearers of this letter have a desire to serve me in the war. I know no one better to commit them to than you. Receive them in my name, and as the need arises use them against Shaddai and his men. Farewell."

So they came, and Captain Anything received the three traitors. He made two of them sergeants, but he made Mr. Man's Invention his standard-bearer.

Chapter Five

HINDRANCES TO PEACE

When the King's captains saw how the battle was going, they retreated to their winter quarters and entrenched themselves there. To the great annoyance of their enemy, however, the camp of Shaddai still made frequent and terrifying assaults against the town. The people of Mansoul could not sleep as securely as they had before, nor could they enjoy their wicked pleasures in peace as they had in times past. They had attack after attack, first at one gate, then at another, and then at all the gates at once. They were attacked when the nights were the longest and the weather coldest. To the town of Mansoul it seemed to be a winter like no other.

Without warning, the captains' trumpets would sound, and the catapults would whirl stones into the town. At other times, ten thousand of the King's soldiers would run around the walls of Mansoul at midnight, shouting and lifting up their voices for battle. Sometimes the townspeople would be wounded, and their weeping and lamenting would be heard throughout the now languishing town of Mansoul. Even Diabolus had his rest disturbed by their distressing cries.

During this time, new thoughts began to possess the minds of the townsmen, and old thoughts began to be contradicted. Some would say, "This is no way to live."

Others would then reply, "This will be over shortly."

Then a third would stand up and answer, "Let us return to the King Shaddai, and put an end to this trouble."

A fourth would come in saying fearfully, "I doubt he will receive us."

Mr. Conscience, who had been the recorder before Diabolus took over Mansoul, also began to speak up. His words were now like great claps of thunder. No sound was as terrible to Mansoul as his voice, not even the noise of the King's soldiers and shoutings of the captains.

At the same time, food began to grow scarce in the town, and the pleasures Mansoul had lusted after were departing from her. The things they had enjoyed in the past were now losing their luster. Wrinkles and evidence of the shadow of death were upon the inhabitants. How glad Mansoul would have been to be able to enjoy quietness and peace of mind in the midst of their poverty and need.

In the deep of this winter, the captains sent a summons to Mansoul to yield up herself to the great King Shaddai. They sent it not only once, but twice, and a third time. They hoped that at some time Mansoul might be willing to surrender if they were given another opportunity. In fact, the town would probably have surrendered to them before now if it had not been for the opposition of old Unbelief and the fickleness of Lord Willbewill. Diabolus also stormed about in a frenzy, and Mansoul remained distressed under these fearful and perplexing conditions.

The King's captains had sent a messenger to Mansoul three times. The first time the trumpeter went with words of peace, telling them that the noble captains of Shaddai felt compassion for the now perishing town and were troubled to see them standing in the way of their own deliverance. He said that if poor Mansoul would humble herself and surrender, her rebellion and notorious treason would be forgiven and even forgotten by their merciful King. He told them to beware lest they oppose their own good and defeat themselves in the end. Then the messenger returned to the camp.

The second time the trumpeter went, he treated them a little more harshly. After sounding the trumpet, he told them that by continuing in their rebellion they were inflaming the spirit of the captains. Now they were resolved to make a conquest of Mansoul or lay their bones before the town walls.

He went the third time and dealt with them even more severely. The trumpeter told the townsmen that since they had been so horribly profane he did not know whether the captains were inclining toward mercy or judgment. He said, "They commanded me to give you a summons to open the gates to them.'' Then he returned to the camp.

These three summons, especially the last two, so distressed the town that they called for a conference. They decided that Lord Willbewill should go up to Ear Gate and call to the captains of the camp for a meeting. So Lord Willbewill sounded the trumpet, and the King's captains came with all their military equipment and their soldiers. The townsmen told the captains that they had considered their summons and would come to an agreement with them. But there were certain conditions given by the order of Diabolus that they were appointed to propose. They said they would consent to be one people with them if the captains agreed to these terms:

1. If, under Shaddai's rule, Lord Unbelief, Mr. Forget-Good, and brave Lord Willbewill remain as governors of the town, castle, and gates of Mansoul.

2. That no man now serving under their great Diabolus be cast out of his house or denied any freedom that he had hitherto enjoyed in the town of Mansoul.

3. That they be permitted to continue the rights and privileges long enjoyed under the reign of their only lord and great defender, Diabolus.

4. That no new law or officers will have any power over them without their own choice and consent.

"These are our conditions of peace. And upon these terms," they said, "we will submit to your King."

When the captains heard Mansoul's feeble offer and their bold demands, Captain Thunder made the following speech:

"O inhabitants of the town of Mansoul, when I heard your trumpet calling for a meeting with us, I can truly say I was glad. When you said you were willing to submit yourselves to our King and Lord, then I was even more glad. But when, by your silly conditions and foolish objections, you placed a stumbling block before yourselves, then my gladness turned to sorrow. My hopes for your return have been dashed.

"I imagine that old Ill-Pause, the ancient enemy of Mansoul, drew up these proposals as terms of agreement. But they do not deserve to be admitted in the hearing of any man who pretends to give service to Shaddai. With the highest disdain we refuse and reject these terms as the greatest of iniquities.

"But, O Mansoul, if you will give yourselves into the hands of our King and trust him, he will make terms with you that will be to your benefit. Then we will receive you and be at peace with you. But if you do not trust yourselves to the arms of Shaddai our King, then things will be as they were before. And we know what we have to do."

Then old Unbelief, the mayor, cried out and said: "O Mansoul, who would be so foolish as to take control out of their own hands and put it into the hands of those they do not know? I, for my part, will never yield to such a proposition. Do we know the nature and temperament of their King? It is said by some that he gets angry with his subjects if they step out of line to the slightest degree. Others have said that he requires much more of them than they can perform.

"O Mansoul, it would be wise to take heed to what you are doing in this matter. For if you yield, you will give yourselves up to another and no longer be your own. To give up yourselves to an unlimited power is the greatest folly in the world. For now you may repent, but you can never justly complain. If you submit to him, you do not know which of you he will kill and which of you he will keep alive. He may cut off every one of us and send new people from his own country to inhabit this town."

This speech by the mayor destroyed all hopes of an accord. The King's captains returned to their trenches, while the mayor returned to the castle and to his king.

Diabolus was waiting for Lord Unbelief because he heard that there had been a debate at the wall. When he came into the chamber of state, Diabolus saluted him and said, "Welcome, my lord. How did it go with you today?"

Lord Unbelief bowed low and then told him the whole matter, saying, "Thus said the captains of Shaddai, and thus said I."

Diabolus was very glad to hear it and said, "My faithful Unbelief, I have proved your fidelity more than ten times already and never yet found you to be false. If we withstand this attack, I promise to promote you to a place of honor, a place far better than mayor of Mansoul. I will make you my universal deputy. Next to me you will have all nations under your power. You will destroy all who resist you, and none of our vassals will walk more at liberty than those who are content to walk under your control.''

Unbelief left feeling as if he had indeed obtained a favor. Going happily to his home, he thought about the time when his greatness would be enlarged.

Although the mayor and Diabolus agreed, this rejection of the brave captains put Mansoul into a mutiny. While old Unbelief was at the castle, the former mayor, Lord Understanding, and the old recorder, Mr. Conscience, found out what had happened at Ear Gate. They had not been permitted to be at the debate, lest they show their support for the King's captains. When they learned what had happened, they were very concerned. Gathering some of the townspeople together, they began to explain the reasonableness of the noble captains' demands and the bad consequences that would follow the speech of old Unbelief. They pointed out how little reverence he showed to the captains and how he had implicitly charged them with unfaithfulness and treachery.

''For what else,'' they said, ''could be made of his speech, when Lord Unbelief said he would not yield to their proposition. The captains then threatened to destroy us, when before they had sent us word that they would show us mercy.''

The multitude was now convinced of the evil that

old Unbelief had done, and they began to run together in groups throughout the streets of Mansoul. At first they muttered among themselves, then they talked openly. After that they ran all about and cried as they ran, "O the brave captains of Shaddai! If only we were under the government of the captains and of Shaddai their King."

When Lord Unbelief learned that Mansoul was in an uproar, he came down to pacify the people. He thought he would silence the disturbance with the mighty show of his appearance. But when they saw him, they came running toward him and would have harmed him if he had not gone back home. Then they attacked his house and would have pulled it down around his ears, but the place was too strong. Unbelief then mustered some courage and spoke to the people from a window. "Gentlemen, what is the reason for such an uproar today?"

Lord Understanding answered: "It is because you and your master have not behaved properly as you should toward the captains of Shaddai. In three ways you are at fault. First, you would not let Mr. Conscience and myself attend the hearing of your speech. Secondly, you proposed terms of peace to the captains that by no means could be granted. You expected them to allow Mansoul to still live in all lewdness and vanity before Shaddai. This would mean that Diabolus would still be king in power, and Shaddai only King in name. Thirdly, after the captains told us the conditions for receiving mercy, you ruined everything with your unsavory, unseasonable, and ungodly speech."

When old Unbelief heard this, he cried out, "Treason, treason! To your arms, to your arms, O trustworthy friends of Diabolus in Mansoul."

Lord Understanding responded to this outburst by saying, "Sir, you may attach to my words any meaning you please, but I am sure that the captains of such a King as theirs deserved better treatment at your hands."

Then old Unbelief said, "But, sir, I spoke for my ruler, for his government, and the quieting of the people whom by your unlawful actions you have turned against us."

Then the old recorder, whose name was Mr. Conscience replied, "Sir, you should not distort what Lord Understanding has said. It is evident that he has spoken the truth and that you are an enemy of Mansoul. Your rude and impertinent language has grieved the King's captains and done damage to Mansoul. If you had accepted the conditions of peace, the alarm of war would have ceased throughout the town. But that dreadful sound remains, and the lack of wisdom in your speech has been the cause of it."

Then old Unbelief said, "Sir, I will take your message to Diabolus and see what he has to say about it! Meanwhile, we will seek the good of the town and not ask for your advice."

To this Lord Understanding quickly replied, "Sir, your prince and you are both foreigners to Mansoul and not natives of the town. And who knows what will happen if things get difficult. When you see that you can only remain safe by fleeing, you will leave us to shift for ourselves. Or you may set us on fire and escape through the smoke, leaving us in our ruins."

Old Unbelief said sternly, "Sir, you forget that you are under a governor and that you should conduct yourself like a subject. When my master hears what you have done today, he will give you what you deserve."

While these gentlemen were chiding one another with these words, Lord Willbewill, Mr. Prejudice, old Ill-Pause, and several of the newly appointed aldermen came down from the wall and asked the reason for this commotion. Then every man began to speak at once, so that nothing could be heard distinctly.

Suddenly silence was commanded, and the old fox Unbelief began to speak. "These two peevish old gentlemen, who as a result of their bad dispositions and through the advice of Mr. Discontent, have tumultuously gathered this crowd together and turned them against me. They have also attempted to stir the town into acts of rebellion against our prince."

Then all the followers of Diabolus who were present stood up and affirmed that these things were true. When those who sided with Lord Understanding and Mr. Conscience perceived that strength and power was on the other side, they came to their aid and relief. So a great company was on both sides. Those on old Unbelief's side wanted to have the two old gentlemen taken away to prison, but those on the other side were opposed to the idea. Then they all began to shout for their party. The Diabolonians proclaimed the greatness of old Unbelief, Forget-Good, the new aldermen, and their great Diabolus. The other party praised Shaddai and the captains, applauding their mercifulness and their ways.

This bickering went on for a while until at last they passed from words to blows. The good old gentleman, Mr. Conscience, was knocked down twice by a Diabolonian named Mr. Apathetic. At the same time Lord Understanding was almost killed with a cannonball, but the one who fired the shot failed to take proper aim.

The other side did not escape without injury either. Mr. Rash-Head, a Diabolonian, had his brains beaten out by Mr. Mind, Lord Willbewill's servant. And it made me laugh to see how old Mr. Prejudice was kicked and tumbled about in the dirt. Although he commanded a company of Diabolonians, he had his head sadly cracked by some of Lord Understanding's party.

Mr. Anything also became active in the brawl, but both sides were against him because he was loyal to no one. He had one of his legs broken, and the one who did it wished it had been his neck. Much more harm was done on both sides before it was all over.

Lord Willbewill, in contrast to his former enthusiasm, now appeared to be indifferent. He did not take one side over another, but he smiled to see old Prejudice tumbled up and down in the dirt. And when Captain Anything came limping up to him, he seemed to take little notice of him.

When the uproar was over, Diabolus sent for Lord Understanding and Mr. Conscience. Both of them were thrown into prison as the ringleaders of this terrible riot. Then the town quieted down, and the prisoners were severely punished. Diabolus was going to do away with them, but the present crisis prevented their execution, for the war was once again at their gates.

Chapter Six

THE MARCH OF PRINCE EMMANUEL

When the King's captains had returned to their camp, they called for a council of war to decide what to do next. "Now," some said, "let us go up and attack the town." But most of them thought it would be better to give Mansoul another opportunity to surrender. They thought this to be best because the town seemed more inclined to submit than before.

"And if," they said, "some of them are inclined to yield, another attack may offend them and push them further away from agreeing to our conditions."

They all agreed to this advice, called for a trumpeter, and gave him the message. When the trumpeter came to the wall of the town, he headed for Ear Gate and sounded his trumpet. The people within the town came to see what was the matter, and the trumpeter made the following speech:

"O hardhearted and deplorable town of Mansoul, how long will you love your sinful foolishness and delight in scorning the King's captains? Do you still despise their offer of peace and deliverance? Will you still refuse the mercy of Shaddai and trust the lies and falsehoods of Diabolus? Do you think when Shaddai has conquered you that the memory of your behavior toward him will yield you peace and comfort? Or do you think your abrasive language can make him afraid as a grasshopper? Does he plead with you because he fears you? Do you think that you are stronger than he? Look to the heavens and consider the stars—how high are they? Can you stop the sun from running its course or hinder the moon from giving its light? Can you count the number of the stars or stop the rain from heaven? Can you call to the waters of the sea and cause them to cover the face of the ground? Can you observe everyone who is proud and humble him? Yet these are some of the works of our King, in whose name we come to you, so that you may be brought under his authority. In his name I summon you to yield yourselves up to his captains."

At this summons the people of Mansoul seemed to be at a standstill and did not know how to answer. Diabolus, therefore, appeared and took matters into his own hands. He turned toward the people of Mansoul and said, "Gentlemen and my faithful subjects, if it is true what this summoner has said concerning the greatness of their King, you will always be kept in bondage and fear. How can you even think of yielding to such a powerful ruler, much less endure to be in his presence? I, your prince, am familiar to you, and you may play with me as you would a lamb. Consider, therefore, what is to your advantage, and remember the freedoms I have granted you.

"If all this man has said is true, why is it that the subjects of Shaddai are so enslaved? No people in Universe are as unhappy or trampled upon as they. Consider, my Mansoul, liberty is yours if you know how to use it. Besides, you already have a king, if you will love and obey him."

After hearing this speech by Diabolus, the town of Mansoul hardened their hearts even more against the captains of Shaddai. The thought of his great power shattered their hopes, and the thought of his holiness sank them into despair.

Following a brief consultation, the Diabolonian party sent word back by the trumpeter that they resolved to stick to their prince and never yield to Shaddai. They said it was in vain to give them any further summons, for they would rather die than yield.

Mansoul now seemed to be out of reach or call. Yet the captains, who knew what their Lord could do, would not give up. They, therefore, sent another summons, more sharp and severe than the last. But the more often a summons was sent to yield to Shaddai, the further the people were from reconciliation. The more the captains called to them, the more the people turned away. They ceased to deal with them in this way any more and met together to think of a new way to gain the town and deliver it from the tyranny of Diabolus.

Noble Captain Conviction stood up and said, "My

brethren, this is my opinion. First, we must continually bombard the town and keep it in continual alarm, terrorizing them day and night. By doing this, we will stop the growth of their rebellious spirit; for even a lion can be tamed by continual harassment.

"Secondly, I advise that we draw up a petition to our Lord Shaddai. We will tell our King the state of affairs in Mansoul and beg his pardon for our having no better success. We will earnestly implore his Majesty's help and ask him to send us reinforcements, along with a gallant commander to lead them. Then his Majesty will not lose the advantage of any progress we have made, and he can then complete his conquest of the town."

Following this speech by Captain Conviction, they consented and agreed that a petition should be drawn up and sent speedily by messenger to Shaddai. The content of the petition was:

"Most gracious and glorious King, the Lord of the world and the builder of the town of Mansoul. We have, dear Sovereign, at your command put our lives in jeopardy. At your bidding we have made war upon the famous town of Mansoul. When we went up against it, we did according to our commission and first offered conditions of peace. But they ignored our counsel and disregarded our reproof. They shut their gates in order to keep us out of the town. They mounted their guns and came out against us, doing what damage they could. But we continued to attack them, retaliating when necessary and effectively destroying parts of the town.

"Diabolus, Unbelief, and Willbewill are our greatest enemies. If we had one substantial friend in the town who would have seconded the sound of our summons, the people might have yielded themselves. But there were only enemies there, and no one would speak in behalf of our Lord to the town. Although we have done all we could, Mansoul still remains in a state of rebellion against you.

"Now, King of kings, please pardon your servants who have made little progress in conquering Mansoul. Lord, please send more forces to Mansoul, so that it may be subdued. And send a commander whom the town can both love and fear.

"We do not speak this way because we are willing to abandon the war. In fact, we are willing to lay down our lives in this place. We desire only that the town of Mansoul be won for your Majesty. We also ask your Majesty to settle this matter quickly, so that after their conquest, we may be at liberty to be sent on other missions for you."

The petition was drawn up and sent to the King by the hand of that good man, Mr. Love-To-Mansoul.

When this petition came to the palace of the King, it was delivered to the King's Son. The contents pleased him, and he added some things to the petition himself. After he made these amendments and additions with his own hand, he carried it to the King.

At the sight of the petition, the King was glad, especially when he saw it was seconded by his Son. It also pleased him to hear that his soldiers were so earnest in their work and so steadfast in their resolve that they had already gained some ground against the town of Mansoul.

When the King called for his Son, Emmanuel answered, "Here I am, my Father."

Then the King said, "You know, as I do, the condition of the town of Mansoul and how we have tried to redeem it. Come, my Son, and prepare yourself for the war, for you must go to my camp at Mansoul. You must prevail and conquer the town."

The King's Son replied: "Your law is within my heart. I delight to do your will. This is the day I have longed for and the work I have long awaited. Give me the forces, and I will go and deliver the perishing town from Diabolus and his power. My heart has often been grieved for the miserable town of Mansoul. But now I can rejoice, now I can be glad!" And with that he leaped for joy, saying:

"I have not thought that anything was too costly for Mansoul. The day of vengeance is in my heart for my dear Mansoul, and am I glad that you, my Father, have made me the Captain of their salvation. Now I will begin to come against all those who have invaded my town. I will deliver it from their hand."

The words the King's Son said to his Father flew like lightning around the court. Everyone was talking about what Emmanuel was going to do for the famous town of Mansoul. The noblemen were impressed with the Prince's decision, and the greatest among them desired to go to help Emmanuel recover the miserable town of Mansoul.

It was decided that messengers should go and tell the camp that Emmanuel was coming to recover Mansoul and bringing with him a mighty and impregnable force. The highest-ranking officials in the King's court went to carry this news to the camp at Mansoul. They told the captains that the King was sending Emmanuel and that it delighted the Son to be sent on this errand by the great Shaddai his Father. The captains were so pleased at the thought of his coming that they gave a shout that made the earth shake. The mountains echoed the sound, making even Diabolus tremble with fear.

When his spies told him what was being planned against him and that Emmanuel would soon come to invade the town, Diabolus was greatly disturbed. There was no man in the court nor nobleman in the kingdom whom Diabolus feared as much as he feared the Prince. Remember, Diabolus had felt the weight of his mighty hand before.

The people of Mansoul, however, were not at all concerned about this new development. They were mainly interested in satisfying their pleasures and lusts.

When the time came for the Prince to set out on his march to Mansoul, he took with him five noble captains, each with a force of ten thousand men.

The first was that famous commander, noble Captain Credence. Mr. Promise was his standard-bearer, and he carried a red banner. His emblem was the Holy Lamb on a golden shield.

Captain Good-Hope was the second captain. His banner was blue, and his standard-bearer was Mr. Expectation. For an emblem he had three golden anchors.

The third was that valiant commander, Captain Charity. His standard-bearer was Mr. Compassion, and the green colors were on his flag. His emblem showed three poor orphans embraced by tender, loving arms.

Captain Innocent, that gallant commander, also led a troop of ten thousand. His standard-bearer was Mr. Harmless, and he waved a white banner. For his emblem he had three golden doves.

The fifth commander was the truly loyal and beloved Captain Patience. His standard-bearer, Mr. Suffer-Long, carried a black banner, showing three arrows through a golden heart.

Along with these brave captains and their men, the Prince began his march to the town of Mansoul. Captain Credence led the troops, and Captain Patience brought up the rear. The other three captains and their men made up the main army, while the Prince rode in his chariot at the head of them all. Accompanying them were some noblemen from the King's court who came as volunteers because of their love for Shaddai and their desire for the deliverance of Mansoul.

Emmanuel took with him forty-four battering rams and twelve catapults. These weapons were made of pure gold and carried in the center of the army's ranks. The Prince's armor was also made of gold, and it shone like the sun in the heavens.

As Emmanuel's vast army marched across the Kingdom of Universe toward Mansoul, their armor glittered, and their colorful banners waved in the wind! They marched until they came within five miles of the town. There they waited until the first four captains from the camp came to acquaint the Prince with the situation. Then they continued their journey to the town of Mansoul. When the soldiers in the camp saw that new forces were joining them, they shouted so loudly that it put Diabolus into a panic.

The Prince's army encamped all around the town, not just before the gates as the other captains had done. The King's soldiers also built up large mounds of earth around the wall of the town. Mount Gracious was on one side and Mount Justice on the other. There were also several small banks, like Plaintruth Hill and No-Sin Slope. Many of the catapults were placed on these mounds. Four were placed on Mount Gracious and four on Mount Justice. The rest were conveniently placed in several areas surrounding the town. Five of the biggest battering rams were placed on Mount Hearken. This mount was firmly built near Ear Gate for the purpose of breaking it open.

The men of the town looked out and saw the multitude of soldiers who were encamped outside the wall. When they saw the rams and catapults mounted around the town, together with the glittering armor and the waving colors, their hearts began to faint. They had thought they were sufficiently protected, but now they began to think otherwise.

Having besieged Mansoul, the good Prince Emmanuel had a white flag hung between the golden catapults on Mount Gracious. He did this for two reasons: to give notice to Mansoul that he would still be gracious if they turned to him, and to leave them without any excuse should he destroy them for continuing in their rebellion.

So the white flag was flown for three days to give them time to consider. But they continued to be unconcerned and made no reply to the favorable signal of the Prince.

Then he commanded that they place on Mount Justice the red flag of Captain Judgment with the emblem of the burning fiery furnace. This also stood waving before them in the wind, but the people of Mansoul carried on in the same manner as when the white flag had been hung out. Still, the Prince did not take advantage of them.

Finally, he commanded that his servants hang out the black flag of defiance with the emblem of the three burning thunderbolts. But Mansoul was as apathetic as before.

When the Prince saw that neither mercy nor execution of judgment could come near the heart of Mansoul, he was touched with compassion and said, "Surely this strange behavior of the town of Mansoul arises from their ignorance of the terms and methods of warfare rather than from a secret defiance and hatred of us. Maybe they know the manner of conducting their own wars, but are unfamiliar with the way we make war against my enemy Diabolus."

Therefore, he sent word to the town of Mansoul to let them know what he meant by the signs and ceremonies of the flag. The messenger was also to find out whether they would choose mercy or the execution of judgment.

All this time Mansoul kept their gates fastened shut with locks, bolts, and bars. Their guards were doubled, and their sentries were heavily armed. Diabolus also mustered up as much backbone as he could to encourage the town to resist.

The townsmen answered the Prince in this way: "Great Sir, your messenger has told us that we must accept your mercy or fall by your justice. But we are bound by the law and custom of this place and can give you no positive answer. For it is against the law, government, and royal prerogative of our king to make either peace or war without him. But we will petition our prince to come down to the wall and give you such treatment as he thinks profitable for us." When the good Prince Emmanuel heard this answer and saw the bondage of the people and how content they were to abide in the chains of the tyrant Diabolus, it grieved his heart.

After the town carried this news to Diabolus and told him that the Prince was waiting for an answer, he huffed as powerfully as he could, but in his heart he was afraid.

Then he said, "I will go down to the gates myself and give him such an answer as I think fit." So he went down to Mouth Gate and addressed himself to Emmanuel. But he spoke in a language that the townspeople could not understand.

"O great Emmanuel, Lord of all the world, I know you and that you are the Son of the great Shaddai! Why have you come to torment me and to cast me out of my possession? This town of Mansoul, as you very well know, is mine for two reasons. It is mine by right of conquest; I won it fair and square. Shall the prey be taken from the mighty or the lawful captive be delivered? The town of Mansoul is mine also by their subjection. They have opened the gates of their town to me. They have sworn fidelity to me and openly chosen me to be their king. They have also given their castle into my hands and put the whole strength of Mansoul behind me.

"Moreover, this town of Mansoul has rejected you. They have cast your law, your name, your image, and all that is yours behind their back. Instead, they have accepted and set up my law, my name, my image, and all that is mine. Ask your captains, and they will tell you that Mansoul has, in answer to all their summons, shown love and loyalty to me. But they have always shown disdain, contempt, and scorn for you and your men. Now, you are the just and the holy one who does no iniquity; depart then and leave me to my rightful inheritance."

Diabolus made this speech in his own language. Although he can speak to all men in their native tongues (otherwise he could not tempt them as he does), still his own language is that of the infernal, black pit. The town of Mansoul did not understand him or see how he crouched and cringed as he stood before Emmanuel their Prince. All this time they thought that Diabolus was a powerful force who could not be resisted. Even while he was pleading with Emmanuel not to take Mansoul from him, the inhabitants were boasting of the giant's valor saying, "Who is able to make war against him?"

Chapter Seven

PROPOSALS AND COUNTERPROPOSALS

When Diabolus had finished speaking, Emmanuel, the Golden Prince, stood up and spoke these words.

"You deceiving one," he said, "you pretend to have a lawful right to this deplorable town, when it is apparent to everyone that your entrance to Mansoul was obtained through your lies and deceit. You lied about my Father, you misrepresented his law, and deceived the people of Mansoul. You pretend that the people have accepted you as their king, their captain, and their lord, but that was also the result of your deceit and trickery. If deceitful cunning, wicked schemes, and all manner of horrible hypocrisy can be taken for equity and right, then I will confess that you have made a lawful conquest. But what thief, what tyrant, what devil is there that does not use these evil methods to conquer?

"But I can make it appear, O Diabolus, that all you have spoken to Mansoul has been lies. Do you think it is right that you made my Father out to be a liar and the greatest deluder in the world? And what do you have to say about perverting the right purpose and intent of his law? Was it good also that you preyed on the innocence and simplicity of the now miserable town of Mansoul? You overcame Mansoul by promising them happiness in their transgressions against my Father's law. Yet you knew from your own experience that disobedience was the way to ruin them. You defaced my Father's image in Mansoul and set up your own in its place. This resulted in great contempt for my Father, the heightening of your sin, and intolerable damage to the perishing town of Mansoul.

"You have not only deluded and ruined this place, but by your lies and fraudulent behavior you have set them against their own deliverance. You have stirred them up against my Father's captains and made them fight against those who were sent to deliver them from their bondage! All these things and many more you have done in contempt of my Father and his law to bring the miserable town of Mansoul under his displeasure forever. I have come to avenge the wrong that you have done to my Father and to deal with you for the way you have made poor Mansoul blaspheme his name. You will pay for all the evil you have done, you prince of the Infernal Cave!

"As for myself, O Diabolus, I have come against you by lawful power to take this town out of your burning fingers. For Mansoul is undoubtedly mine, as all who diligently search the most ancient records will see. I will plead my title to Mansoul, O Diabolus, and prove you to be wrong.

"My Father built and designed the town of Mansoul with his own hands. The palace in the center of that town was built for his own delight. This town of Mansoul, therefore, is my Father's because he is the maker of it. Anyone who denies the truth of this must lie against his soul. You master of the lie, this town of Mansoul is mine.

"I am my Father's heir, his firstborn, and the only delight of his heart. I am coming against you in my own right to recover my inheritance out of your hand. Furthermore, I have a right and title to Mansoul because it was my Father's gift. It was his and he gave it to me. My Father has not taken it from me and given it to you. Mansoul is my desire, my delight, and the joy of my heart.

"Mansoul is also mine by right of purchase. I bought it, O Diabolus, I have bought it for myself. Since it was my Father's gift to me as his heir and since I have also purchased it at a great price, the town of Mansoul is lawfully mine. You, therefore, are a usurper, a tyrant, and a traitor by taking possession of what is mine.

"There is a reason that I purchased this town. Mansoul had trespassed against my Father. My Father had said that the day they broke his law, they would die. Now it is more possible for heaven and earth to pass away than for my Father to break his word. When Mansoul sinned by listening to your lie, I offered myself and became a surety to my Father, body for body and soul for soul. I wanted to make amends for Mansoul's transgressions, and my

Father accepted my offer. So when the appointed time came, I gave body for body, soul for soul, life for life, blood for blood, and I redeemed my beloved Mansoul. My Father's law and justice were involved in the transgression, but both are now satisfied; and he is content that Mansoul should be delivered.

"I have come out against you by the direct command of my Father. He said to me, 'Go down and deliver Mansoul.' Let it be known to you and the foolish town of Mansoul that I have not come against you without my Father's authority.

"And now," said the golden-headed Prince, "I have a word for the town of Mansoul." But as soon as he said that he had a word to speak to the townsmen, the gates were double guarded, and all men were commanded not to listen to him.

But he proceeded and said, "O unhappy town of Mansoul, I am touched with pity and compassion for you. You have accepted Diabolus for your king and have become servants of Diabolus against your Sovereign Lord. You have opened your gates to him but shut them firmly against me. You have listened to him but closed your ears to my cry. He brought to you your destruction, and you received him. I have come to you bringing salvation, but you have ignored me.

"Besides, your sacreligious hands have taken all that was mine and given it to my foe—the greatest enemy my Father has. You have bowed and subjected yourselves to him; you have vowed and sworn yourselves to be his. Poor Mansoul! What should I do to you? Should I crush you and grind you to powder or make you a monument of the richest grace? What should I do to you? Listen, O town of Mansoul; listen to my word, and you will live. I am merciful, Mansoul, and you will find me so. Do not shut me out of your gates.

"O Mansoul, it is not my commission nor inclination to do you any harm. Why do you flee from your friend and stick so close to your enemy? It is true that I want you to be sorry for your sin; that is for your own good. But do not despair! This great army has not come to hurt you, but to deliver you from your bondage and to return you to your place of obedience.

"My commission is to make war upon Diabolus your king and all the Diabolonians with him. For he is the strong man who holds the house, and I will put him out. I must divide his spoils; I must take his armor from him. I must cast him out of his stronghold and make it a habitation for myself. And this, O Mansoul, will happen when Diabolus is made to follow me in chains and when you rejoice to see his capture.

"I could, if I put forth all my might, cause Diabolus to leave you and depart. But I have decided to deal with him in a way that will be seen and acknowledged by all. He has taken Mansoul by fraud, and he keeps it by violence and deceit. But I will make him bare and naked in the eyes of all observers. All my words are true, and I am mighty to save and deliver my Mansoul out of his hand."

This speech was intended solely for the people of Mansoul, but they would not listen to it. They shut up Ear Gate and kept it locked and bolted. They set guards at the gate and commanded that no Mansoulian was to go out to the Prince and no one from the camp was to be admitted into the town. Diabolus enchanted them to do these things against their rightful Lord and Prince. Therefore, no one from the King's army could come into the town or be heard within its walls.

When Emmanuel saw that Mansoul was deeply involved in sin, he called his army together and commanded them to be ready at the appointed time. There was no lawful way to take the town of Mansoul, except to get in at the gates. Therefore, he commanded his captains to bring their battering rams and catapults and place them at Eye Gate and Ear Gate.

After Emmanuel had everything ready to do battle against Diabolus, he sent another messenger to the town of Mansoul. He was to find out if they would yield themselves peaceably or whether they were still determined to try him to the utmost extremity.

In response to Emmanuel's messenger, the townsfolk and Diabolus called for a council of war and compiled certain propositions. Then they had to decide who would be sent to present them for Emmanuel's consideration.

In Mansoul there lived an old man, a Diabolonian whose name was Mr. Loth-To-Stoop. He was an obstinate man and a great doer for Diabolus. They sent for him and told him what he was to say.

Mr. Loth-To-Stoop went to Emmanuel's camp, and a time was appointed for him to have an audience with the Prince. After a Diabolonian ritual or two, he began and said, "Great Sir, so that all men may know how good-natured a prince my master is, he has sent me to tell your Lordship his terms of peace. He is willing, rather than go to war, to deliver into your hands one half of the town of Mansoul. I am sent to know if your Mightiness will accept this proposition."

Emmanuel replied, "The whole town is mine by gift and purchase; therefore, I will never lose one half."

Mr. Loth-To-Stoop said, "Sir, my master has said that he will be content for you to be the nominal Lord of all, if he may possess a part of the town."

Emmanuel answered, "The whole town is mine —not in name and word only. I will either be the only Lord and possessor of all of it, or of none of Mansoul."

Then Mr. Loth-To-Stoop presented another proposal, "Sir, notice the condescension of my master! He says that he will be content to have some private place in Mansoul assigned to him, and you will be Lord of all the rest."

To this the Golden Prince replied, "All whom the Father gives me will come to me. And of all the ones he has given me I will lose none, no, not a toe nor a hair. I will not grant Diabolus the least corner in

90

Mansoul to dwell in. I will have all of the town for myself."

Loth-To-Stoop said again, "But, Sir, suppose my lord should surrender the whole town to you, with one provision. When he comes to visit this country, for old acquaintance sake, will you permit him to be entertained as a guest for two days, ten days, or a month or so? Won't this small request be granted?"

"No," Emmanuel replied, "I will not consent for Diabolus to ever have any resting place there."

"Sir, you seem to be very hard," Mr. Loth-To-Stoop said. "Suppose my master agrees to all your Lordship has said, provided that his friends and kindred in Mansoul are free to trade in the town and enjoy their present residences. Won't that be granted, Sir?"

"No, that is contrary to my Father's will. For all Diabolonians living in Mansoul will not only lose their lands and liberties but also their lives."

Mr. Loth-To-Stoop tried again, "But, Sir, will you allow my master to maintain some kind of friendship with Mansoul, by letters and brief visits, if he will deliver all of the town over to you?"

Emmanuel answered, "No, by no means. If any fellowship, friendship, intimacy, or acquaintance is maintained in any way, it will tend to corrupt Mansoul and alienate their affections from me. This will endanger their peace with my Father."

Mr. Loth-To-Stoop added further, saying, "But, great Sir, my master has many friends who are dear to him in Mansoul. May he not bestow on them some tokens of his love and kindness? Then when he is gone, Mansoul may look on his gifts and remember him who was once their king. They will think of the merry times they enjoyed while they lived together in peace."

Emmanuel replied, "No, for if Mansoul comes to be mine, I will not permit the least shred or dust of Diabolus to be left behind. No tokens or gifts bestowed on anyone in Mansoul will remain to call to remembrance the horrible communion that was between the town and him."

"Well, Sir," said Mr. Loth-To-Stoop, "I have one more thing to propose, and then my mission will be completed. Suppose, after my master is gone from Mansoul, that someone living in the town has important business to discuss with him. Suppose, Sir, that nobody can help in that case as well as my master and lord. May my master be summoned for such an urgent matter as this? Or if he may not be admitted into the town, may he and the person concerned meet in a village near Mansoul and settle their business affairs?"

This was the last ensnaring proposition Mr. Loth-To-Stoop had to propound to Emmanuel on behalf of his master Diabolus. But Emmanuel would not grant it, for he said, "After your master is gone, there can be no case or matter in Mansoul that cannot be solved by my Father. Besides, it would be a great disparagement to my Father's wisdom and skill to permit anyone from Mansoul to go to Diabolus for advice. They are encouraged, in everything by prayer and supplication, to let their requests be made known to my Father. Furthermore, should this request be granted, it would open a door for Diabolus and the Diabolonians in Mansoul to plot traitorous schemes. This would bring grief to my Father and me and result in the utter destruction of Mansoul."

When Mr. Loth-To-Stoop heard this answer, he left Emmanuel's presence saying that he would tell his master all that had transpired. He came and told Diabolus that Emmanuel would not permit him to return to Mansoul once he was gone. He reported that Diabolus would never be allowed to have anything more to do either in or with anyone from the town of Mansoul.

After Mansoul and Diabolus had heard this report, they decided to do everything possible to keep Emmanuel out of the town. They sent old Ill-Pause to tell the Prince and his captains their decision. So the old gentleman came up to the top of Ear Gate and called to the Prince's camp for a hearing.

When they came together, he said, "I have been commanded by my high lord to bid you to tell your Prince Emmanuel that Mansoul and Diabolus have resolved to stand and fall together. It is vain for your Prince to think of ever having Mansoul in his hands, unless he can take it by force."

Immediately, someone ran and told Emmanuel what old Ill-Pause had said.

"I will use the power of my sword!" exclaimed

the Prince. "In spite of all the rebellions that Mansoul has made against me, I will not lift my siege and depart. But I will assuredly take my Mansoul and deliver it from the hand of her enemy."

He then commanded Captain Thunder, Captain Conviction, Captain Judgment, and Captain Execution to march up to Ear Gate with trumpets sounding, banners flying, and with voices shouting for the battle. He also asked Captain Credence to join them. Emmanuel then ordered Captain Goodhope and Captain Charity to post their troops in front of Eye Gate. He asked the rest of his captains and their men to place themselves at the best vantage points around the town. All this was done as he had commanded.

Then he ordered that the battle cry be given forth, and the word at that time was *"Emmanuel."* Then an alarm was sounded, the battering rams were employed, and the catapults whirled stones into the town. Thus the battle began.

Diabolus himself was at every gate directing the townsmen in the war. This made their resistance even more forcible, hellish, and offensive to Emmanuel. The good Prince was engaged in battle against Diabolus and Mansoul for several days.

Captain Thunder made three fierce assaults one after another upon Ear Gate causing its posts to shake. Captain Conviction joined Captain Thunder, and both realized that the gate was beginning to yield. So they commanded that the rams should still be used against it. Captain Conviction came near the gate but was driven back with great force and received three wounds in the mouth.

When the Prince learned of the brave attempts of the two captains, he sent for them to come to his pavilion and commanded that they rest for a while. Captain Conviction's wounds were cared for, and the Prince gave both captains a chain of gold and told them to be of good courage.

Captain Goodhope and Captain Charity also fought well in this desperate battle for Eye Gate. In fact, they had almost broken it open. They also received a reward from the Prince, as did the rest of the captains, because they fought valiantly around the wall of the town.

In this battle several of the officers of Diabolus were slain, and some of the townsmen were wounded. One of the officers who was killed was Captain Boasting. He thought that no one could shake the posts of Ear Gate or cause the heart of Diabolus to tremble. Captain Secure was also slain. He used to say that the blind and lame in Mansoul were able to hold the gates of the town against Emmanuel's army. Captain Conviction killed Captain Secure with a two-edged sword.

Captain Bragman, a very desperate fellow who commanded a band of men who threw firebrands and arrows, received a mortal wound in the breast by the hand of Captain Goodhope at Eye Gate. Mr. Feeling was also killed, but he was not a captain. He made it his job to encourage Mansoul's rebellion. He received a wound in the eye from one of Captain Thunder's soldiers and would have been killed by the captain himself, but he made a sudden retreat. Lord Willbewill was wounded in the leg, and the men in the Prince's army later saw him limping as he walked on the wall.

When the Diabolonians saw the posts of Ear Gate shake, Eye Gate nearly broken open, and their captains slain, many of them lost heart and fell by the shots sent by the golden catapults into the town. Among those killed was a townsman named Mr. Love-No-Good. He received a mortal wound, but he did not die right away.

Mr. Ill-Pause, who sided with Diabolus when he first attempted to take Mansoul, also received a grievous wound in the head. Some say that his skull was cracked. After this he was never able to do the evil to Mansoul that he had done in times past. In the heat of the fighting, old Prejudice and Mr. Anything fled.

After the battle was over, the Prince commanded that the white flag again be set upon Mount Gracious for all the town to see. This would show that Emmanuel still had grace for the wretched town of Mansoul.

When Diabolus saw the white flag, he knew it was not for him but for Mansoul. So he cunningly decided to see if Emmanuel would lift his siege if the town promised to reform. He came down to the gate one evening and called to speak with Emmanuel. The Prince came, and Diabolus said to him:

"I see by the white flag that you are anxious for peace and quiet. I thought I would let you know that we are ready to accept any terms which you propose. I know that you require devotion and that holiness pleases you. I know that your main reason for warring against Mansoul is to make it a holy habitation. Well, remove your forces from the town, and I will lean Mansoul in your direction. First, I will stop all acts of hostility against you and be willing to become your deputy. I will now serve you in the town of Mansoul.

"Furthermore, I will persuade Mansoul to receive you as their Lord. I know that they will do it sooner when they understand that I am your deputy. I will show them how they have erred and that transgression stands in the way of life. I will tell them they must conform to the holy law which they have broken. I will impress on them the necessity for reformation according to your law. So that none of these things fail, I myself will set up and maintain a sufficient ministry in Mansoul. You will receive every year, as a token of our devotion to you, whatever levy you place upon us."

Emmanuel said to him, "You are full of deceit! How often have you changed your mind so that you could keep possession of my Mansoul, although I am the rightful heir of the town? You have already made several proposals and this last one is no better than the previous ones. When you failed to deceive by showing your dark side, you transformed yourself into an angel of light, and now you would become a minister of righteousness.

"But know, O Diabolus, that nothing you propose

will be considered, because everything you do is done to deceive. You have no respect for God or love for the town of Mansoul. Anyone who proposes what he pleases so that he may destroy those who believe him is to be abandoned along with all that he says. If righteousness is so important to you now, why is it that wickedness was so dear to you before?

"You speak now of a reformation in Mansoul and that you will even be at the head of that reformation. But you know, as well as I do, that the keeping of the law and righteousness will not take away the curse from Mansoul. When the law was broken by Mansoul, a curse was pronounced against the town. Obeying the law, however, will never deliver Mansoul from the curse of death. Besides, what kind of reformation could be established in a town where the devil makes himself the reformer of evil? You know that all you have now said in this matter is nothing but guile and deceit. Like your first trick, so is the last card you have to play. Many are able to discern who you are when you show your cloven foot. In your white light of transformation, however, you are seen only by a few. But you will not deceive my Mansoul, O Diabolus, for I still love my Mansoul.

"Besides, I have not come to put Mansoul under the burden of the law. If I did, I would be like you. But I have come that by what I have and will do for Mansoul, they may be reconciled to my Father. Although by their sin they have provoked him to anger, they cannot obtain mercy by the law.

"You talk of subjecting this town to do good, when they have known only evil at your hands. I have been sent by my Father to possess and guide Mansoul into conformity to ways that are pleasing in his sight. I will possess the town and cast you out. I will set up my own standard in the midst of them. I will govern them by new laws, new officers, new motives, and new ways. I will pull down this town and build it again. It will be as though it had never existed, and it will then become the glory of the whole universe."

When Diabolus realized that his deceitful tactics were discovered, he was utterly perplexed. But his fountain of iniquity, rage, and malice against Shaddai and the town of Mansoul increased his determination to give fresh battle to the noble Prince Emmanuel.

Diabolus withdrew from the wall and returned to his forces in the heart of the town of Mansoul. Emmanuel also returned to his camp, and both prepared for the coming battle.

Diabolus, knowing he could not win, resolved to do as much damage as he could to the army of the Prince and to the famous town of Mansoul. It was not the happiness of the silly town that Diabolus desired, but its ruin and overthrow. Therefore, he commanded his officers that they should, when they could no longer hold the town, do as much harm as possible to the men, women, and children. "For," he said, "we must demolish the place and leave it in ruins rather than leave it as a suitable habitation for Emmanuel."

Emmanuel, knowing that the next battle would result in his being made master of the place, gave a royal commandment to all his officers, high captains, and men of war. He told them to fight fiercely against Diabolus and all the Diabolonians, but to be kind and merciful to all the inhabitants of Mansoul. The noble Prince said, "Concentrate the heat of the battle against Diabolus and his men."

Chapter Eight

STORMING THE GATES

When the day of battle came, the Prince's men concentrated their main forces against Ear Gate and Eye Gate. Diabolus resisted with all of his power, and his high lords and chief captains fought fiercely against the Prince's army.

After three or four strong charges by the Prince and his noble captains, Ear Gate was finally forced open. Its bars and bolts were broken into a thousand pieces! Having gained entrance to Mansoul, the captains shouted, the town shook, and Diabolus retreated to his stronghold.

Emmanuel immediately established his command post at the entrance to the gate and from there directed his forces. He commanded that the golden catapults continue to be used against the town and especially against the castle where Diabolus had retreated.

From Ear Gate the main street led straight to the house of the former recorder, Mr. Conscience. Near his house stood the castle which Diabolus had made his filthy den. Using shots from the catapults, the Prince's captains quickly cleared the street and made their way up through the heart of Mansoul. Captain Thunder, Captain Conviction, and Captain Judgment ceremoniously entered the town and marched with flying colors up to Mr. Conscience's house. They knocked and demanded to enter, but the old gentleman kept his gates tightly shut.

When Captain Thunder again demanded to enter and no one answered, he pounded the gate with the battering ram. This made the old gentleman shake and caused his house to tremble and totter. Then Mr. Conscience came down to the gate and with quivering lips asked who was there.

Captain Thunder answered, "We are the captains and commanders of the great Shaddai and Emmanuel his Son. We demand possession of your house for the use of our noble Prince." Then the battering ram shook the gate again, making the old gentleman tremble even more. He finally opened the gate, and the King's forces, led by the three brave captains, marched into the house. Once inside, the captains were very cool toward Mr. Conscience and told him nothing about Emmanuel's plans. So he did not know what to think or what would be the end result of these terrible events.

Soon everyone in the town heard how Mr. Conscience's house had been taken and made the captains' headquarters. Many of the townsmen came to find out what had happened. When they saw the captains in possession of the recorder's house and the battering rams pounding against the castle gates, they were riveted in fear and amazement. Mr. Conscience increased their fears and anxiety by telling them that they must expect nothing but death and destruction from the Prince's army.

The old gentleman said, "You realize that we have all been traitors to that once despised but now victorious Prince Emmanuel. As you can see, he has not only besieged our town, but he has forced his way through our gate. Moreover, Diabolus has fled from him, and my house has been made a garrison against the castle where the giant hides. I have transgressed greatly by keeping silent when I should have spoken; and I have perverted justice when I should have performed it. It is true that I have suffered at the hands of Diabolus for taking sides with the laws of Shaddai. But what good will that do? Will that compensate for the rebellion and treason I have allowed to be committed in the town of Mansoul? Oh, I tremble to think what will happen to us!"

While the brave captains were busy in the house of the old recorder, Captain Execution was active in other parts of the town, securing the side streets and the walls. He hunted down Lord Willbewill and would not permit him to find rest in any corner of the town. The captain pursued him so hard that three of Willbewill's men deserted him. Old Mr. Prejudice, who had been made keeper of Ear Gate by Lord Willbewill, fell by the hand of Captain Execution. Mr. Backward, captain of the two guns mounted on the top of Ear Gate, was also cut down to the ground. Captain Execution killed another officer named Captain Treacherous, in whom Willbewill had put a great deal of confidence. In addition, a large number of Lord Willbewill's bravest soldiers were slaughtered by Captain Execution, and many dangerous Diabolonians were wounded by him. But not a native of Mansoul was hurt.

At Eye Gate, where Captain Goodhope and Captain Charity were in charge, great advances were made. Captain Goodhope with his own hands slew Captain Blindfold, the keeper of that gate. Blindfold had been captain of a thousand men who fought with battle-axes. Many of his men were slain, and even more were wounded. In fact, Diabolonians lay dead in every corner of the town, although many still remained alive in Mansoul.

Mr. Ill-Pause was also at the gate. As the orator for Diabolus, he had done much to spread discord in the town of Mansoul; but he, too, fell by the hand of Captain Goodhope.

Realizing their predicament, Mr. Conscience and Lord Understanding, along with other chiefs of the town, decided to meet together. After consultation, they agreed to draw up a petition to send to Emmanuel who now sat at the gate of Mansoul. Their petition said that the old inhabitants of the now deplorable town of Mansoul confessed their sin and were sorry they had offended his Princely Majesty. They begged that he would spare their lives. But the Prince did not answer this petition.

While this was going on, the captains who were

in the recorder's house continued battering the gates of the castle. After some time one of the gates, called Impregnable, was beaten open and broken into a thousand splinters. This made the way clear for the King's army to go up to the stronghold where Diabolus was hiding.

The news that the castle gate was broken open was sent down to Emmanuel. Throughout the Prince's camp, the trumpet sounded, announcing that the war would soon be ended and Mansoul would be set free. Then the Prince arose, gathered his most able soldiers, and marched up the street of Mansoul toward the old recorder's house.

As the Prince, clad in armor of gold, paraded up the street, the townsfolk came out to see him and were impressed by the glory of his appearance. Yet he kept his countenance reserved, so the people could not tell from his expression whether he felt love or hate for them.

"For," they thought, "if Emmanuel loved us, he would show it by his word or expression. But he has not done so; therefore, Emmanuel must hate us. Now, if Emmanuel hates us, then Mansoul will be destroyed and become a dunghill."

They knew they had transgressed his Father's law and turned against him by siding with Diabolus, his enemy. They also realized that Prince Emmanuel knew all this, for they were convinced that he knew everything that happened on the earth. This made them think that their condition was hopeless and that the good Prince would destroy them. "And," they thought, "what better time to punish us than when he has Mansoul in his hand?"

When they saw him march through the town, the inhabitants could do nothing but cringe and bow before him. They were ready to kiss the dust of his feet and wished a thousand times over that he would become their Prince and protector. They talked among themselves about his magnificent appearance and how his glory and valor exceeded all others. But their thoughts would change from one extreme to another, and their fickle hearts were tossed to and fro like leaves in the wind.

When he came to the castle gates, Emmanuel commanded Diabolus to appear and surrender himself into his hands. But, oh, how the beast hated to appear! He resisted and cowered, but he finally came out to the Prince. Then at Emmanuel's command, they took Diabolus and bound him in chains to reserve him for the judgment appointed for him. But Diabolus pleaded with Emmanuel not to send him into the pit and begged to be permitted to depart from Mansoul in peace.

When Emmanuel had taken him and bound him in chains, he led him into the marketplace. There, before Mansoul, he stripped Diabolus of the armor in which he had boasted. Seeing this, the trumpets of the Golden Prince sounded, the captains shouted, and the soldiers sang for joy. Mansoul witnessed the beginning of Emmanuel's triumph over the deceiver in whom they had trusted in the days when he had flattered them.

After stripping the giant naked in the sight of Mansoul and before the King's commanders, the Prince commanded that Diabolus be bound to the wheels of his golden chariot. Then, Emmanuel rode in triumph over him throughout the town of Mansoul and out of Eye Gate to the plain where the King's army was encamped. You cannot imagine, unless you had been there as I was, the shout that came from Emmanuel's soldiers when they saw the tyrant bound and tied to the Prince's chariot wheels.

The soldiers shouted, "He hath led captivity captive, he hath spoiled principalities and powers. Diabolus is subjected to the power of his sword and made the object of all ridicule."

The King's noblemen, who had come from Shaddai's court to see the battle, also shouted with loud voices. They sang with such melodious notes that the angels looked down from heaven to see the reason for this great celebration.

The people of Mansoul, hearing this beautiful music, felt as if they were being held between earth and heaven. Although they did not know what was going to happen to them, the townsmen were very impressed with the excellent ways of the Prince. Their eyes, their hearts, and their minds were held in awe as they observed Emmanuel's glorious display of power.

When the brave Prince finished his triumph over Diabolus, he turned the tyrant loose in the midst of his contempt and shame. The Prince commanded him to never again try to possess Mansoul. Then the defeated enemy left Emmanuel's camp to inhabit the parched places in the desert, seeking rest but finding none.

The forces of Captain Thunder and Captain Conviction remained in Mansoul to guard the castle gates, in case any of Diabolus' followers should attempt to repossess it. This gave the townsmen an opportunity to view the actions of these fierce and noble captains. Still, the future of Mansoul was in doubt, and the townsmen had no rest, peace, or hope.

The Prince did not move into the town of Mansoul, but he remained living at his royal pavilion in the camp among his Father's forces. At a convenient time, he sent special orders to Captain Thunder to summon all the townsmen into the castle yard. He told the captain to take Lord Understanding, Mr. Conscience, and Lord Willbewill into custody and put them under heavy guard until his final orders concerning them were given.

When this action was carried out, it confirmed the townsmen's fears of the ruin of Mansoul. With anxious hearts, they wondered how and when they would be punished. They were afraid Emmanuel would command that they all be thrown into the deep pit, the place Diabolus had dreaded. Yet, they knew that they deserved it.

The town was greatly troubled about the arrest of their leaders. They believed that if these men were executed, it would be the beginning of the ruin of Mansoul. Therefore, along with the men in prison, they drew up a petition and sent it to Emmanuel by the hand of Mr. Would-Live. So he went to the Prince's quarters and presented the petition.

The petition read, "To the great and wonderful Potentate, Victor over Diabolus, and Conqueror of Mansoul. We, the miserable inhabitants of this town, humbly seek favor in your sight. Please do not remember our former transgressions or the sins of our leaders. Spare us according to your great mercy, and do not let us die but live in your sight. Then we will be willing to become your servants. Amen."

The Prince took the petition and read it, but sent Mr. Would-Live away in silence. This further worried the town of Mansoul, but they did not know what else to do. Therefore, they consulted again and sent another petition, similar to the first one.

When the petition was drawn up, they wondered who would take it. They decided not to send it by Mr. Would-Live because they thought the Prince had taken offense at his manner. They attempted to make Captain Conviction their messenger, but he said that he would neither petition Emmanuel for traitors nor be an advocate for rebels. "Yet," he said, "our Prince is good, and you may attempt to send it by someone from your town, provided he pleads for nothing but mercy."

Because of their fear, they delayed sending the petition as long as possible. But at last they decided to send it by Mr. Desires-Awake, a poor man who lived in a small cottage in Mansoul. When they told him they wanted him to take the petition to the

Prince, Mr. Desires-Awake said, "Why should I not do my best to save so famous a town as Mansoul from deserved destruction?" They, therefore, gave him the petition and told him how to address the Prince.

After he arrived at the Prince's pavilion, he asked to speak with his Majesty. Word was taken to Emmanuel, and the Prince came out to meet the man. When Mr. Desires-Awake saw the Prince, he fell down with his face to the ground and cried out, "O that Mansoul may live before you!" He then presented the petition.

When the Prince read it, he turned away and wept. After composing himself, he turned again to the man (who all this while lay pleading at his feet) and said to him, "Go back to your town, and I will consider your requests."

In the town of Mansoul, the people were anxiously waiting to hear the result of their petition. When at last they saw their messenger coming back, they ran to meet him and asked him what Emmanuel had said. But he replied that he would be silent until he came to the prison where Lord Understanding, Lord Willbewill, and Mr. Conscience were held captive. As he went toward the prison, a multitude followed to hear what the messenger had to say.

When he showed himself at the prison gate, the mayor looked as white as a sheet, and the recorder trembled with fear. But they asked, "Sir, what did the great Prince say to you?"

Mr. Desires-Awake said, "When I came to the

Prince's pavilion, I called, and he came forth. I fell prostrate at his feet, for the glory of his countenance would not allow me to remain standing. As he received the petition, I cried, 'O that Mansoul might live before you!' After he read it, he turned about and said, 'Go back to your town, and I will consider your request.' "

The messenger added, "The Prince to whom you sent me is so beautiful and glorious that whoever sees him must both love and fear him. As for me, I can do nothing else, although I do not know what will happen in the end." Everyone was amazed at the messenger's answer, both the prisoners and the people. But they did not know how to interpret what the Prince had said.

After the throng of people had left, the prisoners began to comment on Emmanuel's words. Lord Understanding, the former mayor, said that the answer did not seem too severe. But Willbewill said it indicated bad things to come, and Mr. Conscience said it was the message of death. The people who remained behind heard only bits and pieces of what the prisoners said, and no one had the right understanding of things. You cannot imagine the disturbance this caused and what confusion there was in Mansoul now.

Those who had heard what was said went about the town, one repeating one thing and another quite the contrary. But both were sure that what they heard was true. One would say, "We will all be killed!" Another would say, "We will all be saved!" A third would say that the Prince was not concerned about Mansoul. A fourth said that the prisoners would suddenly be put to death. Each one was convinced that his version was correct and all the others were mistaken. As a result, Mansoul was thrown into great confusion.

All this chaos came about when Mr. Conscience said that the Prince's answer was a message of death. It was these words that had excited and created the fear in the town. In the past, Mansoul had considered Mr. Conscience as a prophet and everything he said as truth. For this reason, the people were terrified. They now began to feel the effects of their stubborn rebellion and unlawful resistance against the Prince. These effects were the result of the guilt and fear that had swallowed them up.

After a while, when the widespread fear had somewhat diminished, the townsmen took heart and decided to petition the Prince for life again. They drew up a third petition which said:

"Prince Emmanuel, the great Lord of all worlds and Master of mercy, we, your poor, miserable town of Mansoul, confess that we have sinned against your Father. We are no longer worthy to be called your Mansoul, but we should be cast into the pit. We deserve to be destroyed. If you condemn us to the pit, we can only say that you are righteous. We cannot complain about anything you do to us. But let mercy reign! And let it be extended to us! Oh, let mercy take hold of us and free us from our transgressions. Then we will sing of your mercy and your judgment. Amen."

This petition, like the others, was designed to be sent to the Prince. But who would carry it? There was an old man in the town named Mr. Good-Deed, but his nature was quite the contrary to his name. Some were for sending him, but Mr. Conscience disagreed and said, "We now stand in need of and are pleading for mercy. To send our petition by a man with this name will seem to contradict the petition itself. Should we make Mr. Good-Deed our messenger when our petition cries for mercy?

"Besides," the old gentleman continued, "what if the Prince asks him his name? He will say old Good-Deed. Emmanuel would then reply, 'Oh, is old Good-Deed still alive in Mansoul? Then let old Good-Deed save you from your distress.' If this happens, then I am sure we are lost and a thousand old Good-Deeds could not save Mansoul."

After the recorder had given his reason why old Good-Deed should not take the petition to Emmanuel, the rest of the prisoners and leaders of Mansoul also opposed it. So old Good-Deed was rejected, and they agreed to send Mr. Desires-Awake again. They asked him to go a second time with their petition to the Prince, and he readily told them he would. But they told him to be careful not to offend the Prince in any way. "For if you do, you may bring Mansoul to utter destruction," they said.

When Mr. Desires-Awake saw that he must go on this errand, he asked if his neighbor, Mr. Wet-Eyes, could go with him. Wet-Eyes was a poor man with a broken spirit, but one who could speak well. They agreed that he should go with him, and the two men prepared for their mission. Mr. Desires-Awake put a rope upon his head, and Mr. Wet-Eyes followed, wringing his hands together.

As they went this third time, they thought that by coming again they may become a burden to the Prince. Therefore, when they came to the door of his pavilion, they first gave an apology for coming to trouble Emmanuel so often. They said that they came not because they delighted in hearing themselves talk, but they came out of necessity. They said they could have no rest day or night because of their transgressions against Shaddai and Emmanuel his Son. They also thought that Mr. Desires-Awake may have offended his Highness the last time. After they made this apology, Mr. Desires-Awake prostrated himself at the feet of the mighty Prince, saying, "Oh! May Mansoul live before you!" Then he delivered his petition.

The Prince, after reading the petition, turned aside and wept as he had before. Then he came to where the petitioner lay on the ground and demanded to know his name and why he had been chosen for such an errand.

The man said to the Prince, "Oh, my Lord do not be angry. Why do you desire to know the name of such a dead dog as I? The reason the townsmen chose to send me on this errand is known only to them. But it could not be that they thought I had favor with my Lord, for I am even out of sorts with myself. Who then could love me? Yet I desire to live, and I want the townsmen to live also. But we are guilty of great transgressions, and they have sent me in their names to beg my Lord for mercy. May it please you to give us mercy and not ask who we are."

Then the Prince asked, "And who is your companion in this mighty matter?"

Mr. Desires-Awake told Emmanuel that this was his poor neighbor and one of his most intimate associates. "And his name," he said, "is Wet-Eyes. There are many common people by that name in Mansoul. I hope you are not offended that I brought my poor neighbor with me."

Suddenly, Mr. Wet-Eyes fell on his face to the ground and apologized for coming with his neighbor to see the Prince. "O my Lord," he said, "I myself do not know who I am nor whether my name is true or false. Some have said that this name was given to me because Mr. Repentance was my father. My mother called me by this name from the time I was in the cradle. But I do not know whether it was because of the moistness of my brain or the softness of my heart. I see dirt in my own tears and filthiness at the bottom of my prayers. But I beg you," the gentleman wept, "not to remember our transgressions nor take offense at our unworthiness. Mercifully pass by the sin of Mansoul and do not withhold your grace any longer."

At the Prince's bidding, they rose and stood trembling before him. Emmanuel spoke to them and said, "The town of Mansoul has grievously rebelled against my Father by rejecting him as their King and choosing a liar, a murderer, and a renegade as their leader. Diabolus, your pretended prince, rebelled against my Father and me and desired to become a prince and king. But he was discovered and apprehended. For his wickedness, he was bound in chains and thrown into the pit along with his companions. Then he offered himself to you, and you received him.

"For a long time this has been an insult to my Father, so he sent a powerful army to obtain your obedience. But you rebelled and shut your gates against his captains. You went to battle and fought for Diabolus against them. So they asked my Father for more support, and I, along with my men, have come to subdue you. But as you treated my servants, so you treated their Lord. You stood in hostility against me. You shut your gates against me and turned a deaf ear to my words. You resisted as long as you could, but now I have conquered you.

"Did you cry to me for mercy as long as you had hope that you could prevail against me? But now that I have taken the town, you cry. Why did you not cry before when the white flag of my mercy, the red flag of justice, and the black flag that threatened execution were set up to compel you to submit? Now that I have conquered Diabolus, you come to me for favor. Why did you not help me fight against the evil one? Yet, I will consider your petition and answer it in a way that will bring me glory.

"Go tell Captain Thunder and Captain Conviction

to bring the prisoners out here to the camp tomorrow. Tell Captain Judgment and Captain Execution to stay in the castle and keep everything quiet in Mansoul until they hear further from me." Then he turned and went back into his royal pavilion.

The two petitioners left to return to their companions, but they had not gone far when they realized that no mercy had yet been extended by the Prince. These thoughts about what would become of Mansoul were so troublesome that they dreaded delivering their message to their leaders at the prison.

When they came to the gates of the town, Mr. Desires-Awake and Mr. Wet-Eyes found the townsmen eagerly waiting for them. As soon as they saw them, the people cried out, "What news do you have from the Prince? What did Emmanuel say?" But the two messengers said they must first deliver their message to Lord Understanding, Mr. Conscience, and Lord Willbewill. So away they went to the prison with the multitude following them.

At the gates of the prison, they told the first part of Emmanuel's speech to the prisoners. They told how he reflected on their disloyalty to his Father and himself as their King. This made the prisoners turn pale, but the messengers proceeded and said, "The Prince also said that he would consider your petition and give an answer according to his glory."

As these words were spoken, Mr. Wet-Eyes gave a great sigh. All of them were disheartened and did not know what to say. Great fear came upon them, and the look of death could be seen in some of their faces.

Among the townsmen was a sharp-witted fellow, an unprincipled man of high rank named old Inquisitive. This man asked the petitioners if they had told every word that Emmanuel had said. And they answered, "No."

Then Inquisitive said, "I thought so. What else did he say to you?"

The messengers paused for a moment, but at last they told them everything, saying, "The Prince told us to tell Captain Thunder and Captain Conviction to bring the prisoners down to him tomorrow. He said that Captain Judgment and Captain Execution should take charge of the castle and town until they heard further from him." They also told them that after the Prince had given these commands he immediately turned his back on them and went into his royal pavilion.

When the people heard that the prisoners must go out to the Prince in the camp, they cried out with one voice that reached up to the heavens. Each of the three then prepared himself to die. Mr. Conscience said to them, "This was the thing that I feared." The three concluded that by sunset tomorrow they would be tumbled out of the world.

The townsmen figured that in time they must all drink of the same cup; therefore, Mansoul spent that night mourning in sackcloth and ashes.

Chapter Nine

THE TRIUMPHANT ENTRANCE

When the time came for the prisoners to appear before the Prince, they dressed themselves in mourning attire. The townspeople also wore mourning clothes and stood upon the wall hoping the Prince would be moved with compassion when he saw them.

The busybodies in the town ran here and there throughout the streets, creating a commotion and crying out with fear as they ran. Some were shouting one thing, and others were yelling something different.

Captain Thunder and the guards walked in front of the prisoners, and Captain Conviction came behind. The three prisoners, bound in chains, walked along mournfully smiting their breasts and daring not to lift their eyes. They went out at the gate of Mansoul and came into the midst of the Prince's army. The sight and glory of his magnificent forces greatly heightened their affliction. When they could bear it no longer, they cried out, "O unhappy men!

O wretched men of Mansoul!'' The sound of their clanking chains mixed with the mournful cries of the prisoners made the noise even more lamentable.

When they came to the door of the Prince's pavilion, they lay prostrate on the ground. One of the guards went and told his Lord that the prisoners had arrived. The Prince then ascended his throne and sent for the prisoners who, when they came before him, trembled and covered their faces with shame. As they drew near the place where he sat, they threw themselves down before him. The Prince said to Captain Thunder, ''Tell the prisoners to stand on their feet.''

As they stood trembling before him, he asked, ''Are you the men who were the servants of Shaddai?''

''Yes, Lord, yes,'' they answered.

''Are you the men who allowed yourselves to be corrupted and defiled by that abominable one, Diabolus?'' the Prince asked.

They said, ''We did more than allow it, Lord, we willingly chose it.''

The Prince asked further, ''Would you have been content to remain in slavery under his tyranny as long as you lived?''

''Yes, Lord, yes, for his ways were pleasing to our flesh,'' the prisoners answered.

''And did you,'' he asked, ''when I came against this town of Mansoul, heartily wish that I would not have the victory over you?''

''Yes, Lord, yes,'' they said.

"Then," asked the Prince, "what punishment do you think you deserve at my hand for these and your other high and mighty sins?"

They said, "Both death and the pit, Lord, for we deserve no less."

"Do you have anything to say for yourselves?" he asked. "Is there any reason why the sentence you confess you deserve should not be carried out?"

"We can say nothing, Lord. You are just, and we have sinned."

"What are these ropes on your heads?" the Prince asked.

The prisoners answered, "These ropes are to bind us for our execution, if mercy is not found in your sight."

"Are all the men in the town of Mansoul in agreement with this confession?"

They answered, "All the natives, Lord, except for the Diabolonians who came into our town when the tyrant took possession of us. We can say nothing for them."

The Prince then commanded that a herald be sent throughout the camp of Emmanuel to proclaim that the Son of Shaddai had in his Father's name and glory gotten perfect victory over Mansoul. The prisoners were to follow the herald and say, "Amen."

As this was being done, music from the heavens resounded melodiously all around them. The captains who were in the camp shouted, and the soldiers sang songs of triumph to the Prince. The colorful banners waved in the wind, and great joy was everywhere, except in the hearts of the men of Mansoul.

Then the Prince called for the prisoners to come before him again. They came and stood trembling. He said to them, "You and the whole town of Mansoul have committed trespasses and iniquities against my Father and me. But I have power and commandment from my Father to forgive the town of Mansoul, and I forgive you accordingly."

Having said this, he gave them a parchment, sealed with seven seals, on which was written a large and general pardon. He commanded Lord Understanding, Lord Willbewill, and Mr. Conscience to proclaim the pardon throughout the whole town of Mansoul by sunrise tomorrow.

The Prince then stripped the prisoners of their mourning clothes and gave them beauty for ashes, the oil of joy for mourning, and the garment of praise for the spirit of heaviness. He gave jewels of gold and precious stones to each of the three. He took away their ropes and put chains of gold about their necks and earrings in their ears.

When the prisoners heard the gracious words of Prince Emmanuel and saw all that was done for them, they almost fainted away. The grace, the gifts, and the pardon were so sudden and glorious that they staggered in surprise and amazement. Lord Willbewill swooned outright, but the Prince stepped over to him. He put his everlasting arms under him, embraced him, kissed him, and told him to rejoice for everything would be performed according to his word. He also kissed, embraced, and smiled upon the other two, saying, "Take these as further tokens of my love, favor, and compassion for you. And I command you, Mr. Conscience, to tell the town of Mansoul all you have heard and seen."

Then the chains of the pardoned prisoners were broken to pieces before them and thrown into the air. The three men fell down before the Prince, kissed his feet, and wet them with their tears. They cried out with loud voices, saying, "Blessed be the glory of the Lord in this place."

They were told to rise up, go to the town, and tell Mansoul what the Prince had done. He also commanded that musicians with flutes and drums should accompany them all the way into the town of Mansoul.

Then something happened that they never dreamed of nor expected. The Prince called for noble Captain Credence and commanded that he and some of his officers march with banners flying high before these noblemen of Mansoul. At the exact time Mr. Conscience was to read the general pardon, Captain Credence was to enter at Eye Gate with his ten thousand soldiers and march up the high street of the town to the castle gates. He was to take possession of the castle until the Prince came. Captain Judgment and Captain Execution were to leave the stronghold to him, withdraw from Mansoul, and return immediately to the Prince's camp. In this way the town of Mansoul was to be delivered from the terror of the King's first four captains and their men.

I have told you how the prisoners were welcomed

by the noble Prince Emmanuel, how they behaved themselves before him, and how he sent them back to their home in jubilation. All this time the people of the town waited, with great sadness of heart and tormented minds, to hear of the death of their leaders. Their thoughts were filled with many uncertainties, and their hearts trembled with fear.

After anxiously waiting, they looked over the wall of Mansoul and thought they saw a group of people returning to the town. The townsmen wondered who they were and why they were coming. At last they realized that they were the prisoners. Can you imagine how surprised they were, especially when they saw the procession that accompanied them?

The three prisoners had gone to the camp in black, but they came back to the town in white. They had gone down in iron chains, but they returned with chains of gold. They went to the camp looking for death, but they came back with the assurance of life. They had walked to the camp with heavy hearts, but they returned with flutes and drums playing before them.

As soon as the procession arrived at Eye Gate, the poor and feeble town of Mansoul gave such a shout that the captains and the Prince's army were startled by the sound of it. Who could blame them for rejoicing? Seeing their leaders arrayed in such splendor was like seeing them raised from the dead. They had expected the axe and the block, but instead they received such gladness, comfort, and consolation that it was enough to make a sick man well.

When the three noblemen came up to the gate, the townsmen saluted them and said, "Welcome, welcome, and blessed be the one who has spared you. We see it is well with you. But will it go well with the town of Mansoul?"

Then Mr. Conscience and Lord Understanding answered, "Oh! Good news! We bring good tidings of great joy to poor Mansoul!" Then they gave another shout that made the earth ring.

After this the townsmen inquired how things went in the camp and what message they had from Emmanuel for the town. The three men told everything that had happened to them at the camp and everything the Prince did for them. Mansoul was amazed at the wisdom and grace of Prince Emmanuel. Then the noblemen told them what they had received from him for the whole town of Mansoul.

Mr. Conscience delivered the message in these words, *"Pardon! Pardon! Pardon* shall be given to Mansoul tomorrow!" Then he commanded the people of Mansoul to meet together in the marketplace the next day to hear their general pardon read.

What a difference this announcement made in the countenance of the town. No one in Mansoul could sleep that night because of their joy. In every house there was music, singing, and rejoicing.

This is the song they sang: "Oh! More of this at the rising of the sun! More of this tomorrow! Who would have thought yesterday that today would have been such a day? Who would ever have thought that our prisoners would leave in irons but return with chains of gold? They went to be judged, but they were acquitted; not because they were innocent, but because of the Prince's mercy. Is this the common custom of princes? Do they always show such favors to traitors? No! Mercy is given only by Shaddai and Emmanuel his Son."

As morning drew near, Lord Understanding, Lord Willbewill, and Mr. Conscience walked down to the marketplace at the time the Prince had appointed. They wore the attire that the Prince had given them the day before, and the street was illuminated by their glory. At the lower end of the marketplace where public matters were read, the townsfolk eagerly waited to find out what the Prince had to say to them.

Mr. Conscience, the recorder, stood to his feet, beckoned with his hand for silence, and read the pardon with a loud voice. "The Lord, the Lord God merciful and gracious, pardons all your iniquity, transgression, and sin. All manner of blasphemy will also be forgiven." Following this proclamation, the name of every person in Mansoul was read aloud.

When the recorder had finished reading the pardon, the townsmen ran along the wall of the town, leaping for joy. They bowed themselves seven times with their faces toward Emmanuel's pavilion and shouted, "Let Emmanuel live forever!" Then the bells of the town rang, the people sang, and the music was heard in every house in Mansoul.

When the recorder had finished reading the pardon, Emmanuel commanded all the trumpets in the camp to sound and the banners to be displayed, half of them on Mount Gracious and half on Mount Justice. The Prince commanded all the captains to parade through the town, showing all their soldiers and military equipment. Even Captain Credence could not keep silent in such a day. From the top of the castle, he shouted joyfully and waved his banner before Mansoul and the Prince's camp.

At the completion of these joyful ceremonies, the Prince commanded his captains and soldiers to show Mansoul some feats of war. With great agility, dexterity, and bravery, these military men displayed their battle skills to the admiring gaze of Mansoul. They marched and counter-marched; they opened to the right and left; they divided and sub-divided; they closed and they wheeled. They performed twenty other difficult maneuvers, handling their weapons with perfect precision. The people of Mansoul watched in amazement and were thrilled by the marvelous performance of the King's great army.

When it was over, the whole town of Mansoul went to the Prince in the camp to thank and praise him for his abundant favor. They asked him, if it would please his Grace, to come into Mansoul with his men and to take up residence there forever. They did this in a most humble manner, bowing themselves seven times to the ground before him. Then the Prince said to them, "Peace be to you."

With the Prince's consent the townsmen approached his throne and touched the top of his golden scepter. They said that Prince Emmanuel, along with his captains and men of war, could dwell in Mansoul forever. They said his battering rams and slings could be stored there for the service of the Prince and for the protection of Mansoul. "For," they said, "we have room for you and your men. We also have room for your weapons of war and a place to make an armory. Do this, Emmanuel, and you will be King of Mansoul forever. You can govern according to your desire and appoint governors under the captains and men of war. We will become your servants and live by your laws."

They added, "If you withdraw yourself and your captains, the town of Mansoul will die. Our blessed Emmanuel, you have done so much good for us and have shown us great mercy. What will happen if you depart from us? Our joy will be as if it had not been, and our enemies will come a second time with more rage than at first! You are the strength and life of our poor town. Please accept this motion we have made. Come and dwell in the midst of us, and let us be your people. Besides, Lord, many Diabolonians may still be lurking in the town of Mansoul. If you leave us, they will betray us into the hand of Diabolus again. And who knows what tricks, plots, or schemes have already passed between them? We dread falling into their horrible hands again. Please accept our palace as your place of residence, and the houses of our richest men for your soldiers' quarters."

Then the Prince said, "If I come to your town, will you allow me to prosecute my enemies and yours? Will you also help me in such an under-taking?''

They answered, "We do not know what we will do. We never imagined that we would ever be such traitors to Shaddai as we have proved to be. What can we say to our Lord? Let the Prince dwell in our castle and make our town a garrison. Let him set his noble captains and his warlike soldiers over us. Let him conquer us with his love and overcome us with his grace. Then surely he will be with us and help us, as he was and did that morning our pardon was read to us. We will comply with our Lord and with his ways, and we will fall in line with his word against our enemies.

"One more word, and we will no longer trouble our Lord. Oh, Prince, we do not know the depth of your wisdom. Who could have thought that the contentment we now enjoy could have come out of those bitter trials with which we were tried at first? But, Lord, let light go before, and let love come after. Take us by the hand and lead us always by your counsel. Whatever you do will be for our good. Come to Mansoul and do as you please, Lord. Come to Mansoul, keep us from sinning, and make us your servants."

The Prince said to the town of Mansoul, "Go, return to your houses in peace. I will willingly comply with your desires. I will remove my royal pavilion and march my forces into the town. I will take possession of your castle in Mansoul and set my soldiers over you. I will do things in Mansoul that cannot be paralleled in any nation, country, or kingdom under heaven.''

Then the men of Mansoul gave a shout and returned to their houses. They told their families and friends the good things that Emmanuel had promised to do for Mansoul. ''Tomorrow,'' they said, ''he and his men will march into our town and take up residence in Mansoul.''

In preparation for the coming of their Prince, the inhabitants of the town went out to the meadows to gather tree branches and flowers to lay on the streets. They also made flower garlands to show how joyful they were to receive Emmanuel into Mansoul. The townsmen decorated the street from Eye Gate to the castle, the place where the Prince would live. They also prepared music to play before him on his march to the palace.

At the appointed time the Prince approached the town, and the gates were opened wide before him. The leaders and elders of Mansoul saluted him with a thousand welcomes as he and all his soldiers entered Mansoul. The Prince, clad in golden armor, rode in his royal chariot while the trumpets sounded around him and the elders danced before him. Behind him marched his noble captains, leading their divisions with banners flying high. The tops of the city walls were filled with the inhabitants who went up to view the approach of the blessed Prince and his royal army. The windows, balconies, and roofs of the houses were all filled with people waiting to see Emmanuel in all his glory.

When he had come as far as the recorder's house, the Prince sent a messenger to Captain Credence to find out whether the castle of Mansoul was prepared for his royal presence. Word was brought that it was. Then Captain Credence was commanded to come with his troops to meet the Prince and conduct him into the castle. That night, to the joy of Mansoul, the Prince, with his mighty captains and men of war, stayed in the castle.

The next concern of the townsfolk was how the captains and soldiers of the Prince's army should be quartered among them. Their concern was not where they would place them, but how they could fill their houses with them. Everyone in Mansoul had such high esteem for Emmanuel and his men that nothing pleased them more than having enough room to house a captain or soldier in their homes. In fact, they considered it a great privilege to wait on them and to do their bidding like servants.

They finally decided where all the captains and their men were to be quartered. Captain Innocent was housed at Mr. Reason's and Captain Patience at Mr. Mind's residence. It was ordered that Captain Charity should reside at Mr. Affection's house and Captain Good-Hope at Lord Understanding's.

Because Mr. Conscience's house was next to the castle, it was ordered by the Prince that, in case of an enemy attack, he should give the alarm. For this reason, the recorder requested that Captain Thunder and Captain Conviction, along with all their men, take up residence with him.

As for Captain Judgment and Captain Execution, Lord Willbewill housed them and their men. The Prince had reinstated Willbewill as a leader of the town, commanding him to rule for the good of the people instead of for their harm as he had done under the tyrant Diabolus.

Emmanuel's other officers and soldiers were quartered in homes throughout the rest of the town, but Captain Credence and his men resided in the Prince's castle.

The leaders and elders of the town of Mansoul thought they would never have enough of Prince Emmanuel. His person, his actions, his words, and behavior were very pleasing and appealing to them. Although the castle of Mansoul was his place of residence, they asked him to frequently visit the streets, houses, and people of Mansoul. "For," they said, "dear Sovereign, your presence, your appearance, your smile, and your words are the life and strength of the town of Mansoul."

They longed to have, without interruption, continual access to him. For this reason, the Prince commanded that the castle gates remain open. The people could then come and go as they pleased and feel welcome in his royal mansion. Whenever Emmanuel spoke, the townsmen all stopped talking to listen; and when he walked among them, they delighted to imitate his actions.

One day Emmanuel held a feast for Mansoul and invited the townsfolk to come to the castle for his banquet. He fed them with all kinds of fancy food not grown in the fields of Mansoul or in all the Kingdom of Universe. These special delicacies came only from the court of King Shaddai, his Father. Dish after dish was set before them, and they were encouraged to eat freely. Mansoul drank water that had been made into wine and ate angels' food sweetened with honey from the rock.

While they were eating, lovely music filled the banquet hall. I must not forget to tell you that the musicians at this banquet were not from that country or even from the town of Mansoul. But they were masters of the songs sung at the court of Shaddai.

After the feast was over, Emmanuel entertained the townsfolk with some curious riddles presented by his Father's Secretary. These riddles were designed by King Shaddai himself and were about his Son, his wars, and his ways with Mansoul. Emmanuel gave the meaning to some of these riddles himself. And oh, how the people were enlightened! They saw things they had never seen before. They were amazed that such wonders could be contained in so few and in such ordinary words.

As the riddles were explained, the people realized that these were actually a portrait of Emmanuel himself. When they read the book where the riddles were written and looked into the face of the Prince, Mansoul could not help but say, "This is the Lamb, this is the Sacrifice, this is the Rock, this is the Door, and this is the Way."

You can imagine how the people enjoyed this entertainment. They were delighted and filled with wonder as they understood and considered the mysteries Emmanuel had opened to them. Whenever they were at home or in a secluded spot, they could not help but sing of him and his ways. The townsmen were so taken with their Prince that they would sing of him even in their sleep.

It was in the heart of Prince Emmanuel to remodel Mansoul and put it into a condition that would reflect the prosperity and security of the now flourishing town. Because of his love for Mansoul, the Prince also wanted to protect the town against any insurrections at home or any invasions from abroad.

First, he commanded that the great catapults be mounted on the battlements of the castle. Some were to be placed on the new tower built by Emmanuel. He also invented a new weapon that would throw stones from the castle all the way out of Mouth Gate. This weapon could not be resisted by any enemy or fail to miss its mark. It did such wonderful exploits that it was committed to the care and management of brave Captain Credence in case of war.

Emmanuel then called Lord Willbewill and commanded him to take care of the gates, the wall, and towers in Mansoul. The Prince also gave him control of the militia with special orders to withstand all insurrections and disturbances that might be made against the King or the peace and tranquility of the town of Mansoul. He also commissioned Willbewill to apprehend any Diabolonians he found lurking in the corners of the town. He was to keep them in custody until their case could be tried by the court.

Then he called for Lord Understanding, the mayor who had been removed when Diabolus took the town. The Prince reinstated him to his former office, and it remained his position for the rest of his life. Emmanuel told him to build a residence near Eye Gate and design it like a tower for defense. He also told him to read the revelation of mysteries all the days of his life, so he would know how to properly perform his office.

The Prince appointed Mr. Knowledge as the new recorder. He did this, not out of contempt for old Mr. Conscience who had been the recorder before, but because he had another job for Mr. Conscience to do.

Then the Prince commanded that the image of Diabolus be taken down, destroyed, ground down to a powder, and thrown into the wind over the town wall. He ordered the image of Shaddai to be set up again, along with his own, upon the castle gates. His name, Emmanuel, was also to be engraved in the finest gold over the gate to the entrance of the town.

Chapter Ten

TRIAL OF THE DIABOLONIANS

After the town had been restored to its former grandeur and the Prince was reigning in the town, Emmanuel issued a new proclamation. He commanded the apprehension of the three chief Diabolonians—Mr. Unbelief, Mr. Lustings, and Mr. Forget-Good. In addition, the burgesses and aldermen appointed by Diabolus were to be taken into custody by brave Lord Willbewill.

Those arrested were Alderman Atheism, Alderman Hard-Heart, and Alderman False-Peace. The burgesses were Mr. No-Truth, Mr. Pityless, Mr. Haughty, and others equally as evil. These were held under tight security by the jailer, Mr. True-Man, whom Emmanuel had brought with him from his Father's court when he first made war upon Diabolus in Mansoul.

The Prince then ordered that the three strongholds built by the Diabolonians in Mansoul be pulled down and demolished. This took a long time because the strongholds were large and the stones, timber, and all the rubbish had to be carried outside the town. When this was done, the Prince ordered that the Lord Mayor convene a court of justice for the trial and execution of the Diabolonians who were held in custody.

When the time came and the court convened, Mr. True-Man brought the prisoners who were shackled and chained together. After they were presented before the Lord Mayor, the chief magistrate, and the other judges, the jury was impaneled and the witnesses sworn in.

The names of the jury were: Mr. Belief, Mr. True-Heart, Mr. Upright, Mr. Hate-Bad, Mr. Love-God, Mr. See-Truth, Mr. Heavenly-Mind, Mr. Moderate, Mr. Thankful, Mr. Good-Work, Mr. Zeal-For-God, and Mr. Humble.

The names of the witnesses were Mr. Know-All, Mr. Tell-True, Mr. Hate-Lies, and Lord Willbewill.

Mr. Do-Right, the town clerk, said, ''Bring Atheism to the bar.''

Then the clerk said, ''Atheism, hold up your hand. You are indicted by the name of Atheism as an intruder in the town of Mansoul. You have maliciously taught and maintained that there is no God. You have done this against the honor and glory of the King and against the peace and safety of the town of Mansoul. What do you have to say? Are you guilty of this indictment or not?''

''Not guilty,'' Atheism said.

Then the baliff announced, ''Call Mr. Know-All, Mr. Tell-True, and Mr. Hate-Lies into the court.''

When they appeared, the clerk said, "You, the witnesses for the King, look at the prisoner. Do you know him?"

Mr. Know-All said, "Yes, my lord, we know him; his name is Atheism. He has been a troublesome fellow for many years in the miserable town of Mansoul."

"Are you sure you know him?" the clerk asked.

"Know him? Yes, my lord. I have often been in his company. He is a Diabolonian and the son of a Diabolonian. I knew his grandfather and his father," Mr. Know-All answered.

"He stands indicted by the name of Atheism. It is charged that he has maintained and taught that there is no God. What do you, the King's witnesses, say to this? Is he guilty or not?" asked the clerk.

Mr. Know-All answered, "We were once in Villain's Lane together, and he talked about many different philosophies. I heard him say that he did not believe there was a God. He said, 'I can profess to believe and be religious if the company I am in and the circumstances require it.'"

"Are you sure you heard him say this?" asked the clerk.

"By the oath that I have taken, I can honestly report that I heard him make this statement."

Then the clerk turned to Mr. Tell-True. "What do you have to say to the King's judges regarding the prisoner?"

"I was formerly a companion of his, for which now I am truly sorry. I have often heard him arrogantly say that he believed there was neither God, angel, nor spirit."

"Where did you hear him say so?"

"In Blackmouth Lane and in Blasphemer's Row, as well as in many others places."

"What do you know about him, Mr. Tell-True?" the clerk asked.

"I know he is a Diabolonian, the son of a Diabolonian, and a horrible man to deny Deity. His father, Never-Be-Good, had other children besides Atheism. I have no more to say."

"Mr. Hate-Lies, look at the prisoner. Do you know him?" the clerk asked.

"Yes, this Atheism is one of the vilest wretches I ever knew or had to do with in my life. I have heard him say that there is no God. I have heard him say that there is no world to come, no sin, and no punishment hereafter. Moreover, I have heard him say that it was just as good to go to a brothel as to go hear a sermon."

"Where did you hear him say these things?"

"In Drunkard's Row," Mr. Tell-True replied, "just at the end of Rascal Lane at Mr. Impiety's house."

Then the clerk announced, "Take Atheism away and bring Mr. Lustings to the bar."

"Mr. Lustings, you are indicted by the name of Lustings as an intruder in the town of Mansoul. You have devilishly taught by practice and filthy words that it is lawful and profitable for man to give way to his carnal desires. You have said that you will never deny yourself any sinful delight as long as your

139

name is Lustings. Are you guilty of this indictment or not?''

Mr. Lustings said, "Sir, I am a man of high birth and have been accustomed to expensive pleasures and pastimes. I am not, however, accustomed to being scolded for my actions but have been left to follow my own will and desires. It seems strange to me that I should be called into question for that which I and almost all men secretly or openly enjoy."

"Sir," the clerk remarked, "we are not concerned with your greatness; although the higher you were, the better you should have been. But we are concerned about an indictment against you. What do you say? Are you guilty of it or not?"

"Not guilty," Mr. Lustings replied.

"Baliff, call the witnesses to come forward and give their evidence," the clerk instructed.

"Gentlemen, come in and give your evidence for the King against the prisoner at the bar," the baliff proclaimed.

"Mr. Know-All, look at the prisoner at the bar. Do you know him?" the clerk asked.

"Yes, my lord, I know him."

"What's his name?"

"His name is Lustings. He was the son of Beastly, and his mother gave birth to him on Flesh Street. She was Evil-Desire's daughter. I knew the entire family."

"You have heard his indictment. What do you say? Is he guilty of the things charged against him or not?" the clerk asked.

Mr. Know-All replied, "Sir, he has indeed been a great man—a thousand times greater in wickedness than his birthright entitled him."

The clerk further questioned, "But what do you know about his particular actions, especially with reference to his indictment?"

Mr. Know-All answered, "I know him to be a swearer, a liar, and a Sabbath-breaker. I know him to be a fornicator and an unclean person guilty of an abundance of evils. To my knowledge, he has been a very filthy man."

"But where did he commit his wickedness, in private corners or openly and shamelessly?"

"All over the town, my lord," replied Mr. Know-All.

"Mr. Tell-True, what do you have to say for our Lord the King against the prisoner at the bar?" asked the clerk.

"All that the first witness has said I know to be true, and a great deal more besides."

Then the clerk turned toward the bar and asked, "Mr. Lustings, do you hear what these gentlemen are saying?"

Without embarrassment Mr. Lustings answered, "I was always of the opinion that the happiest life a man could live on earth was to deny himself nothing he desired. I have never been false at any time to this opinion of mine, and I have always lived according to my whims. Having found such sweetness in these pleasures, I encouraged others to enjoy them also."

Then the judges proclaimed, "He has condemned himself by his own words. Take him away and bring Mr. Unbelief to the bar."

The clerk began the questioning. "Mr. Unbelief, you are indicted by the name of Unbelief. While you were an official in the town of Mansoul, you feloniously and wickedly rebelled against the captains of the great King Shaddai when they came and demanded possession of Mansoul. You defied the names, forces, and causes of the King. You stirred up and encouraged the town of Mansoul to rebel against and resist the forces of the King. What do you say to this indictment? Are you guilty of it or not?"

Then Unbelief said, "I do not know Shaddai. I love my old prince, Diabolus, and I thought it was my duty to be loyal to him and do what I could to possess the minds of the men of Mansoul. I did my best to resist foreigners and fight against them. I will not change my opinion for fear of persecution, although you are presently in the place of power."

Then the judges said, "This man is incorrigible. He maintains his criminal acts with arrogant words and his rebellion with impudent confidence. Therefore, take him away and bring Mr. Forget-Good to the bar."

The clerk began, "Mr. Forget-Good, you are indicted by the name of Forget-Good. When the affairs of the town were in your hand, you forgot what was good and fell in with the tyrant Diabolus against Shaddai, his captains, and all his hosts. You dishonored and broke his law, endangering the famous town of Mansoul. What do you say to this indictment? Are you guilty or not guilty?"

"Gentlemen," Forget-Good said, "please attribute my forgetfulness to my age and not to my willfulness—to the madness of my brain and not to the carelessness of my mind. Then I hope by your charity to be excused from great punishment, although I am guilty."

The judges replied, "Forget-Good, your forgetfulness of good was not simply the result of weakness, but you deliberately forgot because you hated to keep virtuous things in your mind. Evil things you could retain, but what was good you could not stand to consider. Your age, therefore, and your pretended madness are used to try to blind the court and cover your criminal deeds. But let us hear what the witnesses have to say for the King against the prisoner at the bar. Is he guilty of this indictment or not?"

At this time, Mr. Hate-Lies spoke up, "My lord, I have heard Forget-Good say that he could not bear to think of goodness for even a quarter of an hour."

"Where did you hear him say so?" the clerk asked.

"In All-Base Lane, at a house next door to the sign of the conscience seared with a hot iron."

"Mr. Know-All, what can you say for our Lord the King against the prisoner at the bar?"

"I know this man well. He is a Diabolonian and his father's name was Love-Nothing. I have often heard him say that he considered the very thoughts of goodness the most burdensome things in the world."

"Where have you heard him say these words?"

"In Flesh Lane, opposite the church," replied Mr. Know-All.

Then the clerk said, "Mr. Tell-True, give your evidence concerning the charges brought against the prisoner at the bar."

"My lord, I have often heard him say that he would rather think of the vilest things than of what is contained in the Holy Scriptures."

"Where did you hear him say such grievous words?" the clerk asked.

"In a great many places," answered Mr. Tell-True, "particularly in Nauseous Street, in the house of Mr. Shameless. I also heard it in Filth Lane, at the sign of the reprobate."

The judges said, "Gentlemen, you have heard the indictment, his plea, and the testimony of the witnesses. Bring Mr. Hard-Heart to the bar."

The clerk proclaimed, "Mr. Hard-Heart, you are indicted by the name of Hard-Heart because you wickedly possessed the town of Mansoul with impenitency and stubbornness. You kept them from remorse and sorrow for their sins during their rebellion against the blessed King Shaddai. What do you say to this indictment? Are you guilty or not guilty?"

"Sir, I never knew what remorse or sorrow meant. I am impenetrable. I cannot be pierced with men's griefs, and their groans will not enter my heart.

Whenever I hurt someone or do them wrong, their mourning is music to me.''

"You see the man is a Diabolonian and has convicted himself,'' said the judges. "Take him away, jailer, and bring Mr. False-Peace to the bar.''

The clerk began, "Mr. False-Peace, you are indicted by the name of False-Peace. You satanically kept the town of Mansoul in a false, groundless, and dangerous peace during her apostasy and hellish rebellion. This damnable security brought dishonor to the King, transgression of his law, and great damage to the town of Mansoul. What do you have to say? Are you guilty of this indictment or not?''

Mr. False-Peace replied, "Gentlemen and you appointed to be my judges, I acknowledge that my name is Mr. Peace, but I deny that my name is False-Peace. Send for someone who intimately knows me, like the mid-wife who assisted at my birth or the gossips who were at my christening, and they will prove that my name is not False-Peace but Peace. Therefore, I cannot make a plea to this indictment since my proper name is not written on it. My true name is Peace, and I was always a man who loved to live in quiet surroundings. I thought others loved peace and quiet also; therefore, whenever any of my neighbors were troubled, I endeavored to help them. I can give many examples of my good temperament.''

Mr. False-Peace continued, "When our town of Mansoul turned from the ways of Shaddai, some of the townsmen began to regret what they have done.

It troubled me to see them upset, so I thought of ways to get them quiet again. During the war between Shaddai and Diabolus, I often used some device or another to bring peace to those afraid of destruction. I have always been a man of gracious temperament, as some say a peacemaker is. Then let me, gentlemen, be considered a peacemaker by you. I do not deserve this inhumane treatment but, instead, liberty and license to seek compensation from those who have been my accusers."

Then the clerk said, "Baliff, make a proclamation."

"As the prisoner at the bar has denied his name to be that mentioned in the indictment, the court requires proof of his true name. If there is anyone who can provide information to the court regarding the original and right name of the prisoner, let him come forth and give evidence."

Then two witnesses came into the court and requested to tell what they knew concerning the prisoner at the bar. The name of one was Search-Truth, and the name of the other was Vouch-Truth. The judges asked these men if they knew the prisoner and what they could say concerning him.

Mr. Search-Truth said, "My lord, I——"

"Wait," said the judges, "give him his oath." Then they swore him in, and he proceeded.

"My lord, I have known this man from a child and can attest that his name is False-Peace. I knew his father, Mr. Flattery. His mother was called Miss Soft-Heart before she was married. When these two came together, they had a son and named him False-Peace. I was his playmate, although I was somewhat older than he. When his mother called him home from play, she used to say, 'False-Peace, False-Peace, come home quickly.'

"Yes, I also knew him when he was a baby. Although I was only a child myself, I can remember when his mother used to play with him in her arms. She would call him twenty times in a row, 'My little False-Peace, my pretty False-Peace, my sweet False-Peace.' The gossips also knew this was his name, although he has had the audacity to deny it in open court."

Then Mr. Vouch-Truth was called upon to tell what he knew about False-Peace. So they swore him in.

Mr. Vouch-Truth said: "My lord, everything the former witness has said is true. His name is False-Peace, and I have in former times seen him angry with those who have called him anything other than False-Peace. He would say that they were mocking him. But this happened when Mr. False-Peace was a great man and the Diabolonians were in control of Mansoul."

Then the judges ruled, "Gentlemen, you have heard what these two men have sworn against the prisoner at the bar. And now, Mr. False-Peace, these honest men have sworn that this is your name. As to the plea you made regarding the matter of your indictment—you are not charged with evil-doing because you are a peacemaker among your neighbors.

You are charged with wickedly keeping the town of Mansoul in a false and damnable peace contrary to the law of Shaddai. All that you have pleaded for yourself is that you have denied your name, and we have witnesses to prove that you are the man.

"The peace that you boast of making among your neighbors is not a companion of truth and holiness, but that which is without foundation. It is grounded on a lie and is both deceitful and damnable. Your plea, therefore, has not delivered you from the indictment you are charged with, but rather it has convicted you. But we will be fair. Call the witnesses and see what they have to say for our Lord the King against the prisoner at the bar."

"Mr. Know-All, what do you have to say for our Lord the King against the prisoner at the bar?" asked the clerk.

"My lord, this man has for a long time made it his business to keep the town of Mansoul in a state of sinful quietness in the midst of all her filthiness and turmoil. He has said in my hearing, 'Come, come, let us avoid all trouble, no matter how it comes. Let us seek a quiet and peaceable life, although it may not have a firm foundation.' "

"Mr. Hate-Lies, what have you to say?" asked the clerk.

"My lord, I have heard him say that peace with unrighteousness is better than trouble with truth."

"Where did you hear him say this?"

"I heard him say it in Folly Yard, at the house of

Mr. Simple, next door to the Self-Deceiver. Yes, he has said this twenty times in that place."

Then the clerk proclaimed, "We need no further witnesses since this evidence is clear and plain. Take him away, jailer, and bring Mr. No-Truth to the bar.

"Mr. No-Truth, you are indicted by the name of No-Truth because you endangered the entire town of Mansoul. You attempted to deface and utterly destroy all the reminders of the law and image of Shaddai that remained in Mansoul after her apostasy from her King to Diabolus. What do you say? Are you guilty of this indictment or not?"

"No. Not guilty, my lord."

Then the witnesses were called, and Mr. Know-All gave his evidence against him.

"My lord, this man was present at the pulling down of the image of Shaddai. In fact, he did it with his own hands. I stood by and saw him do it, at the command of Diabolus. Yes, this Mr. No-Truth also set up the horned image of the beast, Diabolus, in the same place. At the bidding of Diabolus, he burned every remainder of the law of the King that he could lay his hands on in Mansoul."

"Who saw him do this besides yourself?" the clerk asked.

Mr. Hate-Lies replied, "I did, my lord, and so did many others. This terrible act was not done in secret but in the open view of all. He chose to do it publicly because he delighted in doing it."

The clerk then asked, "Mr. No-Truth, how could you have the audacity to plead not guilty when you were obviously the perpetrator of all this wickedness?''

"I thought I must say something, so I spoke according to my name. It has always been to my advantage in the past not to speak the truth."

"Take him away, jailer, and bring Mr. Pityless to the bar," said the clerk.

"Mr. Pityless, you are indicted by the name of Pityless because you have traitorously and wickedly suppressed all compassion. You would not allow poor Mansoul to console her own misery when she rebelled against her rightful King. Instead, you turned her mind away from any thoughts that had a tendency to lead her to repentance. What do you have to say to this indictment? Guilty or not guilty?''

"I am not guilty of pitylessness. All I did was cheer up the people, according to my name. For my name is not Pityless but Cheer-Up. I could not bear to see Mansoul inclined to melancholy."

"What?" the clerk asked. "Do you deny your name and say it is not Pityless but Cheer-Up? Call for the witnesses. What do you say to the plea?''

Mr. Know-All spoke up, "My lord, his name is Pityless. He has written the name on all his personal and private documents. But these Diabolonians love to counterfeit their names: Mr. Covetousness hides himself behind the good name of Stewardship; Pride can call himself Mr. Neat or Mr. Handsome when the need arises. All the rest of them do the same."

"Mr. Tell-True, what do you say?" asked the clerk.

"His name is Pityless, my lord. I have known him

150

from a child, and he has done all the wickedness charged against him in the indictment. But there is a group of Diabolonians who are not acquainted with the danger of judgment. Therefore, anyone who has serious thoughts about avoiding judgment is considered melancholy by them.''

"Bring Mr. Haughty to the bar, jailer," said the clerk.

"Mr. Haughty, you are indicted by the name of Haughty because you devilishly taught the town of Mansoul to arrogantly reject the summons given them by the captains of Shaddai. You prompted them to speak contemptuously against their great King and encouraged Mansoul to take up arms against his Son Emmanuel. What do you have to say? Are you guilty of this indictment or not?''

Mr. Haughty replied, "Gentlemen, I have always been a man of courage and valor. Even in the darkest circumstances, I have never been one to hang my head in shame. I hate to see men give up in the face of battle even if their adversaries are ten times stronger. It has never mattered to me who the enemy was or the cause in which I was engaged. It was enough to me if I fought bravely like a man and returned as the victor.''

The judges said, "Mr. Haughty, you are not indicted because you have been a valiant man or for your courage in times of distress. But you have used this pretended valor to draw the town of Mansoul into acts of rebellion against the great King and Emmanuel his Son. This is the crime with which you are charged in the indictment." But Mr. Haughty did not reply to these charges.

When these proceedings were completed against the prisoners at the bar, the judges gave the matter over to the jury with these instructions: "Gentlemen of the jury, you have heard the indictment against these men, their pleas, and the testimony of the witnesses against them. Now you must consider in truth and righteousness the verdict you should bring for the King against them."

Then the jury composed of Mr. Belief, Mr. True-Heart, Mr. Upright, Mr. Hate-Bad, Mr. Love-God, Mr. See-Truth, Mr. Heavenly-Mind, Mr. Moderate, Mr. Thankful, Mr. Humble, Mr. Good-Work, and Mr. Zeal-For-God withdrew themselves. After they were cloistered away, they began to discuss the evidence presented to them.

Mr. Belief, the foreman, began: "Gentlemen, as for the prisoners at the bar, I believe they all deserve death."

"That is right," said Mr. True-Heart, "I agree with your opinion."

"Oh, what a tribute to justice," said Mr. Hate-Bad, "that villains such as these have been apprehended!"

"Yes, yes," said Mr. Love-God, "this is one of the happiest days of my life."

Then Mr. See-Truth said, "I know that if we condemn them to death, our verdict will stand before Shaddai himself."

Mr. Heavenly-Mind said, "When all criminals like

these are cast out of Mansoul, what a pleasant town it will be!"

Then Mr. Moderate said, "It is not my custom to pass judgment with rashness, but the crimes of these men are so notorious and the testimony so concrete that a man must be blind to say the prisoners should not die."

"Blessed be God," said Mr. Thankful, "that these traitors are in safe custody."

"And I join with you in thanksgiving upon my knees," said Mr. Humble.

"I am glad also," said Mr. Good-Work.

Then the warm and true-hearted Mr. Zeal-For-God said, "Execute them for they have corrupted the town and sought the destruction of Mansoul."

Having agreed on their verdict, the jury returned to the courtroom.

Then the clerk said, "Good men, stand up together to give your verdict. Are you all agreed?"

"Yes, my lord," the jury replied.

"Who will speak for you?"

"Our foreman."

The clerk addressed them, saying, "Gentlemen of the jury, you have been impanelled for our Lord the King to serve in a matter of life and death. You have heard the trials of each of the prisoners at the bar. What do you say? Are they guilty of those crimes for which they stand indicted, or are they not guilty?"

"Guilty, my lord," replied the foreman.

The clerk then announced, "Take the prisoners away, jailer."

The verdict was returned in the morning, and in the afternoon they received the sentence of death according to the law. The prisoners were held in the inner prison until the time of execution, which was to be the next morning.

Chapter Eleven

NEW APPOINTMENTS

In the interim between the sentencing and the time of execution, one of the Diabolonian prisoners, Mr. Unbelief, broke out of the prison and escaped. He got outside of the town and lay lurking in ditches and holes waiting for an opportunity to repay Mansoul for their treatment of him.

When Mr. True-Man, the jailer, realized that he had lost one of his prisoners, he was terribly worried because this prisoner was the worst of the gang. He reported the escape to Lord Understanding, Mr. Knowledge, and Lord Willbewill and requested an order to search for him throughout the town. A search was made, but Unbelief could not be found anywhere in Mansoul.

An investigation revealed that he had lurked a while outside the town. Several people had caught a glimpse of him as he made his escape out of Mansoul, and one or two said they saw him running across the plain. Later, it was reported by Mr. Did-

See that Unbelief roamed over the dry places until he met Diabolus on Hellgate Hill.

At that time the old gentleman lamented to Diabolus about the despicable changes Emmanuel had made in Mansoul! Unbelief told how Mansoul had received a general pardon at the hands of Emmanuel. He reported how they had invited the Prince into the town and given him the castle for his possession. He said they had called Emmanuel's soldiers into the town, housed them in their homes, and entertained them with the timbrel, song, and dance.

"But," said Unbelief, "the greatest atrocity is that Emmanuel pulled down your image and set up his own. He expelled your officials and appointed new ones. And Willbewill, who we thought would never turn against us, has obtained great favor with Emmanuel. Willbewill has received a special commission from his master to search for, apprehend, and put to death all Diabolonians that he finds in Mansoul. He has already taken and committed to prison eight of my lord's most loyal friends. By now, they have all been arraigned, condemned, and probably executed. I was the ninth, who would surely have drunk of the same cup; but through my cleverness, I escaped from them."

When Diabolus heard his lamentable story, he yelled and blew fire like a dragon, making the sky dark with his roaring. He swore that he would take revenge on Mansoul for this. Both he and his old friend Unbelief decided to begin planning how they could take the town again.

Back in Mansoul, the day came for the prisoners to be executed, and they were solemnly brought to the gallows by the people of the town. The Prince had said, "The execution must be done by the hand of the townsmen, so I may see their commitment to keep my word and do my commandments. Then I can bless them for doing this deed. Proof of sincerity pleases me. Let Mansoul, therefore, lay their hands upon these Diabolonians and destroy them."

When the prisoners were brought to the gallows, the townsmen had a difficult time putting them to death. These Diabolonians, knowing they must die, strongly resisted, and the townsmen were forced to cry out to the captains for help.

The great Shaddai had a Secretary who deeply loved the people of Mansoul, and he was at the place of execution. When he heard the men of Mansoul crying out against the struggling and unruliness of the prisoners, he rose up and placed his hands on the hands of the townsmen. So they hanged the Diabolonians who had been a plague, a grief, and an offense to the town of Mansoul.

When this good work was done, the Prince came down to comfort the men of Mansoul and strengthen their hands. He said that by this act they had proved their love for him and showed themselves to be overseers of his laws. He told them he would appoint a captain from among the townsmen who would be the ruler of a thousand for the benefit of the now flourishing town of Mansoul.

So the Prince called Mr. Waiting and sent him up

to the castle gate to see Mr. Experience, the assistant to Captain Credence. Now this young gentleman was watching the captain train his men in the castleyard when Mr. Waiting said to him, "Sir, the Prince would like to see you immediately." So he brought Mr. Experience down to Emmanuel.

The men of the town knew Mr. Experience well because he had been born and raised in Mansoul. They knew him to be a prudent man of valor who was handsome, articulate, and very successful in any undertaking. Therefore, the hearts of the townsmen were filled with joy when they saw that the Prince was impressed with Mr. Experience and wanted to make him captain over a band of men.

They bowed before Emmanuel and shouted, "Let Emmanuel live forever!"

Then the Prince said to young Mr. Experience, "I want to confer on you a position of trust and honor in my town of Mansoul." Hearing this, the young man bowed his head and worshipped.

"I am appointing you," said Emmanuel, "as captain over a thousand men."

The new captain exclaimed, "Let the King live forever!"

The Prince gave orders to the King's Secretary to draw up a commission making Mr. Experience captain over a thousand men. "Let it be brought to me," he said, "so I may set my seal upon it." The commission was drawn up, brought to Emmanuel, and he set his seal on it. Then Mr. Waiting took it to the captain.

As soon as the captain received his commission, he sounded his trumpet for volunteers, and young men swarmed to him. The greatest men in the town sent their sons to enlist under his command. Captain Experience's lieutenant was Mr. Skillful, and his standard-bearer was Mr. Memory. He carried the white colors for the town of Mansoul, and his emblem was the dead lion and dead bear.

After the Prince returned to his royal palace, the elders of Mansoul, the mayor, the recorder, and Lord Willbewill went to congratulate him. They wanted to thank Emmanuel for his love, care, and the tender compassion which he had showed to his eternally grateful town of Mansoul. After a time of sweet communion between them, the townsmen solemnly ended their ceremony and returned to their homes.

One day Emmanuel decided to renew Mansoul's charter and enlarge it so that their yoke would be easier. When he had read their old charter, he laid it aside and said, "Now that which decays and waxes old is ready to vanish away." He also said, "The town of Mansoul will have a new and better charter, more gracious and firm by far."

In essence this new charter said:

"Emmanuel, Prince of Peace and great lover of the town of Mansoul, I do in the name of my Father and of my own clemency grant to my beloved town of Mansoul: Free, full, and everlasting forgiveness of all wrongs, injuries, and offenses done by

159

them against my Father, me, their neighbors, or themselves.

"In addition, I give them the holy Law and my Testament for their everlasting comfort and consolation. I also give them a portion of the same grace and goodness that dwells in my Father's heart and mine.

"It is my pleasure to give them the world and everything in it for their good. They shall have power over all and receive the honor of my Father. I grant them the benefits of life and death, of things present and things to come. No other city or town will have this privilege, only my Mansoul.

"Furthermore, I grant them free access to me in my palace at any time to make known their desires to me. When they come, I promise to hear their requests and correct all their grievances. I also give to Mansoul full power and authority to seek out, enslave, and destroy all Diabolonians that are found wandering in or about the town.

"Finally, I grant to my beloved town of Mansoul authority not to allow any foreigner or stranger to freely share in their excellent privileges. All the grants, privileges, and immunities that I bestow on the famous town of Mansoul are only for the true inhabitants and their descendants after them. Diabolonians of every race, country, or kingdom will be barred from sharing in these rights and privileges."

When the town of Mansoul had received their gracious charter from Emmanuel, they carried it to the marketplace where Mr. Knowledge read it in the presence of all the people. Then it was engraved on the castle gates in letters of gold. This was done so that the people would always have it in their view and be reminded of the blessed freedom that their Prince had bestowed upon them. Then their joy would be increased and their love renewed for their great and good Emmanuel.

What joy and comfort now possessed the hearts of the men of Mansoul! The bells rang, the minstrels played, the people danced, the captains shouted, the banners waved in the wind, and the silver trumpets sounded.

When the celebration was over, the Prince sent again for the elders of the town and talked with them about a ministry he intended to establish among them. This ministry would instruct them in things concerning their present and future state.

"For," he said, "without teachers and guides, you will not be able to know or do the will of my Father."

When the elders of Mansoul brought this news to the people, the whole town was pleased. In fact, whatever the Prince did pleased the people. They implored his Majesty to establish this ministry among them to teach them his law, statutes, and commandments so that they could be instructed in all good and wholesome things. Emmanuel told them that he would grant their requests and would appoint two instructors: one from his Father's court and one who was a native of Mansoul.

"The one from the King's court," said he, "is a person of no less quality and dignity than my Father and I. He is the Lord Chief Secretary of my Father's house. He is and always has been the chief dictator of all my Father's law, a person well-versed in all mysteries and knowledge like my Father and myself. Indeed, he is one with us in nature, and he will love and be faithful to the eternal concerns of the town of Mansoul.

"He must be your chief teacher, for only he can teach you clearly about all high and supernatural things. He and only he knows the ways and methods of my Father. Only he can show how the heart of my Father feels at all times, in all things, and on all occasions toward Mansoul. No man knows the things of my Father, except his high and mighty Secretary. Only he can tell Mansoul how and what they must do to keep themselves in the love of my Father. He can also bring lost things to your remembrance and tell you things to come.

"This teacher, therefore, must have preeminence over your other teacher, both in your affection and judgment. His great dexterity will help you draw up petitions to my Father for your help and for his pleasure. His personal dignity and the excellence of his teaching oblige you to love him, fear him, and to take heed not to grieve him.

"This person puts life and vigor into all he says and can also put it into your heart. He can make you prophets who are able to tell what will happen in the future. By this person you must frame all your petitions to my Father and me. Moreover, let nothing enter the town or castle of Mansoul without first obtaining his advice and counsel so as not to disgust this noble person.

"Take heed that you do not grieve this minister, for if you do, he may fight against you. And if he ever sets himself against you in battle array, you will be more distressed than if twelve legions from my Father's court were sent to make war on you.

"But if you listen to him and love him, if you devote yourselves to his teaching and seek to maintain communion with him, you will find him ten times more wonderful than anyone in the whole world. Yes, he will shed abroad the love of my Father in your hearts, and Mansoul will be the wisest and most blessed of all people."

Then the Prince called for Mr. Conscience, the old gentleman who had formerly been the recorder. He was an expert in the laws and government of the town and very articulate in domestic affairs. Therefore, the Prince appointed Mr. Conscience as the minister of all the laws, statutes, and judgments of the famous town of Mansoul.

"And you must," said the Prince, "confine yourself to the teaching of moral virtues and civil duties. You must not presume to be a revealer of those high and supernatural mysteries that are kept close to the heart of Shaddai my Father. For those things no man knows, and no one can reveal them except my Father's Secretary. You are a native of the town of Mansoul, but the Lord Secretary is a native with my

Father. You have knowledge of the laws and customs of the municipality, and he knows the wisdom and will of my Father.

"Mr. Conscience, although I have made you a minister and a preacher to the town of Mansoul, you must still be a student of the things which the Secretary knows and will teach to this people. You must, in all high and supernatural things, go to him for information and knowledge. Although there is a spirit in man, the Secretary's inspiration must give the understanding. You must, Mr. Conscience, keep low, be humble, and remember that the Diabolonians who were not faithful and obedient in their original positions of authority under Shaddai are now prisoners in the pit. Therefore, be content with your assignments.

"I have made you my Father's ambassador on earth in the matters which I have mentioned. You have the authority to teach the people of Mansoul and discipline them if they do not willingly obey your command.

"And, Mr. Conscience, because you are old and feeble, I give permission for you to go to my fountain and drink freely of the juice of my grapes, for my river always flows with wine. By doing this, you will eliminate from your body all sickness and disease. It will also increase your understanding and strengthen your memory for the reception and keeping of everything the King's Secretary teaches."

Mr. Conscience gratefully accepted the office of

minister to Mansoul. Then Emmanuel addressed all of the townsmen.

"Behold," the Prince said to Mansoul, "because I love and care for you, I have appointed preachers to instruct you. My Father's noble Secretary will teach you all the high and sublime mysteries. And this gentleman," pointing to Mr. Conscience, "is to instruct you in all human and domestic matters. In addition, he can relate to you anything he has heard and received from the mouth of the Lord High Secretary, but he must not pretend to be a revealer of these high mysteries himself. Only the Lord High Secretary has the power, authority, and skill to analyze and unveil these mysteries to Mansoul. But he may speak about them, as may the rest of the town, encouraging one another to faithfully adhere to them. I want you to observe and do these things, for it is for your life and the lengthening of your days.

"And one more thing, my beloved Mansoul. You must not dwell on anything Mr. Conscience teaches you as your trust and expectation for the next world. I say the next world because I plan to give another world to Mansoul when this world is worn out. You must rely completely on the doctrines taught you by Lord Secretary. Even Mr. Conscience himself must not look for life from that which he reveals. His dependence must be on the doctrine of the other preacher. Mr. Conscience must also be careful not to receive any doctrine or point of doctrine that is not communicated to him by his superior teacher."

After the Prince had settled these matters in the famous town of Mansoul, he proceeded to give the elders a word of caution regarding the King's high and noble captains.

"These captains," he said, "love the town of Mansoul. They were chosen to faithfully serve in the wars of Shaddai against the Diabolonians for the preservation of the town. I charge you not to behave improperly toward my captains or their men, since they are chosen from among many others for the good of Mansoul.

"They have the hearts and faces of lions when they are called to engage and fight against the King's foes and the enemies of Mansoul. Yet, if any disapproval is cast on them by the town of Mansoul, it will dishearten them and take away their courage. Do not, therefore, O my beloved, act unkindly toward my valiant captains and courageous men of war. Instead, love them, nourish them, and help them; then they will not only fight for you but cause all the Diabolonians who seek your destruction to flee from you.

"If any of my captains should become sick or weak and unable to perform their duties, do not despise them but rather strengthen and encourage them. For they are your fence, your guard, your wall, your gates, your locks, and your bars. When they are weak, they can do only a little and need your help. Yet, when they are well, you know what exploits and warlike achievements they are able to do and will perform for you.

"Besides, if they are weak, the town of Mansoul cannot be strong. If they are strong, then Mansoul cannot be weak. Your safety, therefore, lies in their health and in your encouragement of them. Remember, if they are sick, they caught their disease from the town of Mansoul itself.

"I have said these things to you because I love your welfare and your honor. Take care, therefore, my Mansoul, to be faithful in everything I have given you to do. This responsibility has been given, not only to your town officials and elders, but to you the people. Your well-being depends on the observation of the orders and commandments of your Lord.

"Next, O Mansoul, I warn you that, in spite of the reformation presently taking place, you need to hearken diligently to me. You will soon know that there are still many Diabolonians remaining in the town of Mansoul. These Diabolonians are fierce and anxious for revenge. Even now, they are plotting and scheming how they can bring you to desolation, to a state far worse than that of the Egyptian bondage. They are the loyal friends of Diabolus, so keep on the alert and look around you. They used to lodge with their prince in the castle when Unbelief was the mayor of this town. But since my coming, they live in the walls, where they have made dens, caves, holes, and strongholds for themselves.

"Therefore, O Mansoul, it will be that much more difficult for you to capture them and put them to death according to the will of my Father. You cannot completely rid yourselves of them unless you pull down the walls of your town, which I am by no means suggesting you do. You may ask, 'What should we do then?' Be diligent and act like men; watch their strongholds, find their hiding places, assault them, and do not make peace with them. Refuse any terms of peace they offer you, and all will be well between you and me.

"So that you may be able to distinguish them from the natives of Mansoul, I will give you this brief list of the names of their leaders: Lord Fornication, Lord Adultery, Lord Murder, Lord Anger, Lord Lasciviousness, Lord Deceit, Lord Evil-Eye, Mr. Drunkenness, Mr. Idolatry, Mr. Witchcraft, Mr. Variance, Mr. Emulation, Mr. Wrath, Mr. Strife, Mr. Sedition, and Mr. Heresy. These are some of the chief rascals who seek to overthrow you. But study the law of your King, and you will find a description of the character traits by which these Diabolonians can be identified.

"If these villains are allowed to roam freely about the town, they will, like vipers, eat out your hearts, poison your captains, cut the muscles of your soldiers, break the bars on your gates, and turn your flourishing town into a barren and desolate wilderness. So you may have courage to apprehend these villains wherever you find them, I give you full power and commission to seek out, capture, and put to death every Diabolonian you find lurking within or without the walls of Mansoul.

"In addition to the two ministers I have appointed, my four noble captains can publicly preach good doctrine that will lead you in the way. Yes, they will set up a weekly and, if need be, a daily lecture in Mansoul. They will teach lessons that will be profitable to you if you heed them.

"Now that I have given you the names of the Diabolonian vagrants and renegades, I will tell you that some of them will creep in and try to deceive you. In fact, they will appear to be very sincere and religious. And if you don't watch out, they will do more harm than you can ever imagine. They will disguise themselves in a manner different from their description. Therefore, Mansoul, watch and be sober; do not allow yourselves to be deceived."

When the Prince had reformed the town and instructed them in many important matters, he appointed a day in which he intended to bestow another badge of honor on Mansoul. This badge would distinguish them from all the other people and nations that dwell in the Kingdom of Universe.

It was not long before the appointed day came, and the Prince and his people met in the palace. First, Emmanuel made a short speech and then did as he had promised.

"My Mansoul," he said, "that which I am about to do will make you known to the world as mine and distinguish you in your own eyes from all false traitors that may creep in among you."

Then he commanded his servants, "Bring forth the white and glistening robes that I have provided for my Mansoul." The white garments were brought out of his treasury and laid out for the people to see. He told them to take the robes and put them on. "According," he said, "to your size and stature." So the people were clothed in fine, white linen, pure and clean. Then Mansoul shone as fair as the sun, clear as the moon, and as awesome as an army with many banners.

The Prince said to them, "This, O Mansoul, is the badge by which my people are distinguished from the servants of others. Yes, I give these robes to all who are mine and without one no man is permitted to see my face. Wear them for my sake because I gave them to you and because you want the world to know you belong to me. No other prince, potentate, or mighty one of Universe gives such a distinctive garment to his people.

"And now," he said, "let me give you my commandments concerning these garments, and be sure you heed my words. First, wear them every day lest you should at sometime appear to others as if you were not one of mine. Always keep your robes white, for if they are soiled, it will bring dishonor to me. Lift them up from the ground, and do not let them drag in the dust and dirt. Do not wear them loosely, lest you walk naked, and others see your shame.

"Finally, if you should soil or defile your robes (which would greatly displease me, and make Diabolus glad), then quickly do that which is written in my law. Keep your garments clean, and you will be able to continue to come before my throne. I will not leave you or forsake you but will dwell in the town of Mansoul forever.''

Mansoul and its inhabitants were like the signet ring upon Emmanuel's right hand. Where was there a town, a city, or a municipality that could compare with Mansoul? A town redeemed from the hand and power of Diabolus! A town King Shaddai loved so much that he sent Emmanuel to regain it from the prince of the Infernal Cave. Yes, Emmanuel loved to dwell in Mansoul, and he chose it for his royal habitation. He fortified it for himself and made it strong by the force of his army.

Mansoul now had an excellent Prince, valiant captains, men of war, mighty weapons, and garments as white as snow. Will the town of Mansoul treasure these great benefits and use them according to that end and purpose for which they were bestowed on them?

Chapter Twelve

THE SILENT DEPARTURE

When the Prince had completed the remodeling of the town, he was delighted with the work of his hands. He took pleasure in the good he had done for the famous and flourishing Mansoul and commanded that his banner be placed upon the battlements of the castle.

The Prince also gave the townspeople permission to make frequent visits to the castle. The elders of Mansoul often came to him at his palace, and they walked and talked together of all the great things he had done and promised to do for the town. Emmanuel often visited with the Lord Mayor, Lord Willbewill, and the honest subordinate preacher, Mr. Conscience.

How graciously, how lovingly, how courteously, and tenderly this blessed Prince acted toward the town of Mansoul! Whenever he went into the streets, gardens, orchards, and other places, he showed his love for the people. To the poor he gave his blessing and benediction. He would kiss them, and if they were ill, he would lay his hands on them and make them well. He would daily, and sometimes hourly, encourage the captains with his presence and kind words. A smile from him put more vigor, more life, and strength into them than anything else under heaven.

The Prince would feast with his people and fellowship with them continually. Hardly a week passed without a banquet being held at which they communed together. And he never sent them away empty-handed. He gave each one either a ring, a gold chain, a bracelet, a white stone, or some other special gift. Mansoul was dear to the Prince and lovely in his eyes.

If he did not see the townsmen for a while, Emmanuel would send them an abundance of meat, wine, and bread from his Father's storehouse. Luscious delicacies would cover Mansoul's tables, and whoever saw it would say there was nothing like it in any other kingdom.

When the townsmen did not frequently come to visit him, the Prince would go out into the town, knock at their doors, and ask to come in. If they heard him and opened their doors, he would renew his love for them and confirm it with some new gift or sign of continued favor.

It was amazing to see, in the very place where Diabolus had schemed with his Diabolonians, the Prince of princes eating and drinking with the people of Mansoul. During the feasts, Emmanuel's mighty captains, men of war, trumpeters, and choirs served and entertained the townsmen. Mansoul's cup ran over, and her channels flowed with sweet wine. She ate the finest of the wheat and drank milk and honey out of the rock! The people said, "How great is his goodness! Since we have found favor in his eyes, how honored we have been!"

During this time of tranquility and joy, the blessed Prince ordained a new officer in the town, a good person named Mr. God's-Peace. This man was placed over Lord Willbewill, Lord Mayor, Mr. Conscience, Mr. Mind, and all the natives of the town. Mr. God's-Peace was not a native of Mansoul, but he came with Prince Emmanuel from Shaddai's court. He was an acquaintance of Captain Credence and Captain Good-Hope; some people say they are related.

Mr. God's-Peace was made governor of the town, especially over the castle, and Captain Credence was there to help him. As long as things went according to the will of this sweet-natured gentleman, the town was in a happy condition. There was no quarreling or gossiping in all the town of Mansoul. Everyone minded their own business and did the work they had been assigned. The noblemen, the officers, and the soldiers all observed their proper order. The women and children of the town went about their business joyfully. Everyone worked and sang from morning until night. Throughout the town of Mansoul, nothing was to be found except harmony, quietness, joy, and health. And this lasted all that summer.

In the town of Mansoul there lived a man named Mr. Carnal Security. This man, after all the mercy bestowed by the Prince, brought Mansoul into terrible slavery and bondage.

When Diabolus first took possession of the town of Mansoul, he brought with him a great number of Diabolonians. Among these was Mr. Self-Conceit. Diabolus, perceiving this man to be active and bold, sent him on many desperate missions. He was very successful in his assignments and pleased his lord more than most who served him. Finding Mr. Self-Conceit suitable for his purposes, Diabolus made him second in command to the great Lord Willbewill, of whom we have written so much before.

In those days Lord Willbewill was pleased with Mr. Self-Conceit and his achievements, so he gave him his daughter, Lady Fear-Nothing, as his wife. Now the son of Lady Fear-Nothing and Mr. Self-Conceit was Carnal Security. There were many of these mixed marriages in Mansoul, and it was difficult in some cases to find out who were natives and who were not. Mr. Carnal Security was related to Lord Willbewill on his mother's side, although his father was a Diabolonian by nature.

Carnal Security took after his father and mother. He was self-conceited; he feared nothing; and he was a very busy man. Any new idea, strange philosophy, or unusual entertainment in the town was instigated by him in one way or another. Yet, in the midst of any conflict, he rejected those he considered weak and always sided with the strongest faction.

When Shaddai and Emmanuel made war on Mansoul, Mr. Carnal Security was in town. He was very active among the people, encouraging them in their rebellion and hardening them in their resistance against the King's forces. When the town of Mansoul was taken over by the glorious Prince, Mr. Carnal Security saw Diabolus ousted and forced to leave the castle in great shame. He realized that the town was filled with Emmanuel's captains and weapons of war, so he cleverly wheeled about. In the same way he had served Diabolus, he now pledged his support to the Prince.

Having obtained some information about Emmanuel's plans, Mr. Carnal Security ventured into the company of the townsmen and attempted to chat with them. He knew that the power and strength of Mansoul was great and that it would please the people if he praised their might and glory. Therefore, he exaggerated the power and strength of Mansoul's strongholds and fortifications, saying that the town was impregnable. He magnified the captains and their weapons, assuring the townsmen that the Prince would make Mansoul happy forever. When he saw that some of the people were delighted and taken with his discourse, he made it his business to walk from street to street, house to house, and man to man, convincing them of their safety. Soon they became almost as carnally secure as he was. So from talking, they went to feasting and from feasting to playing.

Mayor Understanding, Lord Willbewill, and Mr.

Knowledge were also taken with the words of this flattering gentleman. They forgot that their Prince had warned them to be careful not to be deceived by any Diabolonian trickery. He had further told them that the security of the now flourishing town did not lie so much in her present fortification as in her desire to have Emmanuel abide within her castle. The true doctrine of Emmanuel was that Mansoul should take heed not to forget his and his Father's love for them. They were also to behave themselves in a way that would keep them in his love.

It was a grievous mistake for them to become infatuated with one of the Diabolonians, especially one like Mr. Carnal Security. They should have listened to their Prince, feared him, and loved him. They should have stoned this carnal mischief-maker to death and walked in the ways of their Prince. Their peace would have been like a river if their righteousness had been like the waves of the sea.

From his residence in the castle, Emmanuel observed what was happening in the town. He realized that by the policy of Mr. Carnal Security, the hearts of the men of Mansoul had turned cold in their love for him. With great sadness he went to his Father's Secretary and said, "Oh, that my people had listened to me and that Mansoul had walked in my ways! I would have fed them with the finest of the wheat and sustained them with honey out of the rock."

Then he said in his heart, "I will return to my

Father's court until the people of Mansoul consider and acknowledge their offense."

His heart was broken because they no longer visited him at his royal palace as they had before. In fact, they did not even notice that he no longer came knocking on their doors. The Prince still prepared the love-feasts and invited them to come, but they neglected his invitations and no longer took delight in his companionship. The people of Mansoul did not seek or wait for his counsel but became confident in themselves, concluding they were now strong and invincible. They believed Mansoul was secure and beyond all reach of the enemy.

Emmanuel realized that, by the craft of Mr. Carnal Security, the town of Mansoul was no longer dependent on him and his Father. Instead, they trusted in the blessings they had received. At first, he grieved over their fallen condition; then, he attempted to make them understand that the way they were going was dangerous. The Prince sent his Lord High Secretary to forbid them to continue in their ways. But twice when he came to them, he found them at dinner in Mr. Carnal Security's house. The Secretary realized that they were not willing to listen to reason concerning their own good, so he went his way grieved in his heart. When he told the Prince about their indifference, Emmanuel was also offended and grieved. So he made plans to return to his Father's court.

During the time he remained in Mansoul before his departure, the Prince kept more to himself than he had formerly. If he came into the company of the townsmen, his conversation was not as pleasant and familiar as it had been before. When the townsmen came to visit him, as now and then they would, he was not as readily available as they had found him to be in the past. Formerly, at the sound of their feet, he would have run to meet them halfway and embrace them in his arms. Now they would knock once or twice, and he would seem not to hear them.

Emmanuel continued to behave this way, hoping the people of Mansoul would reconsider their actions and return to him. But they did not take note of his new ways toward them, and they were not touched with the memory of his former favors.

The Prince, therefore, withdrew himself—first privately from his palace, then to the gates of the town, and finally away from Mansoul. He left the town until they would acknowledge their offense and earnestly seek his face. Mr. God's-Peace also retired from his position and, for the present, no longer performed his duties in the town.

By this time, the people were so hardened in their ways and so indoctrinated by Mr. Carnal Security that the departure of their Prince did not touch their hearts. In fact, they did not remember him after he was gone, and his absence was of no consequence to them.

One day this old gentleman, Mr. Carnal Security, made another feast for the town of Mansoul. At that time there was a man in the town named Mr. Godly-

Fear. He had formerly been quite popular, but now no one noticed him. Old Carnal Security planned to corrupt Mr. Godly-Fear, so he invited him to the feast with his neighbors.

When the day came, Mr. Godly-Fear appeared along with the rest of the guests. Everyone was merrily eating and drinking except this one man. Mr. Godly-Fear sat like a stranger and neither ate nor was merry. When Mr. Carnal Security perceived this, he spoke to him.

"Mr. Godly-Fear, are you not well? You seem to be sick in body or mind or both. I have some tonic, made by Mr. Forget-Good, which will make you feel lighthearted and more relaxed around our feasting companions."

Mr. Godly-Fear discreetly replied, "Sir, I thank you for all your kind hospitality, but I have no desire to drink your tonic. But I do have a word for the natives of Mansoul: Elders of Mansoul, it is strange to see you so jolly when the town of Mansoul is in such a sorrowful state."

Then Mr. Carnal Security said, "You want to sleep, no doubt. If you please, sir, lie down and take a nap. Meanwhile, we will be merry."

Then the good man said, "Sir, if you were not devoid of an honest heart, you could not do as you have done and continue to do."

Mr. Carnal Security asked, "Why?"

"Please do not interrupt me," Mr. Godly-Fear said. Then he continued speaking to the elders of Mansoul: "It is true that the town of Mansoul was strong and impregnable. But you, the townsmen, have weakened it, and we now lie exposed to our enemies. It is not a time to flatter or be silent. Your Mr. Carnal Security has cleverly stripped Mansoul and driven her glory from her. He has pulled down her towers, broken down her gates, and removed her locks and bars.

"From the time that you elders of Mansoul and you, sir, became so important, the Prince has been offended. Now he is gone. If anyone questions the truth of my words, I will answer him with these questions: Where is Prince Emmanuel? When was the last time a man or woman in Mansoul saw him? When did you last hear from him or taste of his dainty morsels? You are now feasting with this Diabolonian monster, but he is not your Prince. Your enemies from outside could not have captured you, but since you have sinned against your Prince, your enemies within have taken over your town."

Then Mr. Carnal Security said, "Now, now, Mr. Godly-Fear, will you never shake off your timidity? Are you afraid of the sky falling in? Who has hurt you? Behold, I am on your side. But you are for doubting, and I am for being confident. Besides, is this a time to be sad? A feast is made to enjoy. Why, then, do you now shamefully break into such melancholy language when you should eat, drink, and be merry?"

Mr. Godly-Fear replied, "I should be sad because Emmanuel has left Mansoul! He is gone, and you, sir, are the man who has driven him away. Yes, he is gone without even notifying the nobles of Mansoul about his departure. If that is not a sign of his anger, then I am not acquainted with the methods of godliness.

"Now, my lords and gentlemen of Mansoul, I am still speaking to you. Your rejection of him provoked the Prince to depart gradually from you. He waited for some time hoping you would come to your senses and humble yourselves before him. But when he saw that no one paid any attention to these indications of his anger and judgment, he went away. And I saw him depart.

"Even now while you boast, your strength is gone. You are like Samson who lost his long locks of hair while he was sleeping. You may shake yourselves and attempt to do as at other times, but without your Prince you can do nothing; and he has departed from you. Now turn your feast into a fast and your joy into mourning."

The subordinate preacher, old Mr. Conscience, was startled at what was said and began to second it.

"Indeed, my brethren," he said, "I fear that Mr. Godly-Fear is telling the truth. I, for my part, have not seen my Prince for a long time. I cannot remember the last day I was with him, nor can I answer Mr. Godly-Fear's questions. I am afraid that all is doomed for Mansoul."

Mr. Godly-Fear replied, "I know that you will not find him in Mansoul for he has departed and gone. He left because the elders rewarded his grace with intolerable unkindness."

Then the subordinate preacher looked as if he would fall down dead at the table. In fact, everyone present, except the man of the house, began to look pale and deathly. Mr. Carnal Security retreated into his drawing room because he disliked depressing situations.

Having recovered a little and agreeing to believe Mr. Godly-Fear and his sayings, the townsmen began to discuss what they should do to punish those who had led them astray and how they could recover Emmanuel's love. They remembered what the Prince had told them to do to any false prophets who tried to deceive the town of Mansoul. So they took Mr. Carnal Security and burned him up in his house because he was a Diabolonian by nature.

When this was over, they began to look for Emmanuel their Prince. They sought him, but they did not find him. Then they were convinced of the truth of Mr. Godly-Fear's words. They began to condemn themselves severely for their vile and ungodly behavior, concluding that the Prince had left because of them.

Then they decided to go to the Lord Secretary, whom they had refused to hear and whom they had grieved with their behavior. Because he was a prophet, they wanted to ask him where Emmanuel was and how they could direct a petition to him. But the Lord Secretary would not admit them to a conference about this matter. He would not even permit them to enter his royal house, nor would he come out to tell them what to do.

It was a dark and gloomy day when the people of Mansoul saw they had been foolish. They realized what the companionship and trickery of Mr. Carnal Security had done. They saw the damage his flattering words had brought to poor Mansoul, but they were ignorant of what it was further going to cost them.

Chapter Thirteen

A DIABOLICAL PLOT

When the Sabbath day came, the people of Mansoul went to hear Mr. Conscience, their subordinate preacher. How he thundered that day! His text was taken from the prophet Jonah: ''They that observe lying vanities forsake their own mercies'' (Jonah 2:8).

The power and authority of that sermon was unlike any they had heard before. It had such an effect on the people that the look of dejection could be seen on their faces. When the sermon was over, the people were hardly able to go to their homes. For days afterward, they were under such heavy conviction that they did not know what to do.

The preacher not only showed the townsmen their sin but trembled before them under the sense of his own guilt. He cried out as he preached to them, ''Unhappy man that I am! I have done such a wicked thing! I, a preacher, whom the Prince appointed to teach Mansoul his law, have been foolish and sinful. I was one of the first to be found in transgression. This transgression fell within my precincts, and I should have cried out against the wickedness. Instead, I let Mansoul lie wallowing in it until it drove Emmanuel from our borders.'' He also accused all the town's elders and noblemen of neglecting their duties.

About this time a terrible disease came upon the town of Mansoul, and most of the inhabitants were greatly afflicted. Even the captains and the men of war were brought to a languishing condition that lasted a long time. In case of invasion, nothing could be done, either by the townsmen or field officers to protect the town. Many pale faces, weak hands, feeble knees, and staggering men now walked the streets of Mansoul. Groaning and moaning could be heard throughout the town, and many lay on their death beds.

The garments that Emmanuel had given the townsmen were in dreadful condition. Some were badly ripped and torn, and some hung so loosely on their emaciated bodies that the wind could blow them away.

After they had spent some time in this sad and desperate condition, the subordinate preacher called for a day of fasting. The people were to humble themselves for being so wicked against the great Shaddai and his son. Captain Thunder was asked to preach.

When the day came, the captain's text was: ''Cut it down; why cumbereth it the ground?'' (Luke 13:7). First, he showed what prompted these words—the fig tree was barren. Then he showed what was contained in this verse—repentance or utter desolation. He then showed by whose authority this sentence was pronounced—by Shaddai himself. Lastly, he showed the reasons for this judgment, and then he concluded his sermon. His application of the truth of this statement was so relevant that he made poor Mansoul tremble. This sermon, as well as the former one, deeply stirred the hearts of the men of Mansoul. It greatly helped to keep awake those who had been aroused by the preaching of Mr. Conscience. Throughout the whole town, there was little or nothing to be heard or seen but sorrow, mourning, and woe.

After this sermon, the people got together and consulted what should be done. "But," said the subordinate preacher, "I will do nothing on my own, without seeking the advice of my neighbor, Mr. Godly-Fear. For he understands more about the mind of our Prince than we do."

They sent for Mr. Godly-Fear and asked his opinion about what they should do. The old gentlemen replied, "It is my opinion that Mansoul should in this day of distress compose and send a humble petition to their offended Prince Emmanuel. Then, in his favor and grace, he may return to you and not remain angry forever."

When the townsmen heard this speech, they all agreed to take his advice. So they composed a petition containing their request.

The next question was, "But who will carry it?"

At last they agreed to send it by the Lord Mayor. He accepted the responsibility and journeyed to the court of Shaddai, where Prince Emmanuel had gone.

When he arrived, the mayor found that the gate was shut and so closely guarded that the petitioner was forced to stand outside for a long time. Then he asked that someone go in to the Prince and tell him who stood at the gate and what his business was. So one of the guards went and told Shaddai and Emmanuel his Son that the Lord Mayor of the town of Mansoul stood at the gate desiring to be admitted into the presence of the Prince. He also told the reason for the Lord Mayor's errand.

The Prince, however, would not come down nor give permission for the gate to be opened for him. Instead, he sent him this answer: "They have turned their backs against me, but now in time of trouble they say to me, 'Arise and save us.' Can they not go to Mr. Carnal Security, to whom they went when they turned from me, and make him their leader, their lord, and their protector in their trouble? Why do they visit me now in their distress, when in their prosperity they went astray?"

This answer made the Lord Mayor cringe. It troubled, perplexed, and grieved him terribly. He now began again to see what it meant to be familiar with Diabolonians like Mr. Carnal Security. When he saw that there was little help to be expected, either for himself or his friends, he smote his breast and returned, weeping all the way over the lamentable state of Mansoul.

When he came within sight of the town, the elders of Mansoul went out at the gate to meet him and find out what happened at court. The mayor told them his tale in such a hopeless manner that they all cried out and wept. They threw ashes on their heads, put sackcloth on their bodies, and went crying throughout the town of Mansoul. When the rest of the townsfolk saw how their leaders grieved, they all mourned and wept. This was a day of rebuke and anguish to the town of Mansoul.

After they had composed themselves, the elders again came together to discuss what they could do. They asked advice from Mr. Godly-Fear, who told them that there was no better way to accomplish their purpose. He told them not to be discouraged about what had happened at the court and not to give up, even if several of their petitions were answered with nothing but silence or rebuke. "For," he said, "it is the wise Shaddai's way to make men wait and exercise patience. And those in need should be willing to wait until he is ready to receive them."

These words encouraged them, and they sent their petitions again and again. Not one day or even an hour passed without a man being sent to the court of the King Shaddai with letters requesting the Prince's return to Mansoul. The road was full of messengers going and returning, meeting one another along the way. Some were coming from the court, and some were coming from the town. This was the work of the miserable town of Mansoul all that long, cold, and tedious winter.

You may remember that many of the old Diabolonians remained lurking about in the town of Mansoul. Some had come with the tyrant when he invaded and took the town. Others were there by reason of their birth and upbringing. Their holes and dens were in, under, and around the wall of the town. Some of their names were: Lord Fornication, Lord Adultery, Lord Murder, Lord Anger, Lord Lasciviousness, Lord Deceit, Lord Evil-Eye, Lord Blasphemy, and that horrible villain, the old and dangerous Lord Covetousness. These, along with many more, resided in the town of Mansoul even after Emmanuel had driven Diabolus out of the castle.

The good Prince had granted a commission to Lord Willbewill and to the whole town to seek, take, and destroy any Diabolonians they could lay their hands on. But the townsmen neglected to search for, apprehend, and destroy these Diabolonians. Therefore, these villains boldly came out of hiding and showed themselves to the inhabitants of the town. Some of the men of Mansoul became too familiar with them, to the sorrow of the municipality.

When the Diabolonian chiefs perceived that Emmanuel had departed from Mansoul, they began to plot the ruin of the town. So they met together at the den of Mr. Mischief and discussed how they could deliver Mansoul into the hands of Diabolus again. Some advised one way, and some another, each according to his own liking.

At last Lord Lasciviousness proposed that some

of the Diabolonians in Mansoul offer themselves as servants to a few of the natives of the town. "For," he said, "if they do so and Mansoul accepts them, they may make the taking of the town easier than it would be otherwise."

Lord Murder stood up and said, "This must not be done at this time because Mansoul is now in great turmoil. Our friend, Mr. Carnal Security, ensnared them and made them offend their Prince. They may try to reconcile themselves to their Lord by capturing our men. Besides, we know that they have been commissioned to take and slay us wherever they find us. Let us, therefore, be wise as foxes because we can do them no harm if we are dead."

After they had tossed the matter about, they jointly agreed that a letter should be sent to Diabolus informing him of the condition of the town. "We should also," some said, "let him know our intentions and ask his advice in this case." So a letter was composed:

"To our great lord, the Prince Diabolus, dwelling below in the Infernal Cave. We, the true Diabolonians still remaining in the rebellious town of Mansoul, cannot endure to witness how you are disgraced and reproached among the inhabitants of this town. In addition, your long absence has been to our detriment.

"We are writing to say that the situation is not entirely hopeless. This town may become your habitation again because it has turned away from Prince

Emmanuel, and he has departed from them. Although they send letter after letter asking him to return, they still receive no word from him.

"Lately, there has been great sickness among them, not only among the poor people of the town, but also among the lords, captains, and chief elders. Only we Diabolonians remain well, lively, and strong. Through the townsmen's great transgression on the one hand and their debilitating sickness on the other, we suspect that they lie exposed to your hand and power. If, therefore, you decide to come and make an attempt to take Mansoul again, send us word; and we will be ready to deliver it into your hands. Or, if you do not consider what we have said to be a good idea, tell us your plan; and we will follow it no matter what the cost."

When Mr. Profane, the messenger, came with his letter to Hellgate Hill, he knocked at the brazen gates for entrance. Cerberus, the keeper of that gate, opened it for Mr. Profane. He presented the letter to Diabolus and said, "Tidings, my lord, from our trusty friends in Mansoul."

From all over the den, Beelzebub, Lucifer, Apollyon, along with their other wicked friends, gathered together to hear the news from Mansoul. After the letter was openly read and the contents were told throughout the den, the command was given to ring Deadman's bell. So the bell was rung, and the princes rejoiced that Mansoul would soon be theirs again. The clapper of the bell sounded the song, "The town of Mansoul is coming to dwell with us; make room for the town of Mansoul."

After they had performed this horrible ceremony, they got together again to discuss what answer they should send to their friends in Mansoul. Some advised one thing and some another. Finally, they decided, because the matter required haste, to leave the whole business to Prince Diabolus. So he drew up a letter, in answer to the one Mr. Profane had brought, and sent it to the Diabolonians in Mansoul.

"To our offspring, the high and mighty Diabolonians, who dwell in the town of Mansoul. Diabolus, the great prince of Mansoul, wishes you a successful conclusion of those many brave enterprises, conspiracies, and designs that you have in your hearts to attempt to do against Mansoul.

"Beloved children and disciples, we have joyfully received your welcome letter by the hand of Mr. Profane. To show how acceptable your tidings were, we rang our bell for gladness. We rejoiced when we perceived that we still had friends in Mansoul who sought our honor and revenge in the ruin of the town. We also rejoiced to hear that they are in a degenerated condition, that they have offended their Prince, and that he is gone. Their sickness also pleases us, as does your health, might, and strength. We would be glad, most horribly beloved, if we could get this town into our clutches again. We will not spare our wit, our cunning, and our hellish inventions to bring your plan to a hasty conclusion.

"Comfort yourselves with the knowledge that we will again surprise Mansoul and take it. We will attempt to slay all your enemies with the sword and make you the great lords and captains of the place. And you need not fear that we will ever be cast out again. This time we will come with more strength and get a firmer hold than we did the first time. Besides, it is the law of Prince Emmanuel that if we get them a second time, they will be ours forever.

"Therefore, our trusty Diabolonians, endeavor to spy out the weakness of the town of Mansoul. Also, attempt to weaken them more and more. Then send word telling us the way you have chosen to attempt to regain the town. Will you persuade them to live a vain and loose life, drive them to doubt and despair, or blow up the town with the gunpowder of pride and self-conceit? O brave Diabolonians, be ready to make a most hideous assault from within, when we come to storm it from without. May you be successful in your attempts, for this is the desire of your great Diabolus, Mansoul's enemy, who trembles when he thinks of judgment to come. All the blessings of the pit be upon you.

"Given at the pit's mouth by the joint consent of all the princes of darkness. To be sent to the forces remaining in Mansoul by the hand of Mr. Profane.

"Signed, Diabolus"

When Mr. Profane returned to Mansoul with this letter, he went straight to the house of Mr. Mischief where the conniving Diabolonians were meeting.

Seeing that their messenger was safe and sound, their hearts were gladdened. They asked Mr. Profane about the welfare of Lord Diabolus, Lucifer, and Beelzebub, along with the rest of their friends at the den.

To this, Profane answered, "Well, my lords, they are well, even as well as can be in their place."

After reading the letter from Diabolus, they were encouraged and began to discuss how to complete their Diabolonian design upon Mansoul. The first thing they agreed upon was to keep Mansoul from discovering their plans. The next thing they determined was how to bring to pass the ruin and overthrow of Mansoul. One said after this manner, and another said after that.

Mr. Deceit stood up and said, "The high ones of the deep dungeon suggested these three ways: destroy Mansoul by making the town loose and vain; ruin the town by driving them to doubt and despair; or demolish them with the gunpowder of pride and self-conceit.

"Now, if we tempt them with pride, that may do something; and if we corrupt them with depravity, that may help. But in my mind, if we could drive them to despair, that would hit the nail on the head. Then they would question the truth of the love of their Prince and that will greatly discourage them. If this works well, it will make them stop sending petitions to him. Then that will be the end of their earnest solicitations for help, and they will conclude that they may as well do nothing as to keep trying without any results." So they unanimously agreed on Mr. Deceit's idea.

The next question they asked was, "How will we bring this project to pass?"

This was answered by the same gentleman. "We must enlist volunteers from among our ranks who are willing to disguise themselves, change their names, and go into the marketplace dressed like foreigners. They must seek employment as servants among the townsmen and pretend to have their masters' best interests at heart. By doing this, they will corrupt and defile the town. Then her Prince will not only be further offended, but he will, in the end, spew them out of his mouth. When this is accomplished, our Prince Diabolus will prey upon them. Then they will easily fall into the mouth of the eater."

As soon as this project was proposed, it was unanimously accepted. All the Diabolonians were eager to engage in this enterprise, but they decided it was best to begin with only a few. They selected Lord Covetousness, Lord Lasciviousness, and Lord Anger to infiltrate Mansoul. Lord Covetousness called himself by the name of Prudent-Thrifty; Lord Lasciviousness took the name of Harmless-Fun; and Lord Anger called himself Good-Zeal.

On market day, these three robust-looking fellows came into the marketplace. They were disguised in sheep's wool as white as the white robes of the townsmen and spoke the language of Mansoul fluently. When they offered to work for the townsmen, they were quickly hired because they asked small wages and promised to serve their masters well.

Mr. Mind hired Prudent-Thrifty, and Mr. Godly-Fear hired Good-Zeal. Now Harmless-Fun was not hired as quickly as the others because the town of Mansoul was observing Lent. But when Lent was almost over, Lord Willbewill hired Harmless-Fun to be both his butler and his footmen.

Once these villains infiltrated the houses of the leaders of Mansoul, they began to do great mischief. Using their filthy and sly ways, they quickly corrupted the families where they were working. Prudent-Thrifty and Harmless-Fun were very effective in contaminating their masters. But Good-Zeal was not as well-liked by his master, who had discovered that his newly-hired servant was a counterfeit rascal. When Good-Zeal realized this, he speedily escaped from the house. If he had not, his master, Mr. Godly-Fear, would probably have hanged him.

When these vagabonds had corrupted the town as much as they could, they met to decide when they should make an attempt to seize Mansoul. They all agreed that a market day would be the best time because the townsfolk would be busy doing business. And this was their rule, "When people are most busy, they least suspect a surprise."

"We will also then," they said, "be able to assemble ourselves together with less suspicion. If we make our attempt and fail, we can hide ourselves in the crowd and escape."

Having agreed on these things, they wrote another letter to Diabolus and sent it by the hand of Mr. Profane.

"The Lords of Looseness send greetings to the great and high Diabolus from our dens, caves, and strongholds in and about the wall of the town of Mansoul. How glad we were when we heard of your readiness to help us carry out our plan to ruin the town. We know that it must be pleasing to you and profitable to us to see our enemies die at our feet. We are still cunningly devising the best way to make this plan a success.

"We considered that most hellishly three-fold project which you proposed to us in your last letter. We have concluded that blowing them up with the gunpowder of pride and tempting them to be loose would help, but contriving to bring them into the gulf of desperation will work best of all.

"We have thought of two ways to do this. First, we will make them as corrupt as we can and then fall upon them with great force. Moreover, of all the nations that are at your beck and call, we think an army of Doubters would be the most likely to attack and overcome the town of Mansoul. Then, the pit will open her mouth, and desperation will thrust the townsmen down into it.

"To accomplish this plan, we have already sent three loyal Diabolonians to live among them. They are disguised in white, have changed their names, and are now accepted by them. Mr. Mind hired

Prudent-Thrifty, alias Covetousness, and the master has become almost as bad as his servant. Lasciviousness calls himself Harmless-Fun and has succeeded in making his master, Lord Willbewill, an undisciplined fool. Anger changed his name to Good-Zeal, but Mr. Godly-Fear suspected him and turned our companion out of his house. In spite of this setback, the plan is going as scheduled.

"Our next project involves your coming to the town on market day when they are in the midst of doing their business. Then they will feel most secure and least suspect that an assault will be made upon them. At such a time, they will also be less able to defend themselves or to hinder you in the prosecution of our designs. When you make your furious assault from outside, we will be ready to attack from within. In all likelihood, we will be able to create utter confusion and swallow them up before they can come to their senses. If your serpentine assistants and highly esteemed lords can find a better way than this, let us know quickly.

"To the monsters of the Infernal Cave, from the house of Mr. Mischief in Mansoul, by the hand of Mr. Profane."

Chapter Fourteen

EXPOSING THE DARKNESS

While the hellish Diabolonians were contriving the ruin of Mansoul, the town itself was in a desperate condition. They had come to this sad state because they had so grievously offended Shaddai and his Son, and their enemies had taken advantage of their weakened condition. Although the townsmen had appealed time after time to Prince Emmanuel and his Father seeking their pardon and favor, they had not received as much as a smile from them. Instead, through the deceitful ways of the domestic Diabolonians, the cloud over the town grew blacker and blacker; and their Emmmauel stood farther and farther away.

The sickness also still raged in Mansoul, both among the captains and the inhabitants of the town. But their enemies were healthy and strong and likely to become the head while Mansoul was made the tail.

The Diabolonian letter containing the plot to recapture Mansoul was carried by Mr. Profane to

Hellgate Hill. When Cerberus met Mr. Profane at the entrance to the Black Den, they discussed Mansoul and the plans devised against her.

"Ah! Old friend," Cerberus said, "are you back at Hellgate Hill again? I am glad to see you."

"Yes, my lord, I have come again concerning the town of Mansoul," replied Mr. Profane.

"Tell me, what is the condition of Mansoul at present?" Cerberus asked.

"In a favorable condition for us because their gladness has greatly decayed, and that's as much as our hearts can desire. Their Lord is far removed from them, and that pleases us well. We already have a foot in the door, and our Diabolonian friends are plotting the overthrow of the town. In addition, a terrible sickness rages bitterly among them; and if all goes well, we hope at last to prevail," said Mr. Profane.

Then the dog of Hellgate said, "There is no time like the present to assault them. I hope that the enterprise is a success for the sake of the poor Diabolonians who live in continual fear of their lives in the traitorous town of Mansoul."

Mr. Profane assured him, "The project is almost finished. The Diabolonians in Mansoul are working day and night."

"I am glad things are at this point," Cerberus said. "Go in, my brave Profane, to my lords. They will grandly welcome you. I have already sent your letter to them."

When Mr. Profane went into the den, Diabolus

met him and saluted him, saying, "Welcome, my trusty servant. Your letter has made me very glad." The other lords of the pit also saluted him.

Then Mr. Profane, after bowing to them all, said, "Let Mansoul be given to my lord Diabolus, and let him be her king forever." Then the yawning gorge of hell gave such a loud and hideous groan (for that is their music) that it made the mountains around it tremble as if they would fall apart.

After they had read and considered the letter, they discussed how they should reply to it. The first to speak was Lucifer.

He said, "The first project of the Diabolonians in Mansoul should be to make Mansoul even more vile and filthy. There is no better way to destroy a soul than this. Our old friend, Balaam, prospered using this plan many years ago. Let this, therefore, be a general rule among us for all ages. Nothing can make this plan fail except grace, which I hope this town has not received.

"But I would debate the matter of attacking them on a market day. If we do not time our attack well, our whole project may fail. Our friends, the Diabolonians, say that a market day is best because Mansoul will be very busy and least expect a surprise. But what if they double their guards on those days? And what if their men are always armed on those days? Then you may, my lords, be disappointed in your attempts and bring our friends in the town to unavoidable ruin."

Then the great Beelzebub stated, "There is something in what my lord has said, but his conjecture may or may not happen. We must be informed whether the town of Mansoul has any knowledge of her decayed state or of the plan devised against her. If so, this would provoke her to put guards at her gates and to double them on market days. But if it is discovered that the people are asleep, then any day will do. But a market day is best.''

Diabolus asked, ''How can we find out this information?''

Someone suggested asking Mr. Profane, so he was called in.

''My lords, so far as I can gather, this is the present condition of the town of Mansoul,'' replied Mr. Profane. ''Their faith and love have decayed, and Emmanuel their Prince has turned his back on them. They often ask him to return, but he has not answered their request. In addition, they have made no attempts to reform their ways.''

''I am glad they are backslidden and lacking in reformation, but I am afraid of their constant petitioning. However, their looseness of life is a sign that there is not much heart in their requests; and without heart, things are worth little,'' said Diabolus.

Then Beelzebub joined in, ''If the situation in Mansoul is as Mr. Profane has described it to be, it will not matter what day we assault it. Neither their prayers nor their power will do them much good.''

When Beelzebub had had his say, then Apollyon began. ''My opinion is that we move cautiously, not doing things in a hurry. Let our friends in Mansoul continue to pollute and defile it by drawing the people into more sin. For there is nothing like sin to devour Mansoul. Once this is done and it takes effect, Mansoul will no longer watch or petition or do anything else that would bring her security and safety. She will forget Emmanuel and no longer desire his company. If she can be made to live like this, her Prince will not hurry to come to her aid.

"Our friend, Mr. Carnal Security, with one of his tricks drove Emmanuel out of the town. So why should not Lord Covetousness and Lord Lasciviousness be able to keep the Prince out of Mansoul? Two or three Diabolonians accepted by the townsmen will do more to help make the town your own than an army of ten thousand.

"Therefore, let this project that our friends in Mansoul have set in motion be strongly and diligently carried on with all the cunning imaginable. Let them continually send fellows under one disguise or another to deceive the people of Mansoul. Then, perhaps, we will not need to make war against them. Or, if that must be done, the more sinful they are, the more unable they will be to resist us. Then the more easily we will overcome them.

"But the worst that could happen is that Emmanuel would come to them again. Cannot the same means be used to drive him from them once more? If they lapse into sin again, can he not be driven from them forever in the same way he was driven from them for a season? And if this should happen, then he will take with him all his battering rams, his catapults, his captains, and his soldiers, leaving Mansoul naked and bare. When this town sees herself utterly forsaken by her Prince, will she not open her gates again to you and make you welcome as in days of old? But this will take time. A few days is too short a time to accomplish as great a work as this."

As soon as Apollyon finished speaking, Diabolus began to plead his own cause. He said, "My lords and powers of the cave, my true and trusty friends, I have patiently listened to your long and tedious orations. But my furious appetite lusts to repossess my famous town of Mansoul, and I can no longer wait to see the end of lingering projects. Without further delay, I must, in any way I can, satisfy my insatiable desire with the soul and body of the town of Mansoul. Therefore, lend me your heads, your hearts, and your help, for I am going to recover my town of Mansoul."

When the lord and princes of the pit saw Diabolus' flaming desire to devour the miserable town of Mansoul, they restrained their objections and consented to lend him any help they could. Although, if Apollyon's advice had been taken, they would have distressed the town of Mansoul far more. But they were willing to help Diabolus since they might need his assistance in the future.

Next, they had to decide how many soldiers Diabolus would need to take the town of Mansoul. After some debate it was concluded, as the letter from the Diabolonians had suggested, that an army of terrible Doubters be used for this expedition. They decided that Diabolus should enlist between twenty and thirty thousand men from the land of Doubting. It was also concluded that the lords of the pit should help him in the war by taking command of the soldiers. So they drew up a letter to send back to the Diabolonians in Mansoul.

"From the dark and horrible dungeon of hell, Diabolus and all the princes of darkness send this letter to our friends in and about the walls of Mansoul. We know you are impatiently waiting for our most devilish answer to your venemous plan against the town. You have invented an excellent method for our proceeding against that rebellious people. In fact, a more effective one cannot be thought of by all the wits of hell.

"After much consultation and debate, we have approved your proposal. Our furious and unmerciful Diabolus is raising more than twenty thousand Doubters to come against the people of Mansoul. They are all stout and sturdy men who are accustomed to war. We desire, therefore, that you continue to carry out your plan, by which you will not lose. Yes, and we intend to make you the rulers of Mansoul.

"It is most important, however, that every one of you use all your power, cunning, and delusive persuasion to draw the town of Mansoul into more sin and wickedness. Then sin will bring forth death. We have concluded that the more vile, sinful, and depraved the townsmen are, the more unlikely it is that Emmanuel will come to their rescue. And the more sinful they are, the weaker and less able they will be to resist our assault upon them. That may cause the mighty Shaddai himself to remove his protection and send his captains and soldiers home, leaving the town naked and bare. Then Mansoul will be exposed to us and fall like a fig into the mouth of the eater.

"As to the time of our attack against Mansoul, we have not yet fully resolved that. But some of us think that a market day will certainly be the best. When you hear our roaring drum outside the wall, be ready to make a horrible confusion within the town. Then Mansoul will be distressed before and behind and not know which way to run for help.

"My Lord Lucifer, Lord Beelzebub, Lord Apollyon, Lord Legion, and Lord Diabolus salute you. May you be as hellishly prosperous as we desire to be ourselves. Sent by the letter carrier, Mr. Profane."

They gave this letter to Mr. Profane who prepared for his return to Mansoul from the horrible pit. As he came up the stairs from the depths to the mouth of the cave, Cerberus saw him and asked how things went concerning the town of Mansoul.

"Things went as well as we can expect. The letter that I carried was highly approved by all my lords, and I am returning to tell our Diabolonian friends. I have an answer to it that will make them glad. This letter encourages them to pursue their

207

plans and be ready to attack from within when they see Lord Diabolus descending on the town of Mansoul.''

"But does he intend to go against them himself?'' Cerberus asked.

"Yes, and he will take along more than twenty thousand men of war from the land of Doubting to serve him in the expedition.''

Then Cerberus was glad and said, "If only I could be put at the head of a thousand soldiers. I would show my valor against the famous town of Mansoul.''

"Your wish may come to pass,'' Mr. Profane said. "You look like one who has enough courage. Diabolus needs those who are valiant and brave. But my business requires haste.''

"Yes, so it does,'' Cerberus replied. "Go quickly to the town of Mansoul with all the evil that this place can give you. And when you come to the house of Mr. Mischief, where the Diabolonians meet, tell them that Cerberus offers them his service and hopes to come with the army against the famous town of Mansoul.''

"I will tell them,'' Mr. Profane said. "And I know that my lords will be glad to hear it.''

After a few more of these kind compliments, Mr. Profane said farewell to his friend Cerberus. With a thousand of their pit-wishes, Cerberus bid him a safe journey back to his masters.

When Mr. Profane returned to the house of Mr. Mischief in Mansoul, he found the Diabolonians assembled and waiting for him. He delivered his letter to them along with this compliment: "My lords from the confines of the pit, the high and mighty principalities and powers of the den, salute you, the true Diabolonians of Mansoul. They extend their deepest regard for the great service, high attempts, and brave achievements that you have devised for restoring the famous town of Mansoul to our Prince Diabolus."

Mansoul did not know the power and industry of the enemy nor how near they were to executing the hellish plot devised against her. The town was somewhat conscious of her sin but unaware that the Diabolonians had seeped into her inner being. She cried, but Emmanuel was gone; and her cries did not bring him back. In fact, she did not know if he would ever return and come to Mansoul again.

The townsmen still sent petition after petition to the Prince, but he answered them all with silence. Although the townsmen cried out for help, they made friends with the Diabolonians and walked the streets with them as their companions. The people did not reform their ways, and that was as Diabolus would have it. He knew if they regarded iniquity in their hearts, their King would not hear their prayers.

The sickness sapped the life from Mansoul, causing the people to grow weaker and weaker. Mansoul's weakness became the strength of her enemies, and the sins of Mansoul gave an advantage to her wicked foes. As the Diabolonians increased and grew, the townsmen diminished greatly. More than eleven thousand men, women, and children died from the sickness that plagued Mansoul.

Within the town lived a man named Mr. Prywell who greatly loved the people of Mansoul. He would often go up and down the streets to see and to hear if there were any plots devised against the town. He was a jealous man who feared that some mischief would befall Mansoul, either from the Diabolonians within or from some power without.

One night as Mr. Prywell was spying here and there, he came upon a place called Vile Hill where the Diabolonians used to meet. He heard voices whispering, so he quietly drew closer to the house. As he listened, someone arrogantly affirmed that it would not be long before Diabolus would again possess Mansoul. They said the Diabolonians intended to kill all the Mansoulians, destroy the King's captains, and drive all his soldiers out of the town. Mr. Prywell also heard them say that Diabolus had more than twenty thousand fighting men ready to accomplish this plan within the next few months.

When Mr. Prywell heard this plot, he believed it was true. He went immediately to the Lord Mayor's house and told him about it. The mayor sent for the subordinate preacher, Mr. Conscience. He was the chief preacher in Mansoul because the Lord Secretary still felt uncomfortable in the rebellious town.

The subordinate preacher sounded the alarm to alert the town. When the bell was rung, the people gathered together, and Mr. Conscience told them

Mr. Prywell's news. "A horrible plot has been devised to massacre us all in one day. This news is not to be taken lightly because Mr. Prywell likes to get to the bottom of matters. He is a reasonable and discriminating man who is not a gossip or false prophet. I will call him, and you can hear his news for yourselves."

Mr. Prywell came and told his tale so accurately that Mansoul was convinced of the truth of what he said.

The subordinate preacher supported him, saying, "Sirs, it is not irrational for us to believe this news because we have provoked Shaddai to anger and our sins have driven Emmanuel out of the town. We have had too much communication with the Diabolonians and have forsaken our former ways. It is no wonder that the enemy both within and without has plotted our ruin. What better way than this for them to act? The sickness in the town has made us weak, many good men are dead, and the Diabolonians grow stronger and stronger.

"Besides," the subordinate preacher continued, "Mr. Prywell reports that several letters have passed lately between the princes of the pit and the Diabolonians in order to devise our destruction."

When Mansoul heard all this, they lifted up their voices and wept. They grieved over their foolishness and doubled their petitions to Shaddai and his Son. They also told this news to the Prince's captains, high commanders, and men of war, entreating them to be strong and prepare themselves to battle Diabolus night and day if he came to attack the town.

Immediately after hearing this, the captains came together to decide how to combat these hellish plans devised by Diabolus and his friends against the now sick, weak, and impoverished town of Mansoul. They agreed upon the following particulars:

1. The gates of Mansoul should be kept shut with bars and locks, and all persons going in or out should be strictly examined by the captains of the guards. "In this way," they said, "the schemers living among us will be uncovered."

2. A strict house-to-house search should be made for all kinds of Diabolonians throughout the whole town of Mansoul. Every house should be searched from top to bottom.

3. It was further concluded that anyone who had housed or harbored the Diabolonians should, to their shame and the warning of others, be publicly reprimanded.

4. They resolved that a public fast and a day of humiliation be observed throughout the whole municipality. The people were to repent for their transgressions against the Prince and Shaddai his Father. It was further resolved that anyone, who did not observe that fast and humble themselves for their sins, would be considered a Diabolonian and punished as such for their wicked deeds.

5. It was further concluded that they would renew their repentance for sin and their petitions to Shaddai for help. They resolved to send a message

to the King's court telling everything that Mr. Prywell had told them.

6. It was also determined that thanks should be given by the town of Mansoul to Mr. Prywell for diligently seeking the welfare of their town. Since he was so naturally inclined to seek their good and to undermine their enemies, they commissioned him as chief scout.

Chapter Fifteen

THE ARMY OF DOUBTERS

The municipality, along with their captains, did as they had determined. They shut up their gates; they searched for Diabolonians; and they publicly reprimanded those who were harboring any of these creatures.

Mr. Prywell faithfully carried out his responsibilities. He gave himself wholly to his duties not only within the town, but he also went outside to do his scouting and spying.

One day he journeyed toward Hellgate Hill into the country where the Doubters lived. There he learned that Diabolus and his army were almost ready to march. So he quickly returned and called the captains and elders of Mansoul together. He told them where he had been, what he had heard, and what he had seen.

Particularly, he told them that Diabolus had made old Mr. Unbelief, who had escaped from prison in Mansoul, the general of his army. He told them that Diabolus intended to bring with him the chief princes of the infernal pit as the captains over the Doubters. In addition, several leaders from the Black Den would ride with Diabolus to force the town of Mansoul to come under the control of their wicked prince.

Mr. Prywell reported that old Unbelief had been appointed as Diabolus' general because no one was more loyal to the tyrant than he. In addition, Unbelief had an adament hatred for the town of Mansoul. "Besides," he said, "this man remembers how Mansoul humiliated him, and he is resolved to get revenge."

When the captains of Mansoul and the elders of the town heard Mr. Prywell's report, they thought it was time to enact the laws their Prince had given them regarding the Diabolonians. A diligent and impartial search for the Diabolonians was made in all the houses of Mansoul. In Mr. Mind's house, Lord Covetousness was found; but he had changed his name to Prudent-Thrifty. In Lord Willbewill's house, Lasciviousness was found; but he was now called Harmless-Fun.

The captains and elders of the town took these two Diabolonians and held them in custody under the keeping of Mr. Trueman, the jailer. He shackled them with irons and handled them so severely that in time they both fell ill and died in the prison.

Their masters, according to the agreement of the captains and elders, were publicly reprimanded as a warning to the rest of the town. Lord Willbewill and Mr. Mind had to openly confess their sins before the people and were strictly instructed to reform their ways.

Then the captains and elders of Mansoul searched for more Diabolonians who were lurking in dens, caves, holes, or vaults around the wall or in the town. The hunters could plainly see the Diabolonian footprints, and they followed their tracks and smells to the mouths of their filthy caves and dens. Yet, they could not capture them because their Diabolonian ways were crooked, their hideouts strong, and their movements swift.

Mansoul now ruled the remaining Diabolonians so severely that these vile creatures were glad to shrink into corners. Once they had walked openly in the daylight, but now they were forced to embrace secrecy and the night. The townsmen had once been their companions, but now they considered the Diabolonians their deadly enemies. This change was the result of the information gathered by Mr. Prywell.

By this time, Diabolus had assembled the army he intended to bring with him for the ruin of Mansoul. He appointed nine captains and field officers, each one more treacherous than his name implied.

Captain Rage was made commander over the Election Doubters. His standard-bearer was Mr. Destructive, and the great red dragon was his emblem.

The second captain was Captain Fury. He commanded the Vocation Doubters, and his standard-bearer was Mr. Darkness. The emblem on his flag was the fiery flying serpent.

Captain Damnation was captain over the Grace

Doubters. Mr. No-Life carried his banner with the emblem of the Black Den.

The fourth captain, Captain Insatiable, led the Faith Doubters. Mr. Devourer was his standard-bearer, and the yawning jaws were his emblem.

Captain Brimstone was captain over the Perseverance Doubters. His banner was carried by Mr. Burning, and his emblem was the blue flame.

The sixth captain, Captain Torment, led the Resurrection Doubters. Mr. Gnaw was his banner-bearer, and he had the black worm for his emblem.

Captain No-Ease commanded the Salvation Doubters. Mr. Restless carried his banner with the emblem of the ghastly picture of death.

The eighth captain was Captain Sepulcher, the captain over the Glory Doubters. Mr. Corruption carried the banner bearing the emblem of a skull and dead men's bones.

Captain Past-Hope was captain of those who are called the Joy Doubters. His bearer was Mr. Despair, and his emblem was the hot iron and the hard heart.

Over these nine captains, the great Diabolus appointed seven superior captains: Lord Beelzebub, Lord Lucifer, Lord Legion, Lord Apollyon, Lord Python, Lord Cerberus, and Lord Belial. At the appointed time, all of Diabolus' captains and their forces gathered at Hellgate Hill and began their march toward Mansoul.

Having been alerted by Mr. Prywell of Diabolus' coming, the townsmen placed watchmen at the gates of Mansoul and doubled the guards. In addition, the catapults were mounted where they could accurately hurl their great stones at the advancing enemy. The Diabolonians in the town, however, were unable to do the harm they had planned because Mansoul was now awake. In spite of these preparations, the townsmen were terribly frightened by the sight of the approaching army and the thunderous pounding of Diabolus' horrible drums.

When Diabolus came to the town wall, he first approached Ear Gate and assaulted it furiously, supposing that his friends in Mansoul had done their part. Lacking the help he had expected from them and finding his army bombarded with stones from the catapults, he was forced to retreat from Mansoul. He entrenched himself and his men in the field beyond the reach of the weapons in the town.

In order to counterattack, Diabolus built four mounts around Mansoul. The first he called Mount Diabolus, in order to frighten the townsmen even more. The other three he called Mount Alecto, Mount Magaera, and Mount Tisiphone; for these are the names of the dreadful tormentors of hell. He began to play his game with Mansoul, making it cringe in terror like a lion does his prey. But the Prince's captains and soldiers resisted so bravely and did so much damage with their stones that they made him retreat. Then Mansoul began to take courage.

Upon Mount Diabolus on the north side of the town, the tyrant set up his banner. It was a fearful thing to behold because it depicted a picture of Mansoul burning in a flaming fire.

Diabolus decided he wanted to meet with the leaders of the trembling town, so he commanded his drummer to approach the town wall and beat his mighty drum fiercely. He was commanded to do it at night because in the daytime the captains annoyed him with their catapults. The drums were to beat every night until the townsmen wearied of the sound and agreed to confer with him.

The drummer did as Diabolus commanded. When his drum was beating, darkness and sorrow covered the town of Mansoul. How Mansoul trembled! They expected to be overcome at any moment by the terrible Diabolus.

After the drummer had beaten his drum, he made this speech to Mansoul. "My master has sent me to tell you that if you will willingly submit, you will be spared. But if you resist, he will take you by force."

The people of Mansoul had taken refuge with the captains in the castle, so there was no one to give the drummer an answer. Therefore, he proceeded no farther but returned again to his master in the camp.

When Diabolus realized that beating the drum would not force Mansoul to do his will, he decided to send the drummer the next night without his drum. He wanted to let the townsmen know that he still desired a meeting since it was his design to force them to give themselves up. But they neither heard nor heeded him because they remembered what it had cost them the first time they had listened to him.

The following night Diabolus sent as his messenger the terrible Captain Sepulcher. When he came to the walls of Mansoul, this fierce captain cried out:

"O inhabitants of the rebellious town of Mansoul! I summon you, in the name of the Prince Diabolus, to open the gates of your town and permit the great lord to come in. But if you still rebel, we will swallow you up when we overtake the town. But if you will obey my summons, say so; and if not, then let me know.

"The reason for this summons," he continued, "is to remind you that my lord is your undisputed prince. Emmanuel may have dealt dishonorably with him, but my lord will not give up his right to attempt to recover that which is his own. Consider then, O Mansoul, what you must do. If you quietly yield yourselves, then our old friendship will be renewed. But if you still refuse and rebel, then expect nothing but fire and sword."

When the languishing town of Mansoul heard this summons, they were more disheartened than before. But they gave Captain Sepulcher no answer at all, so he returned to his camp.

After a discussion among themselves and with some of their captains, the townsmen decided to approach the Lord High Secretary for counsel and advice. This Lord Secretary was their chief preacher, but he felt uncomfortable in the town and kept himself far removed from them. When they asked him to give them a hearing about their miserable condition, he told them he was still ill at ease and could not listen as he formerly had.

The townsmen also desired that he give them his advice concerning Diabolus and his twenty thousand Doubters. They said, moreover, that both the giant and his captains were cruel men, and that they were afraid of them. But to this the Lord Secretary replied, "You must look to the law of the Prince and see what is written there for you to do."

Finally, they requested that his Highness, the Lord Secretary, help them draw up a petition to Shaddai and Emmanuel his Son. "For," they said, "we have many petitions, yet we have received no answer. But a petition signed by you will bring us favor with the Prince."

The only answer he gave to this was that they had offended and grieved Emmanuel. "Therefore, you must reap what you have sown," he said.

This answer from the Secretary fell like a millstone upon the people. It crushed them so much that they did not know what to do. Yet, they would not comply with the demands of Diabolus or his captains. So the town of Mansoul was caught in a dilemma. Her enemies were ready to swallow her up, and her friends refused to help her.

Then the mayor, whose name was Lord Understanding, stood up and began to analyze the Secretary's words, retrieving comfort out of his seemingly bitter statement. He commented on it, saying, "This dilemma unavoidably follows the saying that we must suffer for our sins. But the words sound as if we will be saved from our enemies. It seems to mean that after a few more sorrows, Emmanuel will come and help us."

When the captains heard what the Lord High Secretary had said, they were of the same opinion as the mayor. The captains, therefore, began to take courage and to prepare to make a brave attack upon the enemy's camp. They hoped to destroy all the Diabolonians along with the roving Doubters that the tyrant had brought with him.

The captains longed to fight for their Prince because they delighted in warlike achievements. The next day they came together and resolved to answer Captain Sepulcher with a bombardment of stones. At sunrise, Diabolus ventured to come near the town again, but the stones were flying like hornets. Nothing is so terrible to Diabolus as the stones flung by Emmanuel's catapults. This attack forced Diabolus to retreat farther away from the town of Mansoul.

When the mayor saw what had happened, he commanded that the bells be rung and thanks be sent to the Lord High Secretary. Indeed, it was by his words that the captains and elders of Mansoul had been strengthened against Diabolus.

Diabolus, seeing that his captains, soldiers, and high lords were frightened and beaten down by the stones from the golden catapults, said to himself, "I will try to catch the people of Mansoul with compliments and flatter them into my net."

When Diabolus came down to the wall, he came alone, without his drummer or Captain Sepulcher. He called for the townsfolk to listen and proceeded in his oration, seeming to be a very sweet-mouthed, peaceable prince.

"Oh, the desire of my heart, the famous town of Mansoul!" Diabolus began. "Many nights I have watched, hoping in some way to do a favor for you. Far be it from me to desire to make war against you, if you should willingly and quietly deliver yourselves up to me. Remember when you enjoyed me as your lord and I enjoyed you as my subjects. You had every delight and pleasure that I could give you or invent to make you happy. You never had so many hard, dark, troublesome times as you have had since you revolted against me. You will never have peace again until you and I become one, as we were before. Embrace me again, and I will enlarge your old charter with abundant privileges. You will be free to enjoy everything that is pleasant from the east to the west. None of your offenses against me will be held to your account as long as the sun and moon endure.

"In addition, my Diabolonian comrades who are lurking in dens, holes, and caves in Mansoul will not harm you anymore. Instead, they will be your servants and minister to you in any way they can. You know them and have been delighted by their company in the past. Why then should we be at odds? Let us renew our old acquaintance and friendship again.

"I take the liberty at this time to speak freely to you. The love that I have for you forces me to do it. Let us avoid any further trouble. I will have you again, either by way of peace or war. Do not flatter yourselves with the power and force of your captains or think that Emmanuel will come shortly to your rescue.

"I come against you with a fierce and valiant army led by all the chief princes of hell. Besides, my captains are swifter than eagles, stronger than lions, and more greedy than the evening wolves. How, then, do you expect to escape my power and force?"

Diabolus ended his flattering, deceitful, and lying speech to the famous town of Mansoul. Then the mayor, Lord Understanding, replied to him.

"O Diabolus, prince of darkness and master of all deceit, we have had enough of you and tasted too deeply of your destructive cup already. Should we, therefore, again listen to you and break the commandments of our great Shaddai? If we joined your ranks, our Prince would reject us and cast us off forever. Can the place he has prepared for you be a place of rest for us? Besides, you are empty and void of all truth, and we would rather die by your hand than fall in with your flattering lies."

When the tyrant realized there was little to be gained by speaking with the mayor, he fell into a hellish rage and resolved to assault the town again with his army of Doubters. So he called for the drummer to alert his men to be ready to attack Mansoul.

Captain Cruel and Captain Torment were assigned to Feel Gate and commanded to remain there for the extent of the war. Diabolus also appointed Captain No-Ease to come to their relief if they needed him. At Nose Gate he placed Captain Brimstone and

Captain Sepulcher who were to guard that side of the town. But at Eye Gate he placed grim-faced Captain Past-Hope who set up his banner with the terrible emblem. Finally, Captain Insatiable was appointed to hold in custody any prisoners of war who were captured.

Diabolus especially wanted to bury Mouth Gate because messengers from the town came in and out of it with their petitions to Prince Emmanuel. In addition, Mouth Gate's higher elevation made it a strategic position for the captain's deadly weapons. From the top of this gate, the captains could catapult their stones at Diabolus and his men.

While Diabolus was industriously preparing to make his assault on Mansoul, the King's captains in the town were also busy making preparations. They mounted their catapults, set up their banners, and gave their soldiers orders to be ready at the sound of the trumpet of war.

While all this was going on, Lord Willbewill watched out for the Diabolonians within the town. He did what he could to smother the ones lurking in caves, dens, and holes in the town wall. Ever since he had repented of his foolish mistake, he had showed more honesty and bravery of spirit than anyone in Mansoul. He even apprehended Jolly and Silly, the two sons of his former servant Harmless-Fun.

After their father, Harmless-Fun, was taken to prison, these two sons began to play pranks on Lord Willbewill's daughters. It was rumored that they became too familiar with the girls. When their father heard about it, he appointed spies to find out if the rumors were true. His two servants, Find-Out and Tell-All, then caught the boys in several indecent and immoral situations. Having obtained sufficient evidence, Lord Willbewill took the two young Diabolonians to Eye Gate where he raised up a very high gallows within the view of Diabolus and his army. There he hanged the young villains in defiance of Captain Past-Hope.

Now these executions greatly embarrassed Captain Past-Hope, discouraged the army of Diabolus, and put fear into the Diabolonian renegades in Mansoul. At the same time, it strengthened and encouraged the captains who belonged to Emmanuel. By this act of Lord Willbewill, the enemy realized that Mansoul had resolved to fight and that the Diabolonians within the town could not do as Diabolus had hoped they would.

Prudent-Thrifty, who had been Mr. Mind's servant, also left behind two children. They were named Gripe and Rake-All. When they saw how Lord Willbewill had dealt with Harmless-Fun's two sons, they decided to try and escape from the town. But Mr. Mind was suspicious and held them in his house until morning. Remembering that all Diabolonians were sentenced to die according to the law, he put them in chains and carried them to the place where the other two had been hanged. There, Mr. Mind executed the children of Prudent-Thrifty.

The townsmen were greatly encouraged by this

act and did what they could to capture more of these Diabolonian troublemakers in Mansoul. But the rest of the villains crouched so low and hid so well that they could not be apprehended.

Chapter Sixteen

NOCTURNAL MANEUVERS

Diabolus and his army were embarrassed and discouraged by the hangings of their comrades, but their discouragement quickly turned into furious anger against Mansoul. At the same time, the townsmen and captains had their hopes and expectations heightened, believing that victory would soon be theirs. So they feared Diabolus and his men even less.

On the Sabbath, the subordinate preacher, Mr. Conscience, gave a sermon using the text, "A troop shall overcome him: but he shall overcome at the last" (Genesis 49:19). He showed that the town would be greatly tested at first, but the victory would most certainly be Mansoul's in the end.

The next day Diabolus commanded his drummer to beat the charge to attack the town. At the same time, the King's trumpeters sounded the call to battle. As Diabolus and his army came down to take the town, the captains in Mansoul bombarded them with stones from the catapults at Mouth Gate.

In the camp of Diabolus nothing could be heard except cursing and raging blasphemy, but in Mansoul encouraging words, prayer, and the singing of psalms resounded throughout the town. The enemy's horrible objections and the terrible noise of their drum was answered with the sound of flying stones and the melodious playing of Mansoul's trumpets.

The fight lasted for several days. Now and then, however, they had a brief intermission during which the townsmen refreshed themselves and the captains prepared for another assault. In the town some were hurt, and some were badly wounded. But there was no one in Mansoul to treat the wounded because Emmanuel was absent from the town. Leaves from the trees were used to stop the bleeding and keep the wounded from dying. But their wounds soon became infected and began to smell terribly.

Lord Reason was wounded in the head, and Mayor Understanding was injured in the eye. Mr. Mind received a stomach wound, and the honest subordinate preacher was shot near the heart. But none of these wounds were fatal.

In the camp of Diabolus a considerable number were wounded and slain. Captain Rage and Captain Cruel were injured, while Captain Damnation was forced to retreat and entrench himself farther away from Mansoul. The banner of Diabolus was trampled down; and his standard-bearer Captain Much-Hurt had his brains beaten out with a catapult's stone, bringing grief and shame to his prince.

Many of the Doubters were also killed, although enough of them were left alive to make Mansoul tremble. When the victory that day was turned in Mansoul's favor, the townsmen and captains took on new courage. The next day Mansoul rested, and the mayor commanded that the bells be rung. The trumpets also joyfully sounded, and the captains shouted all around the town.

During the lull in the battle, Lord Willbewill busily searched out the Diabolonians left in the town. He came across Mr. Anything who had persuaded the three foreign fellows from Captain Thunder's troops to enlist under the tyrant and fight against the army of Shaddai. Lord Willbewill also captured a notable Diabolonian named Loose-Foot. He was a scout to the vagabonds in Mansoul and used to carry news back and forth from the town to the enemy's camp. These two traitors were taken to Mr. Trueman, the jailer, with a commandment to keep them locked in irons. Lord Willbewill intended to hang them at a time when it would bring the most discouragement to the enemy.

Although the mayor was somewhat hampered by the wound he had received, he still gave out orders to all the natives of Mansoul. He commanded them to stand watch, be on their guard, and prove themselves as able-bodied men. In addition, Mr. Conscience, the subordinate preacher, did his best to keep all the laws of Emmanuel alive within the hearts of the people.

After a while the captains of the town agreed upon

a time to make an attack upon the camp of Diabolus. They decided to move at night, but this was a great mistake. Darkness is always best for the enemy, but the worst time for Mansoul to fight. Their courage, however, remained high from their last victory, so the captains went ahead with their plans.

When the appointed time came, the Prince's brave captains cast lots to decide who would lead this foolhardy expedition against Diabolus and his Diabolonian army. The lot fell to Captain Credence, to Captain Experience, and to Captain Good-Hope.

When darkness fell, they set out to attack the troops that lay in seige against them. But instead they came upon the main army of the enemy. Diabolus and his men, being expertly accustomed to night-work, were as ready to defend themselves as if word of an attack had been sent ahead. The battle ensued and blows were hard on every side. The hell-drum beat furiously while the trumpets of the Prince sweetly sounded. As the battle raged, Captain Insatiable watched and waited to receive some fallen prey from Mansoul's ranks.

The Prince's captains fought bravely, beyond what could be expected of them. They wounded many and forced the whole army of Diabolus to retreat. Then something terrible happened.

As brave Captain Credence, Captain Good-Hope, and Captain Experience were pursuing and cutting down the enemy, Captain Credence stumbled and fell. He was hurt so badly that he could not get up until Captain Experience helped him. This created great disorder among their troops. The captain was in such pain that he could not help but cry out. This unnerved the other two captains who supposed that Captain Credence's wound was fatal. Greater confusion ensued, and their soldiers had no heart to continue fighting.

As Diabolus' forces were retreating, he observed that his pursuers had slowed their advance. Assuming that the captains were either wounded or dead, he called for his forces to halt and make an about-face. His troops then began to attack the Prince's army with as much fury as hell could give them. When Diabolus found Captain Credence, Captain Good-Hope, and Captain Experience, he pierced them dreadfully. Yet, in spite of their wounds and the great loss of blood, they were able to return to their troops.

When the Prince's army saw what had happened to these three captains, they thought it best to retreat as fast as they could. So they returned to the town and put an end to this untimely action.

Diabolus, pleased with this night's work, promised himself an easy and complete conquest over the town of Mansoul within a few days. The next day, he boldly came up to the wall of the town and demanded they deliver themselves over to his control.

But Mayor Understanding replied, "You will have to take the town by force. As long as Emmanuel is alive, we will never consent to yield Mansoul to another."

Then Lord Willbewill stood up and said, "Diabolus, you master of the den and enemy to all that is good, we poor inhabitants of the town of Mansoul are well acquainted with your rule and government. We know what will happen if we submit to your rule. When we did not know better, we allowed you to control us. We were like the bird that did not see the snare and fell into the hands of the fowler. Since then we have been turned from darkness to light and have been turned from the power of evil to God. Although we have sustained much loss and plunged ourselves into great perplexity, we still refuse to give up, lay down our arms, and yield to a horrible tyrant like you. We would rather die than submit. Besides, we are hopeful that deliverance will come from the King's court; therefore, we will continue to wage war against you."

These brave speeches by Lord Willbewill and the mayor somewhat dampened Diabolus' boldness, but at the same time it kindled the fury of his rage. The elders' firm determination encouraged the townsmen and captains and was like medicine to brave Captain Credence. Such a bold declaration of their allegiance to the Prince could not have come at a better time.

While the captains and soldiers had been out fighting Diabolus on the battlefield, the Diabolonians within the town had thought, "Now is our time to stir up trouble and make an uproar in Mansoul." They had hastily formed a mob and ripped through the town like a whirlwind. But Lord Willbewill and his men had taken this opportunity to attack, cutting and slashing them with the edges of their swords. The Diabolonians had quickly dispersed and run for their holes.

Many of the Diabolonians were wounded: Lord Quibble, Lord Brisk, Lord Pragmatic, and Lord Murmur. Lord Willbewill also maimed several of the lower-ranking villains, although it is difficult to say how many were actually killed.

This brave act somewhat avenged the wrong done by Diabolus to the three captains. It also let their enemy know that Mansoul would not be defeated by the loss of a victory or two.

Diabolus then resolved to have another bout with Mansoul. "For," he thought, "since I beat them once, I can beat them twice." Therefore, he commanded his men to be ready at a certain hour of the night to make a fresh assault against the town. They were to engage all their forces against Feel Gate and attempt to break into the town that way.

"And," Diabolus said, "those who break in must cry out with a loud voice until nothing is heard in the town except, 'Hell-fire, hell-fire, hell-fire!' " The drummer was also to beat his drum without ceasing, and the standard-bearers were to display their horrible banners. The soldiers were to bravely muster their courage and attack the town with full force.

When night came, the tyrant made a sudden assault upon Feel Gate because he knew it was weak and vulnerable. After his forces had struggled for a while, the gate yielded and burst open wide.

Diabolus then stationed his captains, Torment and No-Ease, at the gate. He attempted to press forward, but the Prince's captains came down on him and made his entrance more difficult than he expected.

The Prince's three best and most valiant captains, however, were wounded and incapable of helping the town. At the same time, all the other captains had their hands full with the Doubters and the captains of Diabolus. Finally, the Prince's men were overpowered and could not keep the enemy out of the town. So the captains and their men fled to the castle, the stronghold of the town, partly for their own security and partly to protect the town. But mostly they wanted to preserve the castle of Mansoul because it was Emmanuel's royal palace.

After the captains had fled into the castle, the enemy, without much resistance, took possession of the rest of the town. They spread themselves into every corner and cried out as they marched, "Hell-fire, hell-fire, hell-fire!" For a while nothing could be heard throughout Mansoul except this dreadful shouting and the roaring of Diabolus' drum. The clouds hung black over Mansoul because ruin seemed imminent.

To make matters worse, Diabolus quartered his soldiers in the houses of the town's inhabitants. The subordinate preacher's house was overflowing with outlandish Doubters; and the mayor's and Lord Will-bewill's houses were also packed. Where was there a corner, a cottage, a barn, or a pigsty that was not full of these vermin? They even turned the men of the town out of their own houses, slept in their beds, and sat at their tables. The people of Mansoul were realizing the fruits of their sin and the poison in the flattering words of Mr. Carnal Security!

The soldiers of Diabolus made great havoc of whatever they laid their hands on. They set fires in several places. Many young children were torn to pieces, and they destroyed the unborn in their mother's wombs. It could not be otherwise, for what conscience, what pity, what compassion can anyone expect at the hands of uncivilized Doubters? Many of the women in Mansoul, both young and old, were ravished and abused, until they fainted and miscarried. Many of them lay dead in the streets and alleys of the town.

Mansoul seemed to be nothing but a den of dragons, an emblem of hell, and a place of total darkness. The town was like a barren wilderness; nothing but briars, thorns, weeds, and dying flesh covered Mansoul.

These Diabolonian Doubters wounded, tortured, and beat many of the townsmen. In fact, most if not all of them were terribly maimed. The wounds that Mr. Conscience received became so infected that he had no relief day or night and suffered in pain continually. The Diabolonian barbarians abused Mayor Understanding until they almost put out his eyes. If Lord Willbewill had not gotten into the castle, they intended to chop him to pieces because they considered him to be one of Diabolus' worst enemies.

You could have walked for days in Mansoul and not seen anyone who looked like a righteous man. Oh, the fearful state of Mansoul now! Every corner swarmed with barbaric Doubters. Gangs of red-coats and black-coats walked the town and filled the houses with hideous noises, vain songs, lying stories, and blasphemous language against Shaddai and his Son. The Diabolonians who used to lurk in the town wall now openly caroused with the Doubters. They strolled along the streets, haunted the houses, and showed themselves more boldly than any of the rightful inhabitants of the now miserable town of Mansoul.

But Diabolus and his outlaws were not satisfied in Mansoul because they were not entertained as the captains and forces of Emmanuel had been. They were not given anything, and all their provisions were seized against the townsmen's will. The poor inhabitants were their captives, and for the present their captives they were forced to be. But the townsmen opposed them as much as possible and showed their dislike as often as they could.

From the castle, the captains continually agitated the villains with stones from their catapults. Diabolus made many attempts to break open the gates of the castle, but he was stopped by Mr. Godly-Fear, the gatekeeper. He was a man of such courage, conduct, and valor that their attempts were in vain as long as life lasted within him. All of Diabolus' attacks against him were fruitless.

The town of Mansoul remained in this tragic and

miserable condition for about two and a half years. The people of the town were forced into hiding, and the glory of Mansoul was laid in the dust. What rest or peace could the inhabitants have, and how could the sun ever shine on the town again?

The main part of the town became the seat of the war. If the enemy could have been kept outside of Mansoul, they would have easily been defeated. But once they were within the walls, the town became their fortress against the Prince's castle and served as their defense. Mansoul was in this sad and lamentable condition for a long time because the petitions they presented to the Prince were to no avail.

Then one day the elders of Mansoul gathered together. After lamenting over their miserable state and this judgment that had come upon them, they agreed to draw up another petition and send it to Emmanuel. But Mr. Godly-Fear stood up and said that he knew the Prince would never receive a petition unless the Lord Secretary's signature was on it. "This," he said, "is the reason you have not succeeded all this time."

They, therefore, decided to draw up a petition and get the Lord Secretary to sign it. But Mr. Godly-Fear answered that the Lord Secretary would not sign any petition that he himself had not been involved in composing. "And besides," said he, "the Prince knows the Lord Secretary's handwriting, and he cannot be deceived. My advice is that you go to his Highness and implore him to give you his help."

The elders heartily thanked Mr. Godly-Fear, took his advice, and did as he had told them.

The Lord Secretary was still living in the castle where all the captains and men-at-arms had taken refuge. When the townsmen went to him and asked if he would please draw up a petition to Emmanuel, the Secretary questioned them, "What petition do you want me to draw up for you?"

The elders replied, "You know how we are backslidden and degenerated from the Prince. You also know who was against us and how Mansoul is now the seat of the war. You know how our men, women, and children have suffered at the hands of our enemies and how the Diabolonians walk the streets with more boldness than the townsmen. Therefore, my Lord, according to the wisdom of God that is in you, please draw up a petition for us to our Prince Emmanuel."

The Lord Secretary answered, "I will draw up a petition for you and sign it also."

Then they asked, "But when should we come and get it?"

He answered, "You must be present at the writing of it and put it in your own words. The handwriting will be mine, but the ink and paper must be yours. Otherwise, how can you say it is your petition? I do not need to petition for myself because I have not offended the Prince."

To this he added, "No petition goes from me in my name to the Prince unless the people who are chiefly concerned join in heart and soul in the matter."

The elders heartily agreed with the Lord Secretary, and a petition was drawn up for them. But who should carry it? That was the next decision. The Secretary suggested Captain Credence for he was a very articulate man. They called for him and explained what he was to do.

"Well," said the captain, "I gladly accept this responsibility. Although I am lame, I will do this business for you with as much speed and as well as I can."

The contents of the petition were as follows:

"Our Lord and Sovereign Prince Emmanuel, the long-suffering Prince, grace is poured into your lips and to you belong mercy and forgiveness. We have rebelled against you and are not worthy to be called your Mansoul or fit to partake of your benefits. We beseech you to do away with our transgressions. We confess that we do not deserve your mercy, but for your name's sake show us your great compassion. We are surrounded on every side, Lord, and our own backslidings reprove us. The Diabolonians within our town frighten us, and the army of the prince of the bottomless pit distresses us. Your grace can be our salvation, and we have no place to go but to you.

"Furthermore, O gracious Prince, we have weakened our captains, and they are discouraged and sick. Lately, some of them have been grievously defeated on the battlefield by the forces of the tyrant. Some of our captains in whom we formerly put our confidence are now wounded men. Besides, Lord, our enemies are strong. They are haughty and threaten to divide us among themselves. They have also brought with them many thousands of grim-faced, unmerciful Doubters who tempt us to defy you as our Prince.

"Our wisdom and our power are gone because you have departed from us. We have nothing we can call our own except sin, shame, and confusion. Take pity upon us, O Lord. Take pity on your miserable town of Mansoul and save us from the hands of our enemies. Amen."

This petition was signed by the Lord Secretary and carried to the King's court by the brave and valiant Captain Credence. He left the town by way of Mouth Gate and went to Emmanuel with the town's plea for mercy.

Chapter Seventeen

EMMANUEL'S MESSAGE

Somehow it reached the ears of Diabolus that a messenger had been sent to Prince Emmanuel. The tyrant was furious and stormed the town of Mansoul, saying, "You rebellious and stubborn Mansoul, I will make you stop sending these petitions!" He also knew that Captain Credence was the messenger who carried the petition to the Prince, and this made him both angry and afraid.

Diabolus commanded that his terrible drum be beat again, a sound which the people of Mansoul could not bear to hear. When the drummer thundered, the Diabolonians gathered together. Diabolus said to them, "O brave Diabolonians, I must tell you that there is treachery devised against us in the rebellious town of Mansoul. Although the town is in our possession, these miserable Mansoulians have dared to send another petition to the court of Emmanuel for help. I am telling you this so you will know how to treat this wretched town. O my loyal Diabolonians, I command you to distress this town even more. Ravish their women, slay their children, assault their leaders, set fire to their houses, and do any other mischief that you can. Let this be their reward for rebelling against me.''

This was the order issued by Diabolus, but something came between the command and the carrying out of the order. In fact, little more than ranting and raving was accomplished by the Diabolonians.

The next day, Diabolus went up to the castle and demanded that the gates be opened to him and his men. To this Mr. Godly-Fear replied that the gates would not be opened for him or the men who followed after him. He also said, ''When Mansoul has suffered a while, she will be made perfect, strengthened, and settled.''

Diabolus further demanded, ''Deliver over to me the men who have petitioned against me, especially Captain Credence. Deliver that rascal into my hands, and I will depart from the town.''

Then a Diabolonian named Mr. Fooling added, ''My lord has offered you a fair choice. It is better that one man perish than for all of Mansoul to be destroyed.''

But Mr. Godly-Fear gave him this answer, ''How long will Mansoul be kept out of the dungeons after she gives up her faith to Diabolus? If we lose Captain Credence, the town will be lost anyway. For if one is gone, the others must follow.'' To this Mr. Fooling said nothing.

Then Lord Understanding said, ''O you devouring tyrant, we will not listen to your words. We are resolved to resist you as long as a captain, a man, or a stone to throw can be found in the town of Mansoul.''

Diabolus answered, "Do you wait, hoping for help and deliverance? You have sent your petition to Emmanuel, but your wickedness clings too close to let innocent prayers come out of your lips. Do you think that you will prevail and prosper in this plan? You will fail in your wish, and you will fail in your attempts. For not only I, but your Emmanuel, is against you. Yes, he has sent me against you to subdue you. So then why do you hope, or by what means will you escape?''

The mayor replied, "We have sinned indeed, but that will not help you. Our Emmanuel has said in great faithfulness, 'And him that cometh to me I will in no wise cast out.' He has also told us that all manner of sin and blasphemy will be forgiven the sons of men. Therefore, we dare not despair, but we will still look, wait, and hope for deliverance.''

By this time Captain Credence had returned from the court of Emmanuel and gone to the castle of Mansoul. When the mayor heard that Captain Credence had come, he withdrew from the roaring of the tyrant and left him yelling at the castle gates. Lord Understanding came to the captain's lodgings, saluted him, and with tears in his eyes asked what had happened at the King's court.

The captain said, "Cheer up, my lord, for all will be well in time." And with that he laid an envelope on the table. The mayor took this as a positive sign and sent word to all the captains and elders of the town who were in the castle or at their guardposts. They were told that Captain Credence had returned from the court and had something special to communicate to them. So they all came up to him, saluted him, and asked him about his journey and the news from the court. After the captain had saluted them, he opened his envelope and took out several notes.

The first note was for Mayor Understanding. It said that Prince Emmanuel had observed the mayor's true and loyal fulfilling of his office and the great concern he had for the people of Mansoul. He had also noted the mayor's boldness for his Prince and how he had engaged so faithfully in his cause against Diabolus. At the close of the letter, the Prince indicated that the mayor would soon receive his reward.

The second note was for the noble Lord Willbewill. In essence it said that his Prince understood how valiant and courageous he had been for his honor when Emmanuel's name was held in contempt by Diabolus. His Prince had also noticed that he had been keeping strict watch over the people of Mansoul and a tight reign around the necks of the Diabolonians still lurking there. The Prince wrote that he was aware that Lord Willbewill had with his own hand executed some of the chief rebels, bringing great discouragement to the enemy and showing a good example to the whole town of Mansoul. He also promised that his lordship would have his reward.

The third note was for Mr. Conscience, the subordinate preacher. His Prince was pleased that he had so faithfully performed his office and executed the trust committed to him by his Lord. He noted how he had exhorted, rebuked, and warned Mansoul according to the laws of the town. It had been brought to the Prince's attention how the subordinate preacher had called the town to fasting with sackcloth and ashes when Mansoul was under revolt. His reward would come soon.

The fourth note was for Mr. Godly-Fear. Emmanuel had observed that he was the first of all the men in Mansoul to detect Mr. Carnal Security as the one who had instigated the defection and decay of goodness in the blessed town. Moreover, his Prince still remembered Mr. Godly-Fear's tears and mourning over the condition of Mansoul. Emmanuel noticed that this reverend person, Mr. Godly-Fear, had stood firmly at the castle gates thwarting all the threats and attempts of the tyrant. He had encouraged the townsmen to make their petition to their Prince in a way that he would accept. It was declared that he would receive his reward.

After all this, there was a note written to the entire town of Mansoul. Their Prince was aware of the many petitions they had sent to him. He said that they would see more of the fruits of their labors in time to come. Their Prince also told them that he was pleased that their hearts and minds were at last fixed on him and his ways. Although Diabolus had made inroads, Emmanuel was sure that neither flatteries nor hardships could make them yield to serve his cruel designs. At the bottom of this note, the Prince wrote that the town of Mansoul was in the hands of the Lord Secretary and under the conduct of Captain Credence. He said, "Yield yourselves to their authority, and in due time you will receive your reward."

After the brave Captain Credence had delivered his notes, he retired to the Lord Secretary's quarters and spent time conversing with him. These two knew more about how things would go with Mansoul than the townsmen did. The Lord Secretary also loved Captain Credence dearly. After some time of talking together, the captain went to his chambers to rest. Not long after, the Lord Secretary sent for the captain again.

When he arrived, the captain asked the Lord Secretary, "What does my Lord have to say to his servant?"

The Lord Secretary took him aside and said, "I am appointing you as the Prince's lieutenant over all the forces in Mansoul. From this day forward, all men in Mansoul will be under your authority. You will manage the war for your Prince and for the town of Mansoul against the forces and power of Diabolus. The rest of the captains will be under your command."

The townsmen began to realize what influence the captain had with the court and also with the Lord Secretary in Mansoul. No one had been able to bring such good news from Emmanuel as he. The people of the town were sorry they had neglected his assistance during the time of their distress. They sent the subordinate preacher to the Lord Secretary to request that everything be put under the government, care, custody, and conduct of Captain Credence.

So their preacher did as they requested and received an answer from the Lord Secretary. He said that Captain Credence was to be the leader of the King's army against their enemies and the guardian of Mansoul. The preacher bowed to the ground, thanked his lordship, and returned to tell the news to the townsfolk. All this was done with great secrecy because their enemies were still strong in the town.

After Diabolus' confrontation with the mayor and brave Mr. Godly-Fear at the castle gates, he went into a rage and called a council of war in order to take revenge against Mansoul. All the princes of the pit came together along with old Unbelief and all the captains of his army. The discussion of the council that day was how they could take the castle. They decided it was impossible for them to be the masters of the town as long as their enemies possessed the castle. So one advised this way, and another advised that. But when they could not agree on a verdict, Apollyon, the president of the council, stood up.

"My brotherhood," he said, "I have two things to propose to you. First of all, we must withdraw from the town and return to the plain again. Our presence here will do us no good because the castle is still in our enemy's hands. It is impossible for us to take it as long as so many brave captains are inside and this bold fellow, Godly-Fear, is the keeper of the castle gates.

"When we have withdrawn to the plain, they will relax and let down their guard. Then of their own accord they will begin to neglect their Prince and bring a bigger blow than we can possibly give them ourselves. If that should fail, our leaving the town may draw the captains out after us. You know what it cost them when we fought them in the field before. Besides, if we draw them out into the field, we can set an ambush behind the town. Then when they come out, we will rush in and take possession of the castle."

But Beelzebub stood up and replied, "It is impossible to draw them all away from the castle. Some will surely remain there to guard it. Such an attempt would be in vain unless we could be sure they will all come out." He concluded that some other means must be employed. The most likely means they could invent was that which Apollyon had advised before—to get the townsmen to sin again.

"For," Beelzebub continued, "it is not our being in the town or in the field. It is not our fighting or our killing of their men that can make us the masters of Mansoul. As long as one in the town is able to lift up his finger against us, Emmanuel will take their side. And if he takes their side, we know what will happen to us. In my opinion, the only way to bring them into bondage is to invent a way to make them sin.

"If we had," he said, "left all our Doubters at home, we would have done as well as we have done now—unless we could have made them the masters and governors of the castle. Doubters at a distance are like objections repelled with arguments. If we can only get them into the castle and make them possessors of it, the day will be ours. Let us, therefore, withdraw ourselves into the plain, assuming that the captains in Mansoul will not follow us. But before we do, let us consult with our loyal Diabolonians and set them to work to betray the town to us. They must do it, or it will be left undone forever."

Beelzebub convinced the whole conclave that the way to take the castle was to get the town to sin. Then they discussed what means they could invent to do this.

Lucifer stood up and said, "The counsel of Beelzebub is pertinent. The way to bring this to pass, in my opinion, is this: Let us withdraw our forces from the town of Mansoul. Let us not terrify them anymore, either with summons, threats, the noise of our drum, or in any other startling manner. For these means only alarm them and put them on their guard. Instead, we will lie in the field at a distance and act as if we take no notice of them.

"I also have another strategy in my head," Lucifer continued. "Mansoul is a market town that delights in commerce. What if a few of our Diabolonians disguise themselves as foreigners and bring some of our wares to sell in the market at Mansoul? It won't matter if they sell their wares for half the worth. We must choose fellows to trade in their market who are clever and true to us. Two come to my mind that I think will be perfect for this work. They are Mr. Pennywise-Poundfoolish and Mr. Big-Time-Spender. Let them engage in this business for us.

"Let Mansoul be so taken up in business that they grow rich and fat. This is the way to gain ground against them. Remember, we prevailed against Laodicea in this way; and how many do we presently hold in this snare? Now when they begin to grow fat, they will forget their misery and fall asleep. Then they will neglect guarding their town and their castle, as well as their gates.

"Yes, in this way we will so encumber Mansoul with possessions that they will be forced to make their castle a warehouse instead of a garrison fortified against us. If we can get our goods and commodities inside, then the castle is more than half ours. If we made a sudden assault upon them, it would be hard for the captains to take shelter there because of all the merchandise stored in the castle. Do you not know the parable, 'The deceitfulness of riches choke the word'? There is also a saying, 'When the heart is over-charged with surfeiting and drunkenness and the cares of this life, all mischief comes upon them unaware.'

"Furthermore, my lords," he said, "when people are taken up with things, they always acquire some of our Diabolonians as servants in their houses. Where is there a Mansoulian concerned with the things of this world who does not have servants like Mr. Profuse, Mr. Prodigality, Mr. Voluptuous, Mr. Pragmatical, Mr. Ostentation, or some other Diabolonians? These fellows can take the castle of Mansoul and blow it up or make it unfit as a garrison for Emmanuel—any of these will do. In fact, they can accomplish more than an army of twenty thousand men. My advice is to quietly withdraw ourselves without any further forcible attempts upon the castle. Instead, let us begin our new project and see if that will not make them destroy themselves."

This advice was highly applauded by them all and considered the very masterpiece of hell. The plan was to choke Mansoul with the cares of this world and to indulge her heart with expensive things. As this Diabolonian council was breaking up, Captain Credence received a letter from Emmanuel saying that he would meet him on the third day in the field outside Mansoul.

"Meet me in the field," read the captain. "What does my Lord mean by this? I do not know what he means by meeting me in the field." So he took the note to the Lord Secretary to ask what he thought about it.

After reading it, he paused and said, "The Diabolonians have met today to decide how to destroy the town. The result of their council is to set Mansoul on a course which, if taken, will surely cause her to destroy herself. They are getting ready for their departure from the town, intending to settle in the field where they will wait to see whether their project will work or not.

"On the third day, be in the plain with the Prince's army ready to fall on the Diabolonians. By that time, the Prince will be in the field. In fact, he will be there before the break of day with a mighty force of his own. Emmanuel's army will be in front of them, and your forces will be behind them. Then the Diabolonians will be trapped, and their army will be destroyed."

Having heard this, Captain Credence went to tell the other captains about the message he had received from Emmanuel. He told them what must be done for their Lord, and the captains were glad. Captain Credence commanded that all the King's trumpeters ascend to the battlements of the castle and play the most joyous music before Diabolus and the town of Mansoul.

When Diabolus heard this joyous music, he was startled and said, "What can be the meaning of this? Their trumpeters are not sounding the charge for battle. What do these madmen mean by being so merry and glad?"

One of the Diabolonians answered him, "They are rejoicing that their Prince Emmanuel is coming to relieve the town of Mansoul."

The townsmen were also greatly concerned about the melodious charm of the trumpets. They answered one another, saying, "This can mean no harm will come to us."

The Diabolonians asked, "What should we do?" Someone answered that it was best to leave the town.

Another of them said, "This is in accordance with our plan, and by leaving we will be better able to battle the enemy if an army comes against us."

On the second day, the Diabolonians withdrew from Mansoul to the plains and firmly encamped before Eye Gate. They would not remain in the town because they did not possess the castle stronghold.

They said, "It will be more convenient for fighting and also for fleeing if we are encamped in the open plains." Besides, the town would have been a grave for them rather than a place of defense if the Prince came and enclosed them within it. In the field they would also be out of the reach of the catapults which had annoyed them all the time they were in the town.

While the Doubters and Diabolonians were withdrawing from Mansoul, the King's captains were eagerly preparing themselves for action. The night before, Captain Credence had told them they would meet their Prince in the field the next day, making them even more eager to engage the enemy. The words, "You will see the Prince in the field tomorrow," were like oil to a flaming fire. It had been a long time since the captains had seen their Prince, and they yearned to be near him once again.

Chapter Eighteen

THE KING OF GLORY

Before daybreak, Captain Credence and the rest of the men of war marched their forces out of the town. Captain Credence went to the head of the army and sounded the battlecry: "The sword of the Prince Emmanuel and the shield of Captain Credence." (In the Mansoulian tongue this means, "The Word of God and faith.") Then the captains and their troops began to surround Diabolus' camp.

They left Captain Experience in the town because he was still recovering from the wounds which the Diabolonians had given him in the last battle. But when he realized that the captains were fighting, he called for his crutches, got up, and went out to the battle, saying, "Will I lie here while my brothers are fighting and Emmanuel the Prince is showing himself in the field to his servants?"

When the enemy saw him with his crutches, they were dismayed even more. "For," they thought, "what spirit has possessed these Mansoulians that they fight against us even on their crutches?"

The captains bravely handled their weapons, still crying out and shouting as they fought, "The sword of the Prince Emmanuel and the shield of Captain Credence!"

When Diabolus saw that the captains were so valiantly surrounding his men, he expected nothing from them but blows and the slashes of their two-edged swords. He, therefore, attacked the Prince's army with deadly force. In the battle, Diabolus first confronted Captain Credence on the one hand and Lord Willbewill on the other.

Willbewill's blows were like the blows of a giant because he had a strong arm. He attacked the Election Doubters because they were Diabolus' bodyguards, and a bloody battle ensued. When Captain Credence saw Lord Willbewill engaged in this heated combat, he also attacked the Election Doubters.

At the same time, Captain Goodhope engaged the Vocation Doubters in a fierce conflict. Captain Experience sent him some aid, forcing the Vocation Doubters to retreat. Both armies were hotly engaged on every side, and the Diabolonians fought with strong determination.

The Lord Secretary commanded that the catapults from the castle be employed so his men could throw stones at close range. After a while, the Diabolonians who had retreated began to rally and attacked the rear of the Prince's army. The Prince's forces were weakening until they remembered they would soon see Emmanuel's face. Then they took courage, and a very fierce battle was fought.

The captains shouted, "The sword of the Prince Emmanuel and the shield of Captain Credence!" Hearing this, Diabolus thought that more aid had come. But Emmanuel had not yet appeared. The outcome of the battle was still in doubt since retreat had been made on both sides. Captain Credence bravely encouraged his men to stand firm, and Diabolus did the same.

"Gentlemen soldiers," Captain Credence said, "I rejoice to see this valiant army and such faithful lovers of Mansoul fighting for our Prince. You have shown yourselves to be men of truth and courage against the Diabolonian forces. Now be courageous and show yourselves strong one more time. After the next engagement, your Prince will show himself in the field. But we must make this second assault against Diabolus, and then Emmanuel will come."

As soon as Captain Credence finished making this speech to his soldiers, Mr. Speedy came to tell him that Emmanuel was at hand. The captain communicated this news to the other field officers, and they passed it on to their soldiers and men of war. Like men raised from the dead, the captains and their troops arose, marched against the enemy, and cried out, "The sword of the Prince Emmanuel and the shield of Captain Credence!"

The Diabolonians also rallied and resisted as much as they could. But in this last engagement the Diabolonians lost their courage, and many of the Doubters fell down dead to the ground.

In the heat of battle, Captain Credence lifted up his eyes and saw that Emmanuel was coming. The Prince came with banners flying, trumpets sounding, and the feet of his men hardly touching the ground. With great swiftness they marched toward the King's captains who were engaged in the battle with Diabolus and his army.

Then Captain Credence headed his men toward the town and gave Diabolus the field. Emmanuel besieged Diabolus' army at the rear, trapping the enemy between the two forces. After a terrible battle, the armies of Emmanuel and Captain Credence met, trampling down the enemy soldiers as they came.

When the captains saw that the Prince had come and attacked the Diabolonians on the other side, they shouted again, "The sword of Emmanuel and the shield of Captain Credence!"

Diabolus saw that he and his forces were severely beaten by the Prince and his princely army, so he and the lords of the pit made an escape. They forsook their army, leaving them to fall by the hand of Emmanuel and noble Captain Credence. All were slain by the Prince and the royal army; there was not one Doubter left alive. Dead men lay spread over the field like fruit drying in the sun.

When the battle was over, order was restored in the camp. The captains and elders of Mansoul came out of the town to salute Emmanuel. They welcomed him with a thousand welcomes because they were so glad he had come to the borders of Mansoul again. He smiled on them and said, "Peace be to you."

Then they all prepared to go into the town—the captains, the elders, the Prince, and the new forces he had brought with him to the war. All the gates of the town were opened to receive him because they were so glad for his blessed return.

The elders posted themselves at the gates of the town to salute the Prince when he entered. As he drew near and approached the gates, they said, "Lift up your heads, O ye gates; and be ye lifted up, ye everlasting doors; and the King of Glory shall come in."

With one voice they cried out, "Who is this King of Glory?"

Then they answered themselves and said, "The Lord strong and mighty, the Lord mighty in battle. Lift up your heads, O ye gates; even lift them up, ye everlasting doors; and the King of Glory shall come in."

As Emmanuel entered the town, the elders and the rest of the men of Mansoul cried out, "They have seen thy goings, O God; even the goings of my God, my King, in the sanctuary!"

The captains escorted the Prince as he entered the gates of Mansoul. Captain Credence went first along with Captain Good-Hope. Captain Charity came behind with his companions, and Captain Patience followed after them. The rest of the captains, some on the right hand and some on the left, accompanied Emmanuel into Mansoul. All the while the banners were displayed, the trumpets sounded, and continual shoutings went up from among the soldiers. The Prince, wearing his armor of beaten gold, rode majestically through the gates in his silver-trimmed chariot.

When the Prince came into Mansoul, he found all the streets strewn with flowers and decorated with branches from the trees that grew throughout the town. Every doorway was filled with people who had adorned the front of their houses with beautiful ornaments in his honor. As Emmanuel passed by, the townsfolk welcomed him with shouts and acclamations of joy, saying, "Blessed be the Prince who comes in the name of his Father Shaddai!"

All the way from the town gates to the castle, his blessed Majesty was entertained with songs by Mansoul's best singers and musicians. The singers went before the Prince, while the musicians and damsels playing their timbrels followed him up to the castle gates.

At the castle gates, the elders of Mansoul—Lord Understanding, Lord Willbewill, Mr. Conscience, Mr. Knowledge, Mr. Mind, and other gentry— saluted Emmanuel again. They bowed before him and kissed his feet. They thanked, blessed, and praised his Highness for having compassion on them in their misery and showing them mercy.

The Prince was escorted into the castle because it was the royal palace and the place where His Honor was to dwell. The castle had been prepared for his Highness by the presence of the Lord Secretary and the work of Captain Credence.

Then the people of the town of Mansoul came to Emmanuel at the castle to mourn and lament for the wickedness which had forced him out of the town. They bowed themselves to the ground seven times and wept aloud, asking forgiveness of the Prince and praying that he would confirm his love for Mansoul once again.

Seeing their repentance, the great Prince replied, "Weep not, but go your way; eat the fat, drink the sweet, and send portions to them for whom nothing is prepared, for the joy of your Lord is your strength. I have returned to Mansoul with mercy, and my name will be exalted and magnified." Then Emmanuel drew the people close to himself and kissed them.

To the elders and to each town officer he gave a chain of gold and a signet ring. He also sent their wives earrings, bracelets, and other valuable jewels. Upon all the true-born children of Mansoul he bestowed many precious gifts.

After Prince Emmanuel had done all these things for the famous town of Mansoul, he said to them, "Wash your garments, then put on your ornaments, and come to me in the castle."

As they washed in the fountain that had been prepared for them, their garments became white. Then they went again to the Prince in the castle and stood before him.

Music and dancing filled the town of Mansoul because their Prince had again granted them his presence and the light of his countenance. The bells rang, and the sun shone comfortably upon them for many days.

The town now began to diligently seek the destruction and ruin of all the remaining Diabolonians hiding in the walls and dens in the town. Some had managed to escape from the hand of their suppressors in Mansoul. Lord Willbewill was a greater terror to them now than he had ever been before. His heart was even more determined to seek them out and put them to death. He pursued these Diabolonians night and day causing them great distress.

After things were put in order in Mansoul, the blessed Prince Emmanuel ordered that the townsmen go out into the plain to bury the dead killed by the sword of Emmanuel and Captain Credence. He knew that the smell from the decaying bodies could infect the air and annoy the famous town. In addition, the Prince realized it was important to remove any thought or memory of Mansoul's enemies from the minds of the inhabitants.

The order was given by the Lord Mayor for the people to take care of this necessary business. Mr. Godly-Fear and Mr. Upright were to oversee the people working in the fields burying the dead. Some were to dig the graves, and some were to bury the dead. Others were to search throughout the plains and around the borders of Mansoul for any Doubters' skulls, bones, or pieces of bone found anywhere near the town wall. The searchers were ordered to set up a marker so that those appointed to bury them could find the bones. It was important that the children born in Mansoul never see a skull or a bone of a Doubter.

In the plains around Mansoul, they buried the Election Doubters, the Vocation Doubters, the Grace Doubters, the Perseverance Doubters, the Resurrection Doubters, the Salvation Doubters, and the Glory Doubters.

They were buried along with their cruel instruments of death—their arrows, darts, axes, and firebrands. They also buried their armor, their banners, the flag of Diabolus, and whatever else they could find that smelled like a Diabolonian Doubter. However, the captains of their forces and the princes of the pit, as well as Diabolus and the seven heads of his army—Lord Beelzebub, Lord Lucifer, Lord Legion, Lord Apollyon, Lord Python, Lord Cerberus, and Lord Belial—all these escaped along with old Unbelief their general.

After their defeat, Diabolus and his old friend Unbelief had returned to Hellgate Hill and descended into the den. There they mourned over their misfortune and the great loss they had sustained against the town of Mansoul. But their grief soon turned to a burning desire for revenge.

They immediately assembled a council to decide what was to be done against the famous town of Mansoul. Their yawning paunches could not wait to see the result of Lord Lucifer's and Lord Apollyon's advice. Every day they eagerly craved to be filled with the body and soul, the flesh and bones of Mansoul. They resolved to make another attempt on the town by using an army made up of Doubters and Bloodmen.

The Doubters' name reflects their nature and the kingdom where they were born. Their nature is to question every one of Emmanuel's truths. Their country is the land of Doubting which lies farther north, between the land of Darkness and the valley of the Shadow of Death. Although the land of Darkness and the Shadow of Death are sometimes thought to be the same place, they are actually two different countries.

The Bloodmen derive their name from their savage nature and the fury that rages within them against the town of Mansoul. Their land lies under the Dog Star, by which they govern their actions. The name of their country is the province of Loathgood. The remotest part of it is a great distance from the land of Doubting, but it borders Hellgate Hill. These Bloodmen are in league with the Doubters, and both question the faith and fidelity of the men of Mansoul. This makes them exceptionally qualified for the service of their prince, Diabolus.

From these two countries, Diabolus raised another army of twenty-five thousand strong to come against Mansoul. Ten thousand Doubters and fifteen thousand Bloodmen were led by several captains. Old Unbelief was again made general of the army.

As for the Doubters, their captains were five of the seven captains from the last Diabolonian army. Their names were Captain Beelzebub, Lucifer, Apollyon, Legion, and Captain Cerberus. Some of

264

the other captains were made lieutenants and standard-bearers in the army.

Diabolus did not consider these Doubters his most reliable men because they had failed so miserably in the last war against Mansoul. He only brought them along to increase the ranks and to help in a pinch. But he put his trust in the Bloodmen because they were all rugged villains who had done daring feats of war before.

The Bloodmen were under the command of Captain Cain, Captain Nimrod, Captain Ishmael, Captain Essau, Captain Saul, Captain Absalom, and Captain Judas.

Captain Cain was over two battalions: the zealous and the angry Bloodmen. The insignia on his flag was the murdering club.

Captain Nimrod was captain over the tyrannical and encrouching Bloodmen; the great bloodhound was his emblem.

The mocking and scorning Bloodmen were commanded by Captain Ishmael. His emblem was a picture of one mocking Abraham's Isaac.

Captain Essau commanded the Bloodmen who begrudged another's blessing. He was captain of the Bloodmen who executed their private revenge on others. His insignia showed one attempting to murder Jacob.

Captain Saul was captain over the groundlessly-jealous and the devilishly-furious Bloodmen. His emblem was three bloody spears thrown at harmless David.

Captain Absalom was captain over the Bloodmen who will kill a father or a friend for the glory of this world. The insignia he carried was of a son pursuing his father.

The Bloodmen who will sell a man's life for money and those who will betray their friend with a kiss were led by Captain Judas. His emblem was thirty pieces of silver.

Diabolus put great confidence in this army of Bloodmen because he had proved them often. Besides, he knew they were like watchdogs that would attack anyone—father, mother, brother, sister, governor, or even the Prince of princes. What encouraged him most was that they had once before forced Emmanuel out of the Kingdom of Universe. "And why," he thought, "can they not also drive him from the town of Mansoul?"

Chapter Nineteen

PRISONERS OF WAR

When Mr. Prywell, Mansoul's chief scout, went out of the town to spy, he saw Diabolus' great army approaching. He returned immediately to report this news to Mansoul. The townsfolk promptly shut their gates and put themselves in a posture of defense against these new Diabolonians who were coming against the town.

Diabolus brought up his army and surrounded the wall of Mansoul. The Doubters were placed at Feel Gate, and the Bloodmen encamped before Eye Gate and Ear Gate. At the same time, Unbelief sent a summons demanding that Mansoul surrender. He threatened to burn down the town if they resisted. But the Bloodmen were not so much in favor of having Mansoul surrender as they were in having the town destroyed. Even if Mansoul were to surrender, the thirst of these Bloodmen would not be quenched. They must have blood—the blood of Mansoul—or else they would die.

When the townsmen received this threatening

summons, they did not know what to do. Finally, they all agreed to take it to the Prince, which they did. At the bottom of the summons, they wrote, "Lord, save Mansoul from the Bloodmen."

So the Prince read it and took note of the short petition that the men of Mansoul had written at the bottom of it. He sent for the noble Captain Credence and asked him to take Captain Patience with him to secure that side of Mansoul beleaguered by the Bloodmen.

Then he commanded Captain Good-Hope, Captain Charity, and Lord Willbewill to take charge of the other side of the town. "And I," said the Prince, "will set my banner upon the battlements of your castle while you three watch out for the Doubters."

The Prince then commanded that brave Captain Experience bring his men to the marketplace and parade them daily before the people of the town. This siege lasted a long time, and the enemy made many fierce attempts against Mansoul. Captain Self-Denial, who commanded the forces at Ear Gate and Eye Gate, made many sneak attacks against the Bloodmen. Captain Self-Denial was a young townsman like Captain Experience. As a hardy man of great courage, he was willing to venture out for the good of Mansoul. Every now and then, he would creep upon the Bloodmen and have brisk skirmishes with them. Some of these warriors were even killed by him. But this was no easy task, and he carried several of their marks on his face and other parts of his body.

After some time was spent in the battle for the faith, hope, and love of Mansoul, Prince Emmanuel called his captains and men of war together. He divided them into two companies and commanded them to go out and attack the enemy. He said, ''Let half of you attack the Doubters, and half of you the Bloodmen. Those of you who go out against the Doubters are to kill as many of them as you can lay your hands on. But those who go out against the Bloodmen are not to kill them but to take them alive.''

In the morning at the appointed time, the captains went against the enemies of the Prince. Captain Good-Hope, Captain Charity, Captain Innocent, and Captain Experience went out against the Doubters. Captain Credence, Captain Patience, Captain Self-Denial and the rest went out against the Bloodmen.

Those who went out against the Doubters assembled on the plain and marched toward the battle. But the Doubters, remembering their last encounter, retreated and fled. The Prince's men pursued the Doubters and killed many of them, but they could not catch them all. Some who escaped went back to the land of Doubting. The rest wandered up and down the countryside doing their Diabolonian mischief among the villagers who lived there. These poor people did not take up arms against the Doubters but allowed themselves to be enslaved by them.

The Prince's captains who went out against the Bloodmen did as they were commanded. They refrained from slaying any of them but tried to surround and capture as many as possible. When the Bloodmen saw that Emmanuel was not in the field, they concluded that Emmanuel was not in Mansoul either. They considered the captains' attempts the fruit of their wild and foolish imaginations, and they despised them rather than feared them. But the captains went about their business, and at last surrounded the Bloodmen. The other captains who had defeated the Doubters came to their aid.

After some struggling, the Bloodmen tried to run away, but it was too late. Although they are mischievous and cruel when they are winning, all Bloodmen are chicken-hearted when they meet their equals on the battlefield! So the captains captured them and brought them to the Prince.

After questioning them, the Prince found the Bloodmen to be from three different counties, although they all came from the same land. One group of them came from Blindmanshire, and everything they did was done out of ignorance. Another bunch of them came from Blindzealshire, and all their actions were determined by superstition. The third lot of them came from the town of Malice in the county of Envy, and everything they did was done out of spite.

When the men from Blindmanshire saw that it was the Prince against whom they had fought, they trembled and cried. Many of them asked him for mercy, and he touched their lips with his golden scepter.

Those who came from Blindzealshire did not ask

for mercy. Instead, they argued that they had a right to do what they had done because Mansoul was a town whose law and customs were different from the people living around them. Very few of these fellows could be brought to see their sinfulness. But those who did repent and ask for mercy also obtained favor from the Prince.

The Bloodmen from the town of Malice in the county of Envy neither wept, disputed, or repented. Instead, they stood before the Prince, gnashing their teeth in anguish and madness because they could not have their way with Mansoul.

The Prince detained these unrepentant fellows, along with all the others who would not ask pardon for their faults. A great inquest was held, and each man was called to answer before our Lord the King for what they had done against Mansoul. And that was the end of the second great army that Diabolus had sent against Mansoul.

There remained, however, four Doubters who had retreated during the battle and had been aimlessly wandering throughout the countryside. When they realized there were still Diabolonians lurking in the town, they decided to go to Mansoul to find them. These Doubters went to the house of an old Diabolonian named Evil-Questioning. He was a great enemy to Mansoul and a great worker among the Diabolonians there. When the Doubters arrived, he welcomed them and pitied their misfortune. After they got acquainted, this old Evil-Questioning asked the four Doubters if they were all from the same town. They answered, "No, nor of one county either."

"For I," said one, "am an Election Doubter."

"I," said another, "am a Vocation Doubter."

The third said, "I am a Salvation Doubter."

And the fourth said he was a Grace Doubter.

"Well," the old gentleman replied, "no matter where you come from, I am persuaded that you are one with my heart. You are welcome to stay." So they thanked him and were glad that they had found a refuge in Mansoul.

Then Evil-Questioning said to them, "How many of your company came with you to the siege of Mansoul?"

They answered, "There were only ten thousand Doubters in all, for the rest of the army consisted of fifteen thousand Bloodmen. But we have heard that every one of them was captured by Emmanuel's forces."

"Ten thousand Doubters?" asked the old gentleman. "That's a large company. But how did it happen that so many of you fainted and were unable to fight your foes?"

"Our general," they said, "was the first man who ran for it."

"Who was this cowardly general?" asked Evil-Questioning.

"He was the former mayor of Mansoul," they said. "But do not call him a cowardly general, for no one has done more service for our prince Diabolus than has Lord Unbelief. Besides, if Emmanuel's men had caught him, they would certainly have hanged him. And hanging is bad news.''

Then the old gentleman said, ''I wish that all ten thousand Doubters were now well-armed in Mansoul, and I was at the head of them. I would see what I could do.''

''Yes,'' they said, ''it would be good if we could see that happen. But wishes! What are they?''

''Well,'' said old Evil-Questioning, ''be careful not to talk too loud. You must be quiet while you are here, or I assure you, you will be arrested.''

''Why?'' asked the Doubters.

''Why?'' repeated the old gentleman. ''Because both the Prince and Lord Secretary, and their captains and soldiers are all present in Mansoul. The town is full of them. Besides, one named Willbewill, a most cruel enemy of ours, has been made keeper of the gate. The Prince has commanded him to diligently look for, search out, and destroy all Diabolonians. And if he finds you, down you will go.''

While all this was going on, one of Lord Willbewill's faithful soldiers, Mr. Diligence, stood listening under old Evil-Questioning's window. He heard the whole conversation between this Diabolonian traitor and the Doubters staying in his house.

Mr. Diligence was a man greatly trusted and dearly loved by Lord Willbewill. He was a man of courage who was untiring in his search for Diabolonians. This loyal soldier went straight to Lord Willbewill to tell him what he had heard.

''And are they still there?'' asked Willbewill. ''I

know Evil-Questioning well because he and I were great friends during the time of our apostasy. But I do not know where he lives now."

"But I do," said Diligence, "and if your lordship will go with me, I will show you the way to his den."

When they came to Evil-Questioning's house, Willbewill broke open the door. He rushed into the room and caught all five of them together, just as Diligence had told him. Lord Willbewill apprehended them, led them away, and handed them over to Mr. Trueman, the jailer, who put them into prison.

In the morning, Mayor Understanding was told what Lord Willbewill had done overnight, and his lordship rejoiced at the news. He was glad not only because Doubters were apprehended, but because old Evil-Questioning was captured. This villain had caused a lot of trouble in Mansoul and been a source of irritation to the mayor. Evil-Questioning had often been hunted, but no hand could ever be laid on him until now.

Preparations were made to bring these five criminals to trial. So the day was set, the court convened, and the prisoners brought to the bar. Lord Willbewill could have executed them when he first captured them, but he thought it would bring more honor to the Prince, more comfort to Mansoul, and more discouragement to the enemy if they were publicly tried.

Mr. Trueman brought the prisoners in chains to

the town hall, for that was the place of judgment. The jury was impaneled, the witnesses sworn, and the prisoners tried for their deeds. The jury was the same one that had tried Mr. No-Truth, Pityless, Haughty, and the rest of their companions.

Old Evil-Questioning himself was brought to the bar first because he was the one who had harbored these Doubters. He was told to listen to the charges against him and that he could object if he had anything to say for himself. So his indictment was read.

"Mr. Questioning, you are indicted by the name of Evil-Questioning as an intruder in the town of Mansoul because you are a Diabolonian by nature and a hater of Prince Emmanuel. You are also indicted for supporting the King's enemies after laws were made to the contrary. You have questioned the truth of Mansoul's doctrines. You are accused of receiving and harboring Mansoul's enemies. What do you have to say to this indictment? Are you guilty or not guilty?"

"My lord," he said, "I do not know the meaning of this indictment because I am not the man you are accusing. The man accused of these charges is called Evil-Questioning. I deny that is my name, since I am Honest-Inquiring. The one sounds like the other, but you know there is a wide difference between these two. Surely a man even in the worst of times and among the worst of men can make an honest inquiry about things without running the risk of death."

Then Lord Willbewill spoke because he was one of the witnesses. "My lord and the honorable magistrates of the town of Mansoul, you have all heard that the prisoner at the bar has denied his name and hopes to evade the charges of the indictment. But I know he is the right man and that his proper name is Evil-Questioning. I have known him more than thirty years, for we, I am ashamed to say, were acquaintances when Diabolus governed Mansoul.

"I testify that he is a Diabolonian by nature, an enemy to our Prince, and a hater of the blessed town of Mansoul. In the time of the rebellion, he stayed at my house for three weeks. We used to talk then as he and his Doubters have recently been heard talking. It is true that I have not seen him for a while. I suppose that the coming of Emmanuel to Mansoul made him change his residence, just as this indictment has driven him to change his name. But this is the man, my lord."

Then the judge said to him, "Do you have any more to say?"

"Yes," said the old gentleman. "Everything that has been said against me has been by the mouth of this witness. And it is not lawful for the famous town of Mansoul to put any man to death by the word of one witness."

Then Mr. Diligence stood up and said, "My lord, when I was on watch one night at the head of Bad Street in this town, I heard some whispering within this gentleman's house. So I went up close to listen, thinking that I might uncover some Diabolonian conspiracy. As I drew nearer, I realized that there were treacherous foreigners in the house. But

I was able to understand their speech for I have been a traveler myself. When I put my ear up to the window, I heard old Mr. Questioning ask these Doubters who they were, where they came from, and what their business was in these parts. He also asked how many of them there were, and they told him ten thousand men. This old Evil-Questioning wished that all ten thousand Doubters were now in Mansoul and that he was the head of them. He then told them to be careful and quiet lest they be captured.''

The judge said, "Mr. Evil-Questioning, here is another witness against you, and his testimony is complete. All this evidence indicates you are a Diabolonian. For if you had been a friend of the King, you would have apprehended these traitors.''

Evil-Questioning replied, "To the first of these I answer that the men who came into my house were strangers, and I took them in. Is it now a crime in Mansoul for a man to entertain strangers? It is also true that I gave them food, but why should my hospitality be blamed? As for the reason I wished ten thousand of them in Mansoul, I never told it to the witnesses or to anyone. I may have been wishing they would be captured, so my wish might be good for Mansoul. I did tell them to be careful not to fall into the captain's hands because I did not want anyone to be killed. It was not because I wanted the King's enemies to escape.''

Lord Understanding said, "Although it is a virtue to entertain strangers, it is treason to entertain the King's enemies. By what you have said, you are only trying to evade the charges and defer the execution of judgment. But if the only charge proved against you was that you are a Diabolonian, then by law you must die. It is even worse to be a harborer of other Diabolonians who are intent on destroying Mansoul.''

Then Evil-Questioning muttered, ''I see how your court works. I must die for my name and my hospitality.'' Then he held his peace.

Next, they called the treacherous Doubters to the bar. The first to be arraigned was the Election Doubter. Because he was a foreigner, the substance of his indictment was told to him by an interpreter. He was charged with being an enemy of Emmanuel the Prince, a hater of the town of Mansoul, and an opposer of her laws.

The judge asked him how he would plead. He confessed he was an Election Doubter and that it was the only religion he had known from his childhood. Then he said, ''If I must die for my religion, I will die a martyr.''

The judge replied, ''To question election is to overthrow a great doctrine of the gospel and cast doubt on the omniscience, power, and will of God. Questioning election weakens the faith of the town of Mansoul and makes salvation depend on works and not on grace. It also contradicts the Word and disturbs the minds of the men of Mansoul. Therefore, according to the law, he must die.''

Then the Vocation Doubter was called to the bar. His indictment was basically the same as the others, only he was particularly charged with denying the calling of Mansoul.

The judge asked him what he had to say for himself.

The Vocation Doubter replied, "I never believed there was any such thing as a distinct and powerful call of God to Mansoul. I thought the voice of the Word only exhorted them to abstain from evil and to do that which is good."

To this the judge responded, "You are a Diabolonian and have denied one of the most fundamental truths of the Prince of the town of Mansoul. For he has called, and she has heard a most distinct and powerful call from her Emmanuel. By this call Mansoul has been quickened, awakened, and possessed with heavenly grace to desire to have communion with her Prince—to serve him, to do his will, and to look for her happiness by doing what pleases him. Because of your hatred for this good doctrine you must be put to death."

Then the Grace Doubter was called, and his indictment was read. He replied that although he was from the land of Doubting, his father was the offspring of a Pharisee who had been a good man. "He taught me to believe that Mansoul will never be saved freely by grace."

The judge said, "The law of the Prince is plain: 'Not of works but by grace you are saved.' Your religion counts on the works of the flesh; for the works of the law are the works of the flesh. You have robbed Shaddai of his glory and given it to a sinful man. You have robbed Emmanuel of the necessity and the sufficiency of his undertaking and have given both over to the works of the flesh. You have despised the work of the Lord High Secretary and have magnified the will of the flesh and the legal mind. You are a Diabolonian and the son of a Diabolonian. You must die for your Diabolonian beliefs.''

The court sent out the jury who promptly returned with the sentence of death. Then the magistrate stood up and addressed himself to the prisoners: ''You, the prisoners at the bar, have been indicted and found guilty of high crimes against Emmanuel our Prince and against the welfare of the famous town of Mansoul. These are crimes for which you must be executed.''

The five Diabolonians were sentenced to death by hanging at the place where Diabolus had assembled his last army against Mansoul. Old Evil-Questioning, however, was hanged at the top of Bad Street, just across from his own house.

Chapter Twenty

A GLIMPSE INTO PARADISE

After the town of Mansoul had executed many of their enemies and troublemakers, the Prince ordered Lord Willbewill to continue to search for and apprehend any Diabolonians left alive in Mansoul. Several of the villains captured were: Mr. Fooling, Mr. Let-Good-Slip, Mr. Slavish-Fear, Mr. No-Love, Mr. Mistrust, Mr. Flesh, and Mr. Sloth.

Lord Willbewill was commanded to apprehend Mr. Evil-Questioning's children and demolish his house. The children that he left behind were: Mr. Doubt, Legal-Life, Ungodly, Wrong-Thoughts-Of-Christ, Clip-Promise, Carnal-Sense, Live-By-Feeling, and Self-Love. All these he had by his wife, No-Hope, the niece of old Unbelief. When her father died, Unbelief raised her and then gave her to old Evil-Questioning to be his wife.

Lord Willbewill carried out his commission with the help of his assistant, Mr. Diligence. He took Mr. Fooling in the streets and hanged him in No-Wits Alley. Lord Willbewill also captured Mr. Let-Good-

Slip one day as he was busy in the market. He executed him according to the law.

Mr. Let-Good-Slip had had a great deal of wealth in Mansoul, but at Emmanuel's coming it had been confiscated. The Prince now gave it to Mr. Meditation, an honest, poor man who had been ignored during the time of the apostasy. This wealth was also to be enjoyed by his son, Mr. Think-Well, and Mrs. Piety, his wife, who was the daughter of Mr. Conscience.

After this, Lord Willbewill apprehended Mr. Con-Artist, a notorious villain who had cheated many people out of their money. He was arraigned and sentenced to the pillory where he was publicly whipped by all the children and servants in Mansoul. Then he was hanged until he was dead. Some wondered at the severity of this man's punishment, but the honest merchants in Mansoul knew the damage one swindler could do to a town in a short time.

Mr. Carnal-Sense was also captured, but he broke out of prison and escaped. This bold villain remained in Mansoul, lurking in the Diabolonian dens during the day and haunting good men's houses at night. A proclamation was posted in the marketplace in Mansoul, signifying that anyone who apprehended and killed Carnal-Sense would be admitted daily to the Prince's table and made keeper of the town treasury. Many townsmen found him, but no one could capture and kill him.

Mr. Wrong-Thoughts-Of-Christ, however, was successfully arrested and put in prison where he eventually died after a lingering illness. Self-Love was also taken into custody. But he had many allies in Mansoul, so his judgment was deferred.

Finally, Mr. Self-Denial stood up and said, "If such villains as these are winked at in Mansoul, I will give up my commission." He then took Self-Love from the crowd and had his soldiers beat this villain's brains out. Some in Mansoul muttered to themselves about the severe execution of Self-Love, but none of them complained openly because Emmanuel was dwelling in the town.

When this brave act of Captain Self-Denial came to the Prince's attention, he promoted him to a higher position. Lord Willbewill also obtained great commendations from Emmanuel for what he had done for the town of Mansoul.

Lord Self-Denial was encouraged by his success and set about helping Lord Willbewill pursue the Diabolonians. They seized Live-By-Feeling and Legal-Life, keeping them in the dungeon until they died. But Mr. Ungodly was a nimble fellow, and they could never catch him, although they attempted to do so many times. He, therefore, and some of the more subtle Diabolonians remained in Mansoul, but they were kept in their dens and holes. If one of them did appear or happen to be seen in the streets, the whole town would chase after them, trying to stone these villains to death.

A measure of peace and quiet settled upon Mansoul. Her Prince abided within her borders while her captains and soldiers did their duties. The townsfolk went about their business, manufacturing goods and trading with other countries.

One day Mansoul received a message from the Prince, saying he wanted to meet with all the people and give them instructions concerning their future safety and comfort. When the appointed time came, the townsmen met together. Emmanuel came in his chariot with his captains attending him on the right hand and the left. After the call was given for silence and some expressions of love were shown, the Prince began to speak:

"You, my Mansoul and the beloved of my heart, many and great are the privileges that I have bestowed on you. I have singled you out from others and chosen you for myself; not because of your worthiness, but for my own sake. I have also redeemed you; not only from the dread of my Father's law, but from the hand of Diabolus. I have done this because I love you and I have set my heart to do you good.

"So that nothing may hinder your way to the pleasures of Paradise, I have purchased you for myself. The price I paid was not with corruptible things like silver and gold, but a price of blood—my own blood which I freely spilled upon the ground to make you mine. So I have reconciled you to my Father and built mansions for you in the royal city. Eye has not seen nor has entered into the heart of man the things my Father and I have prepared for you there.

"Besides, O my Mansoul, you have seen what I

have done and how I have taken you out of the hands of your enemies. You had seriously rebelled against my Father and were content to be possessed and destroyed by the enemies of your soul. I came to you first by my law and then by my gospel, to awaken you and show you my glory.

"You know what you were, what you said, what you did, and how many times you rebelled against my Father and me. Yet, I did not leave you, but I bore your rejection of me, waited for you to change, and accepted you merely because of my grace and favor. I would not allow you to be lost as you most willingly would have been. I encompassed you on every side that I might make you weary of your ways. My only desire was your good and happiness. When I had completed my conquest over you, I turned it to your advantage.

"You have also seen the great company of my Father's forces which I have lodged within your borders: captains and rulers, soldiers and men of war. They are my servants and yours, too, Mansoul. The natural tendency of each of them is to defend, purge, strengthen, and prepare you for my Father's presence, blessing, and glory. You, my Mansoul, were created for this purpose.

"You know how I have forgiven your backslidings and have healed you. Indeed, I was angry, but I turned my anger away from you because of my love for you. My anger and indignation ceased in the destruction of your enemies, O Mansoul. It was not your goodness that caused me to return to you after I hid my face from your transgressions and withdrew my presence from you. The way of backsliding was yours, but the way and means of your recovery was mine. I invented the way for your return. It was I who made a hedge and a wall about you when you were beginning to turn to things in which I did not delight.''

"It was I who made your sweet become bitter, your day night, and your smooth way thorny. I confounded all who sought your destruction. I set Mr. Godly-Fear to work in Mansoul. I stirred up your conscience and understanding, your will and affections after your miserable decay. I put life into you, O Mansoul, so that in me you would find your own health, happiness, and salvation. It was I who removed the Diabolonians the second time from Mansoul; I overcame them and destroyed them before your eyes.

"And now, my Mansoul, I have returned to you in peace, and your transgressions against me are as if they had not been. Things will not be like they were in the past, but I will do better for you than at the beginning. After a little while, I will take this famous town of Mansoul down to the ground. But do not be troubled by what I am saying. I will carry the stones, the timber, the walls, the dust, and the inhabitants into my own country, the Kingdom of my Father. There, I will set up the town in such strength and glory, as it never had in the kingdom where it is now situated.

"I will establish Mansoul for my Father's habitation, because it was first erected for that purpose in the Kingdom of Universe. There I will make it a spectacle of wonder, a monument of mercy, and an admirer of its own glory. The natives of Mansoul will see things there that they have never seen here. In my Father's Kingdom you will be equal to those to whom you were inferior before. And there you, O my Mansoul, will have greater communion with me, with my Father, and with your Lord Secretary than is ever possible to be enjoyed here.

"In Paradise, you will no longer be afraid of murderers or Diabolonians and their threats. No more plots or evil designs will be devised against you, O my Mansoul. You will no longer hear evil tidings or the noise of the Diabolonian drum. No Diabolonian weapons will be mounted against you there, and no wicked emblems will be set up to make you afraid. There, you will not need captains, armor, soldiers, or men of war. You will not have any more sorrow or grief. It will not be possible for any Diabolonian to burrow into your walls or be seen within your borders all the days of eternity. Life there will last longer than you are able to desire it would, yet it will always be sweet and new without any interruption.

"O Mansoul, you will meet many in Paradise who have been like you and partaken of your sorrows. They have also been chosen, redeemed, and set apart for my Father's court and royal city. All of them will be glad for you; and when you see them, you will rejoice in your heart.

"In Paradise there are marvelous things provided by your Father and me that have never been seen since the beginning of the world. These things are kept with my Father and sealed up in his treasury until you come there to enjoy them.

"I told you before that I would remove my Mansoul and set it up elsewhere. In that place there are those who love you and rejoice in you now; but how much more will they rejoice when they see you exalted to honor. My Father will send them to escort you, O my Mansoul, and you will ride on the wings of the wind. They will come to convey, conduct, and bring you to your desired haven.

"I have showed you what will happen hereafter, if you can hear and understand. Now I will tell you what you must do until I come and take you to myself, as it is related in the Scripture of truth.

"First, I charge you to keep clean the garments which I gave you. These robes are made of fine linen, and you must keep them white and pure. When your garments are white, I will be delighted by your ways; and the world will recognize you as mine. Then your movements will be like a flash of lightning that will dazzle the eyes of those who see you. Adorn yourselves as I have said and make your pathways straight for my feet. Then your King will greatly desire your beauty, for he is your Lord. Worship him.

"So that you may keep clean, I have provided an open fountain where you can wash your garments. Wash often in this fountain, and do not wear defiled robes. When you walk about in filthy garments, it brings me dishonor and disgrace and causes you discomfort. Do not let the garments I gave you be defiled or spotted by the flesh. Keep your garments always white, and let your head lack no ointment.

"My Mansoul, I have often delivered you from the designs, plots, attempts, and conspiracies of Diabolus. And for all this I ask nothing of you except that you do not render to me evil for my good. But keep in mind my love and the continuation of my kindness toward you. This will inspire you to walk according to the benefits bestowed on you.

"In ages past, the sacrifices were bound with cords to the horns of the golden altar. Consider what is said to you, O my blessed Mansoul. I have lived, and I have died. I live and will not die for you again. I live that you may not die. Because I live, you will live also. I have reconciled you to my Father by the blood of my cross, and you will live through me. I will pray for you; I will fight for you; I will do good for you.

"Nothing can hurt you except sin; nothing can grieve me except sin; nothing can defeat you except sin. Therefore, be on your guard, my Mansoul.

"Do you know why I still allow Diabolonians to dwell in the town walls? It is to keep you alert, to try your love, to make you watchful, and to cause you to prize my noble captains, their soldiers, and my mercy. It is also to make you remember your once deplorable condition when all the Diabolonians lived, not in your walls, but in your homes and in your stronghold.

"O my Mansoul, if I were to slay all the Diabolonains within your walls, many others would come from without and bring you into bondage. If all those within were cut off, those without would find you sleeping and would swallow you up in a moment. I, therefore, left them within the town—not to harm you (although they will if you listen to them and serve them) but to do you good. I want you to know that whatever they tempt you to do, it is my purpose that they drive you, not farther off but nearer to my Father. In his presence, you will make your petitions, learn about warfare, and be kept humble in your own eyes.

"Show me your love, my Mansoul, and do not let those within your walls take your affections away from him who has redeemed your soul. Let the sight of a Diabolonian heighten your love for me. I came to save you from the poison of those arrows that would have brought about your death. Stand for me, your friend, against the Diabolonians, and I will stand for you before my Father and all his court. Love me in spite of temptation, and I will love you in spite of your weaknesses.

"O my Mansoul, remember what my captains, my soldiers, and my weapons have done for you. They have fought for you; they have suffered because of you; and they have endured much at your hands to do you good, O Mansoul. If you had not had them to help you, Diabolus would certainly have crushed you. Nourish them, therefore, my Mansoul. When you do well, they will be well; when you do poorly, they will be sick and weak. Do not make my captains sick, O Mansoul. If they are sick, you cannot be well; if they are weak, you cannot be strong; if they are faint, you cannot be brave and valiant for your King. You must not live by your feelings and senses, but you must live upon my Word. You must believe, O my Mansoul, when I am away from you, that I still love you and carry you in my heart forever.

"Remember, O my Mansoul, that you are my beloved. As I have taught you to watch, to fight, to pray, and to make war against my enemies, so now I command you to believe that my love is constant. O my Mansoul I have set my heart and my love upon you. Watch and hold fast to my words until Paradise becomes your eternal home."